WATER UNDER THE BRIDGE

Chris Crowther

By the same author
BLADESTRIKE
WATERPROOF
STILL WATERS
THE WATER FROLIC

British Library Cataloguing in Publication Data.
A catalogue record is available from the British Library.

ISBN 978 0 903094 27 6

First published this edition in 2012
by

Hamilton Publications,
9 Marine Parade,
Gorleston on sea,
Norfolk. NR 31 6DU.

www.chriscrowther.co.uk

Printed in Great Britain by
Barnwell Print Ltd, Dunkirk, Aylsham, Norfolk. NR11 6SU

Cover photos by Lord Paul Sergent www.lordofsealand.co.uk
Sketches by Sarah Rogers www.broads-art.co.uk

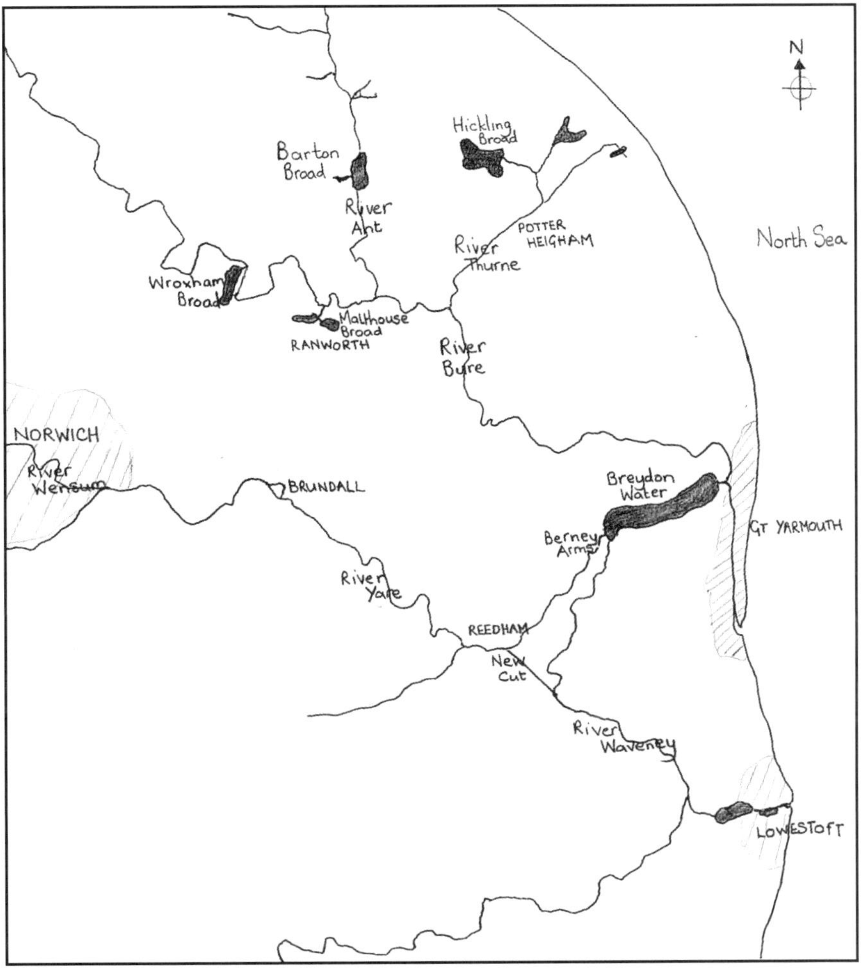
N
Barton Broad
Hickling Broad
River Ant
POTTER HEIGHAM
North Sea
River Thurne
Wroxham Broad
Malthouse Broad
RANWORTH
River Bure
NORWICH
River Wensum
BRUNDALL
Breydon Water
GT YARMOUTH
Berney Arms
River Yare
REEDHAM
New Cut
River Waveney
LOWESTOFT

O what a tangled web we weave,
When first we practice to deceive!

Sir Walter Scott
1771 - 1832

Chapter One

Frank Brooker leaned out from the starboard doorway of *Nordic Princess*'s wheelhouse and gave a thumbs-up. Waiting ready up in the bows, Jack Fellows acknowledged the signal, let go the heavy mooring line from the boat's for'ard Samson post and lowered it down on to the quay heading below. With a gentle evening breeze and an ebb tide flowing past the old trip boat's hull, the gap between bow and shore began to widen immediately, her sternward movement held only by a fore-spring aft. As the angle between vessel and quay opened, another signal from Frank had Jack casting that line off also, leaving *Nordic Princess* totally free. A rumble from below, a short belch of diesel exhaust from the funnel, a momentary vibration and then the boat was gliding into the stream and the trip had begun.

As he made his way to rejoin Frank in the wheelhouse, Jack cast his mind back just a few days to that glorious sailing picnic with Audrey and how it had led to the invitation for this evening's experience.

* * *

That had been a similarly beautiful day, when the gentle slap of water on clinkered planks and a slight movement of the hull had brought him out of a deep and contented sleep. It had taken a few pleasant seconds of semi-consciousness to remember where he was: stretched out on the side bench of a wooden half-decker with his cap blanketing the rays of the afternoon sun. Almost reluctantly, he'd eased himself up onto his side and glanced out across sparkling water. They were still where he'd dropped anchor before lunch: in a secluded bay, sheltered by reedbeds and just off the main broad. Reclining on the other side of the boat, his wife Audrey had put down her book and smiled.

'Don't pretend you haven't been asleep, Jack Fellows,' she laughed. 'Your snoring gave you away.' Audrey unscrewed the top of a flask, poured a cup of steaming-hot tea and handed it across. 'Here, you'll be ready for this.'

'Thanks love, I don't usually drop off during the day.' Jack took the plastic cup and a few welcome sips. 'How long have I been asleep?'

'About two hours. I've almost finished my book, but it's good to see you so relaxed. It was a great idea of yours to hire this boat from Frank.'

'Well, it's a way of helping him out. The yard seems to be pretty lean on customers right now.'

Frank Brooker was the owner of Brookerboats, a small traditional boatyard a mile downriver. The yard had been in his family for generations, but Jack knew times were tough these days and it was an uphill struggle trying to make it pay. He liked Frank, a hardworking grafter of the old school, and hiring one of his sailing day-boats seemed the least he could do to support him. So, a perfect summer's day and a fair breeze had brought them to the broad and provided a morning of exhilarating sailing up and down its length. Being a balanced lugsail, there was no jib for Audrey to work and, though she enjoyed the sensation of sailing, she'd been quite content to sit back and watch Jack handling tiller and mainsheet as the old boat churned its way through the rippled water. Until recently, Jack's navigation ranger job, patrolling the waterways in one of the Broads Authority's launches, had been full-time with little opportunity to enjoy a day's sailing.

'We should do this again, soon Jack. Now you're working fewer hours, you can't say you don't have the time.'

Like the rest of the country, the Broads Authority had not been immune to cost-cutting and Jack had willingly had his own hours reduced to make way for younger rangers.

'Yep, sailing is certainly good for the soul…' he nodded towards the empty plates and glasses on the centre thwart, '… but I'm not sure about the waistline.'

Having eaten a lunch of individual homemade cheese and leek tartlets, rolls and a ready-prepared salad, plus three glasses of *Shiraz*, the tranquillity of the setting together with the gentle movement of the boat, had soon lulled Jack into that blissful post-prandial snooze. Now it was mid-afternoon, and the cup of tea was going down just right.

'This is such heaven,' said Audrey, pouring herself a second cup and cutting two slices of lemon cake. 'I can't understand why Frank has boats lying idle on a day like this.'

Jack took his slice and licked the sugary topping from his fingers. 'Because his boats are old and, let's face it, pretty tatty.'

'I know,' conceded Audrey, 'but Brookerboats' motor cruisers do have a certain period charm and they are cheap to hire compared to other craft these days.'

'Yep, and many people love traditional wooden boats,' agreed her husband, finishing his cake and glancing at his empty cup, 'but even traditionalists expect gleaming hulls and brass oil-lamps, not peeling paint and faded varnish. Okay, Frank's boats are basically sound and it wouldn't need a lot of cash to bring them up to scratch, but light bookings mean there's not much of that right now.'

'Or time either, seeing as Frank tries to do all the work himself, poor chap,' replied Audrey, passing the flask to her husband. 'I can't see how he keeps the yard going from week to week.'

Jack poured himself more tea. 'He wouldn't if it wasn't for the *Princess*,' he explained, spooning in some sugar. 'That boat is the only real earner he's got.' *Nordic Princess* was Brookerboats' passenger trip vessel, bought from a defunct operator in the north of England the previous year. Built in the 1930s, she had originally been a steamer and, although now diesel-powered, still retained her old funnel and classic lines. Jack shrugged. 'The public might hesitate hiring an old cruiser, but they do seem to like the nostalgia of an organised trip on a bygone boat.'

'I wonder why he only runs charters and special evening cruises?' queried Audrey. 'You'd think a boat like that should be sailing every day.'

'He's got enough on his plate without making more work for himself, Aud. It'd take quite a bit of his time and money to prepare *Nordic Princess* for daily sailings and, on top of that, he'd need to employ a regular skipper and stewardess. As it is, just doing pre-booked sailings when he's available to operate it, with guaranteed passengers, keeps the old girl in the black.'

'I've heard his local history and ghost cruises are really popular,' recalled Audrey. 'They're always a sell-out.' She brightened at a thought. 'Perhaps we should take one ourselves. We have the time now.'

'Good idea, but, talking of time,' said Jack glancing at his watch, 'it's gone three, and we've a mile or so to go.' He swigged the rest of his tea, shook any remaining dregs over the side, and handed back the cup. 'Spike will be needing his walk and…' he glanced at the burgee atop the mast, '… this hot day is creating a sea breeze now. We should make the best of a fair wind while we can.'

So, while Audrey cleared away crockery and food, Jack sprang to the main halyard and started hoisting the lugsail. Soon the yard was aloft and the big four-sided sail luffing and billowing. Now the boat was swinging at its cable, as if keen to get moving. Jack made his way to the bow and, hand over hand, hauled in the wet and dripping anchor rope. They were in shallow water and the mudweight soon broke surface.

'Take the tiller and bear away,' shouted Jack as he swung the heavy weight back and forth to wash off the last vestiges of bottom mud before humping it onboard and dashing back to the stern sheets, where Audrey was just wondering what to do next. 'Okay, love, I've got her,' reassured Jack, midshipping the tiller and hardening the mainsheet. As a relieved Audrey moved back to her coolbag, the flapping mainsail filled to silence, and there came a chuckle from the bows as the clinker hull picked up speed and once more cleaved the waters of the broad. They were heading home.

* * *

'This sea-breeze is handy for taking us back, but it will keep us on our toes,' warned Jack with a grin, as he once more hauled in the mainsheet to gybe around yet another bend in the narrow waterway.

Like all rivers, it twisted and turned along its way, with only short straight reaches between each bend. The old wherrymen had given every single Broadland reach a name of its own and Jack had vowed one day to try and learn them all but, for now, he had his work cut out just navigating each one in turn. A wind astern and a run home was certainly good for speed, but the turning river meant the wind was constantly on one side of the sail or the other which meant hauling and easing the sail to prevent an accidental gybe.

'Am I doing all right, Jack?' asked Audrey, letting out a relieved sigh as the river ahead straightened out for a while and she was able to centre the tiller.

'You're doing just fine. Steady as she goes.' Jack had handed over the tiller to his not-very-experienced wife, enabling him to concentrate on the mainsheet. 'Just keep her going straight down this reach.'

'Thank goodness for that.' Audrey's hand eased its grip on the tiller and slowly the colour returned to her fingers. Once again she could sit back and enjoy the passing scene.

And a unique scene it was. This stretch of the waterway was less a river lined with banks, but more a marked channel through the marshes. On either side the reedbeds were interspersed with areas of shallow open water that provided a wonderful natural habitat for Broadland birdlife. Audrey was glad to see the wind-strength dropping now, especially as they were nearing yet another bend to port. But Jack's words were added reassurance.

'Relax now, love. This turn will only bring us more into the wind. We won't be gybing, so I'll take the helm again.'

'With pleasure,' breathed Audrey, only too happy to hand over the tiller to her husband before making her way back to the for'ard end of the boat, where she lay back contentedly listening to the chuckle of water beneath their bow.

They were round and into the next short reach when something seen earlier, as they made their way upriver that same morning, once again caught Jack's attention. 'That weird boat's still there.'

Audrey sat up, rubbed her eyes and peered ahead into the lowering sun, reflecting off the shimmering waters. 'So it is.'

There, on the east bank, moored by rhond anchors, was a singularly strange craft. It had obviously started life as some sort of motor cruiser, but extra accommodation space had since been added with little concern for aesthetics. Now, this somewhat top-heavy and angular cabin ran virtually the full length of the boat, with only the smallest of open wells in the stern. All was painted bright yellow, even to the stubby mast near the bow. It was a colour-scheme broken only by the rust of a rickety chimney poking up amidships and the name painted in red italics on her side: *Fisher of Men.*

Audrey shrugged her shoulders. 'Not the most handsome boat on the river, but it's got a nice name.'

'... and river tolls, thankfully,' added Jack, as they came abeam. He made a mental note of the strange boat's registration. 'I've never seen her before today; I wonder who she belongs to?'

As if in answer, a figure emerged from the cabin into the aft well to watch them glide past. If Audrey had been asked to imagine the owner of this eccentric craft, her description wouldn't have been far short of reality. He was a rather thin man, fortyish, with shoulder-length, lank dark hair and a rather scruffy beard. Despite his rather unkempt appearance, he gave a broad smile and returned Audrey's wave as they passed.

'Well, at least he's friendly.'

'Maybe,' acknowledged her husband with obvious reservation, 'but I'll ring the office tomorrow and find out who he is.'

Audrey knew better than to protest at this intrusion of work into their leisure hours. Years as a senior detective at Scotland Yard had given her husband an indefinable instinct for the dubious, and clearly this boat and its owner had struck such a nerve. Inwardly groaning at Jack's total inability to let things go, she simply said, 'He *looked* amiable enough, Jack.'

'We'll see,' grunted her husband as he steered for the next corner and glanced again at his watch. 'Fifteen minutes will see us back.'

*   *   *

Frank Brooker looked up from re-varnishing a section of *Nordic Princess*'s guardrail, as Jack and Audrey sailed back into the basin. The trip-boat was too big to enter here and lay at permanent moorings outside on the main river. There wouldn't be room for it anyway, for the basin was filled with the rest of his hire-fleet, comprising three motor cruisers and a couple of day-sailers, that lay moored around the perimeter. They should all have been out on hire by this stage of the season, but streaks of grime, faded paint and peeling varnish were evidence enough that they hadn't moved for a year. Frank was well aware of the work and attention these boats needed, but it was only the trip boat that generated any real return, so it was on her that he felt his time best spent. Even the *Princess* had a wooden wheelhouse and a fair amount of wooden trimming, but keeping that and the brasswork bright and shining gave this vessel the gleaming appearance the public loved. He certainly wouldn't say it about the rest of his fleet, but Frank Brooker was proud of *Nordic Princess*.

Jack had been careful to give Frank's pride and joy a wide berth, and now he quickly dropped the sail and ghosted towards the slot he'd left vacant that morning. Once alongside, he was soon springing ashore with the lines, making fast to the quayside bollards and avoiding holes in the walkway.

'However does this yard keep going?' Audrey was voicing her husband's thoughts, as she gathered their picnic gear and prepared to join him on the quay.

'Leave that for now, love,' said Jack, returning the yard owner's slightly forlorn wave. 'Let's go and have a chat with Frank. I reckon he could do with a bit of cheering up.'

They wandered along rotting walkways to where *Nordic Princess*'s seventy-foot length lay on her berth. Frank Brooker looked down and smiled between brushstrokes. 'Had a good day, Jack?'

'Lovely thanks.' Jack nodded at the glass like finish of the guardrail capping. 'Plenty there to keep you busy, Frank.'

'Yep…' the yard-owner glanced towards his idle hire-fleet, '… I wish they looked as good, but…' Frank Brooker shrugged weary shoulders, '…the trouble is, I'm a few decades behind the times. These days, the public want all the home comforts, which you don't get on traditional boats like these.'

'I think there are a lot of people who *love* traditional boats, Frank, but you need to smarten your fleet to attract them.'

The yard-owner nodded. 'You're right, but time's the problem. It would take a lot of man-hours to bring those old cruisers back up to scratch.'

'Can't you hire someone to help?'

Frank Brooker shook his head. 'All the good chaps are with other yards this time of year and I couldn't afford to pay anyone anyway, even part-time.' He slapped a section of guardrail still to be varnished. 'As it is, what time I've got has to be spent on this old girl. At least she brings in some profit.'

Jack took in *Nordic Princess*'s immaculate black hull, gleaming superstructure and the brass-ringed buff of her raked funnel. 'She certainly looks good.'

'Thanks. She takes a lot of work, but she's worth it.' Frank glanced at the quickly drying varnish and then at the setting sun. 'I'd love to show you round, Jack, but…'

'That's okay, I understand… some other day when it's convenient.' They needed to get home to Spike now anyway, but first Jack took out his wallet. 'How much do I owe you, Frank?'

But the tedium of financial matters had never been Frank Brooker's strong point and his lack of interest in the business-side of running a yard was probably the root of his present problems. He gave a dismissive wave. 'Don't worry for now, Jack. Just call in and settle up when you're next around…' he paused as an idea presented itself, '… in fact, why don't you both come along on our ghost cruise on Saturday evening. Then I could really show you the *Princess* in her element and… there's something I want to chat to you about anyway.'

Jack glanced at Audrey, got her beaming smile of approval and said, 'We'd love that, Frank.'

'Excellent. See you both then. We sail at seven.'

Ten minutes and they were driving out of the yard, Jack glancing behind at the dereliction that was Brookerboats. 'It'll be nice to go on a river-cruise with someone else at the wheel, but we'll certainly pay for our passage. Frank's got enough cash problems without giving away tickets.'

'Yes of course…' agreed Audrey, '… but I wonder what it is he wants to talk to you about?'

‘I wonder.’ Jack couldn’t even imagine, but Saturday evening would surely bring the answer.

*   *   *

Chapter Two

'Neatly done, skipper.' Casting off complete, Jack was back in the wheelhouse with Frank.

'Thanks to my good deckhand.' The yard-owner pushed his white-topped cap to the back of his head and smiled. 'Bit of a luxury having someone to handle the lines again, Jack. Just lately I've had to look after the for'ard ones while Jenny handled them aft.'

Jenny was the stewardess, a personable teenager in white uniform shirt and black trousers who, together with skipper Frank, half an hour earlier had cheerfully welcomed them all aboard for this Saturday evening's ghost cruise. While Audrey and the fifty-odd other passengers mingled about the deck, Frank, as promised, had taken Jack for a quick tour of the vessel, starting down below in the engine room, noisy with the big single diesel already turning its warming revs. Topsides again, they briefly looked into the wood-panelled saloon, where the clink of glasses and aroma of newly-percolated coffee was already drawing some passengers into its cosy interior. Finally, they went for'ard past the funnel and into the wheelhouse. Here, the immaculate tradition of varnished ship's wheel, brass clock and barometer, sat in sharp contrast to the modern necessities of engine instrumentation, VHF radio, public address and stereo systems. The shining brass of an engine-room telegraph seemed almost historical.

'I thought you had direct control of the diesel from here, Frank?'

'We do.' Frank pointed to the single-lever engine control, 'but when she was converted from steam, they obviously thought this too much a part of the old ship to remove and left it … and I'm right glad they did.' He gave the brass handle a couple of affectionate jingling "orders" before adding, 'Good job we don't have a manned engine-room now though. Hard enough to make ends meet with just us three crew without having to pay a black-gang as well.'

'So don't you have a deckhand?' asked Jack, who'd already noticed Frank checking the moorings himself.

'We did 'til a few weeks ago, but found we could make do and save a few quid.'

'I could handle the ropes tonight if it would help,' offered Jack.

Frank Brooker raised appreciative eyebrows. ‘Well, it would certainly ease my load, Jack, but I didn’t like to ask, when you’re here to relax.’

‘Sitting back doing nothing isn’t really my thing, Frank,’ explained the ranger without mentioning that a quick glance at the boat’s Station Bill, posted in the saloon, had shown the requirement for *four* crew on evening trips. He had no intention, this pleasant evening, of slipping into officialdom, but if he could help this hard-working owner stay within the letter of the law, so much the better. ‘Tell me what you want and I’ll be glad to do it.’

‘Right…’ Frank quickly explained the boat’s routine for getting underway and coming alongside, ‘… we don’t have the luxury of a bow-thruster, Jack, so we use the ropes to spring off and on just like they did in the old days.’ He glanced at his watch. ‘Five minutes to go… time for the passenger safety briefing. Where’s Rebecca?’

As if on cue, a young woman appeared at the wheelhouse door. Slim, black-haired and in her early thirties, she too was wearing uniform shirt and trousers, but radiating a poise and assurance that spoke of more than mere cabin duties. ‘Evening, skipper. Ready for me to do the briefing?’

‘Yes please, Rebecca, and meet Jack; he’s looking after the deck for us this evening.’

‘Good to meet you.’ Her smile was sincere and voice perfectly modulated, but even as she took the ranger’s hand, there was a glint of recognition in those big blue eyes that mirrored Jack’s own. No time now though for small talk. ‘Right, let’s get them briefed.’ Rebecca took a leadless microphone from the wheelhouse shelf and gave a short test transmission. ‘I’ll do it on the remote from the saloon; that way I can keep eye-contact with the passengers.’

‘Seems a competent girl,’ said Jack, as Rebecca disappeared back down the deck.

‘The best,’ agreed the skipper. He glanced towards the public-address microphone, hung just to one side of the wheel. ‘I hate having to talk on that thing, but Rebecca’s into acting and a natural at it, so she does all the announcements when she’s on board.’

And with that, the small speaker overhead crackled to life and that clear voice said, ‘Ladies and gentlemen, welcome aboard *Nordic Princess* for this evening ghost cruise. I’m Rebecca Smith, your ghost guide for this evening. We’ll be underway very shortly but, before then, I just want to give you a short safety briefing…’

Jack had to make an effort to listen to the full briefing, because he was still trying to recall just why this articulate girl seemed somehow familiar. Perhaps Audrey would know.

* * *

But his wife was also struggling to think why Rebecca Smith looked so familiar. Perhaps later there would be an opportunity to chat and find out where their paths may have crossed but, for now, with the boat underway, Rebecca was busy telling her intent audience something of Broadland's spooky history. Fascinating it was too, delivered with a combination of convincing sincerity and entertaining drama. With the evening shadows lengthening and *Nordic Princess* gliding between ever-expanding reedbeds, Audrey found herself captivated by these tales of ghost wherries, phantom soldiers and spectral voices. Being a staunch Anglican, she had always chosen to regard the paranormal as something to be accepted but not dabbled in. Of course, much of what Rebecca was regaling them with was pure local myth and superstition, but who, after all, wasn't secretly intrigued by the paranormal?

But this evening was meant to be just fun and, being on a boat, though just a few metres from the shore, did so effectively separate you from all the worries of day-to-day life. Audrey wished Jack could be here relaxing and enjoying the evening with her, but she knew just as surely that her husband would be more content in the wheelhouse with Frank. The change would do him good, she thought, as she made her way to the saloon bar and ordered a gin and tonic. Back on the main deck, she found a comfortable seat and sat back to enjoy the commentary as Rebecca, remote mike in hand, wandered amongst her fascinated audience, entertaining them with ghostly tales of each passing location.

'Just off to your starboard side,' she was saying now and pointing to a small patch of open bank between the reeds, 'is where a little old man has often been seen fishing. Not unusual on the Norfolk Broads, you might think, except that sometimes, when holiday-makers have waved to him, he's simply disappeared before their eyes. And not only that…' she continued, building up the ethereal atmosphere, '… many boats passing this spot have experienced unexplained incidents. I wonder,' she continued, in suitably ominous tones, 'what might happen to us tonight?' If there had been chit-chat before amongst passengers, there was certainly silence now, as the spot in question glided silently by. Only

Nordic Princess's diesel exhaust could be heard above the evening stillness and even that seemed to provide a fittingly sinister rumble as all on board waited for…

Suddenly, a shrilling blast broke the stillness, causing all to jump with fright, before dissolving into relieved laughter as everyone realised the source.

'Sorry folks; the skipper's just testing the boat's whistle,' explained Rebecca with a mischievous grin. 'Now, just coming up on the port side…'

* * *

'We always do that there,' explained Frank Brooker with a smile, taking his hand from the whistle cord. Hands back on the wheel, he turned a few spokes to ease *Nordic Princess* around the next lazy bend in the river.

'Well, it certainly got their attention,' chuckled Jack, who had been enjoying the commentary through the PA speaker in the wheelhouse. 'Young Rebecca can certainly spin a tale.'

'Which is all these haunting stories are really,' admitted Frank, 'but the public seem to enjoy them.' They were easing out of the turn now and heading up the next short reach. With *Princess* settled on her new heading, the skipper took his hands from the wheel and turned to Jack. 'Want to have a go?'

'Love to.' Jack took the wheel and gingerly made a few inputs, finding *Nordic Princess* a pleasingly responsive vessel, but also remarkably stable directionally and quite happy to pursue an arrow-straight course when left to her own devices. 'What a lovely old lady. She's a dream to handle.'

'Yeah, they knew how to build 'em those days.' The next sharper bend was fast-approaching and Jack wondered if Frank would be retaking the wheel, but the skipper nodded ahead and said, 'Take her round this next one, Jack, but remember there's a lot of stern swinging out there in the turn.'

'Right, I'll give her plenty of room.'

The distance from the bank was opening up slightly anyway as the river wound its way. Jack eased in some helm, at the same time glancing at the rudder indicator to ensure he wasn't over-steering into the turn. Slowly and surely, *Nordic Princess*'s bow followed the river's meander while the next short reach opened up before them.

'That's perfect, Jack…' Frank was glancing back to check their counter-stern was well clear of the bank, '… but you'll find she keeps swinging, so start taking wheel off sooner than you would in your launch.'

'Aye aye, sir.' Jack brought the wheel amidships and noticed how the bow kept turning a full point before even starting to stabilise on heading and, even then, required a little opposite rudder to get her running straight. There was only a short stretch of river ahead and already he was mentally planning the next turn to starboard but, before that, something else was catching his eye. 'She's still there.'

Ahead of them and still moored to the starboard bank, was the bright yellow *Fisher of Men*.

'You certainly can't miss that one,' joked Frank Brooker, shaking his head and laughing as they drew closer. 'Been there a while now. I wonder who owns her?'

'Some chap called Harold Searby.' Jack had duly checked the registration with head office. 'Apparently our rangers on the southern rivers knew him and his boat quite well. Seems he cruised those waters all year round doing gospel work, but now he's apparently made his way to this neck of the woods.'

'Ah well, a bit of divine help's no bad thing,' commented Frank with a grin as *Fisher of Men* passed by with no sign of her, seemingly curious, owner.

'Absolutely, but we don't want him setting up permanent moorings there.'

Throughout the Broads, many people, for various reasons, chose to live on boats. Some cruised continually, others kept their boats in marinas dedicated to "liveaboards", while just a few put down moorings on any remote bit of riverbank that took their fancy. It was the latter who were actively discouraged by the Broads Authority. Apart from contravening river by-laws, the reality was that some itinerants turned their patch of riverbank into an unsightly tip and, although *Fisher of Men* didn't appear to be in this category, she would need to be investigated just the same. 'I'm on duty Monday,' said Jack, glancing back at the boat now drawing fast astern and rocking slightly in their wake, 'so I'll pay Mr Searby a little visit.'

Perhaps there was a good reason for this unusual boat and its owner to be staying in that one spot. Next week he'd find out. For now Jack concentrated on the bend ahead that would bring them into the last long reach to the broad.

* * *

Audrey had also noticed *Fisher of Men* passing by and looked to see if this Harold Searby was on deck. He wasn't but, learning from Jack of his evangelical work, she'd already made up her mind that he must be a pretty decent type. She'd hoped that Jack would be similarly sympathetic, at the same time realising from long experience that anything deviating from "the norm" was always bound to rouse her husband's suspicion. Jack was the fairest man she had ever known and would bend over backwards to help anyone, but only after assuring himself that their intentions were definitely on the "straight and narrow". Hopefully, despite appearances, Harold would prove as such.

Now they were entering the big broad and Rebecca was telling them of a young soldier drummer boy who, in the Napoleonic Wars, had set off from his camp across the frozen water to see his sweetheart on the other side. He had never arrived and only after the thaw had his body been found in the water. Now local legend had it that in winter months his drumming could still be heard, mournfully disturbing the remote splendour of this bleak expanse. Everyone listened but, on this peaceful summer's evening, the only sound was their own wake breaking across the open broad and the squawking of a flight of greylag geese passing overhead.

But that mention of drumming had triggered Audrey's recall of where she'd previously known Rebecca. Soon they would be at the far end of the broad and have turned for home. Then she would have the chance for a chat with this vivacious girl and confirm her suspicions. She couldn't wait.

*　　*　　*

'Glad you like the old boat, Jack.'

'I think she's great, Frank.' Jack glanced across the expanse of this big broad and thought how different it looked from this slightly elevated position. On either side, bow and quarter waves rolled out across the gently rippling water. The boat herself was causing only a slight disturbance, and little noise other than the reassuring throb of her diesel. Apart from the odd cruiser lying at anchor and a solitary dinghy enjoying a late evening sail, there was little boat traffic to avoid and even the wildlife seemed to accept this mild intrusion with indifference. Jack looked across at *Nordic Princess*'s owner. 'I envy you, Frank.'

'Not my overdraft, you wouldn't.'

‘Things getting tight, are they?’ Jack never liked to enquire into the financial affairs of the boatyards, but Frank Brooker seemed as though he wanted to talk.

‘You could say that.’ He shook his head. ‘Hard times, Jack, and the banks aren’t helping. Not only are mine refusing to extend my overdraft, they’re also talking of calling in the loan I have on *Princess*.’

‘But she’s your only real money-maker,’ protested Jack. ‘Talk about biting off the hand that feeds them…’

‘I know, but the bank’s offloading all their risky investments and *Nordic Princess* is the only security I’ve got against mine.’

‘How about the yard? Surely that’s worth a lot…’

‘… if it wasn’t mortgaged up to the hilt as well.’ The despair in Frank’s voice was evident and Jack searched desperately for some comforting words of his own.

‘You need to get your hire-fleet out on the water again, Frank. Some cash coming in from the boats would surely make the bankers happier?’

The skipper nodded. ‘Probably, but getting them back into reasonable order would take a lot of manhours and, with no spare cash, hiring another hand is out of the question.’

‘I see your problem.’

‘There is one possible solution,’ hinted Frank in slightly hushed tones, ‘which is what I wanted to talk to you about…’

‘If it’s a loan, I don’t have that sort of money,’ Jack interrupted, wanting to lay his cards on the table before this owner’s hopes were falsely raised.

‘No, not that sort of help,’ assured Frank, anxious to avoid misunderstanding, ‘but, before I tell you what, I reckon we could both do with a good cup of tea. Normally the stewardess brings one up about now, but she’ll be pretty busy with this crowd on board, so if you’re happy with the boat?…’

‘I am if you are.’

‘Right… see you soon.’ And then he was gone leaving Jack wondering just what proposal Frank Brooker had in mind, but also very content to have this big boat to himself, conning it down the fairway as the sun began to set.

By the time they reached the far-end of the broad, it was almost dark, the lights of the village already twinkling beyond the encircling reedbeds. Along a short dyke lay several hire-cruisers, snug for the night beside the waterside pub, whose rustic charm was somewhat at odds with the live music within. Jack, however, was allowing none of this to distract him from the rather daunting task of turning *Nordic Princess* around.

He'd half-expected Frank to return to the wheelhouse for this critical manoeuvre, but there was still no sign of skipper or tea, so it seemed a case of just getting on with it. The marked channel widened slightly here, but it was still a reasonably confined area in which to turn a seventy-foot vessel through one-eighty degrees. With no twin screws or bow-thruster to help, the slower the better, thought Jack, as he pulled the engine control to STOP and then even further back to ASTERN. With a welter of churning wash coming from her reversed propeller, *Nordic Princess* gradually slowed until she was barely idling through the water. Back to STOP on the engine and, with the last of the way, Jack eased over to the far side of the channel. Time to turn. Luckily, no other boats were entering or leaving the public moorings, but he still gave two three-second blasts on the whistle before turning the wheel hard-a-port. HALF-AHEAD now on the engine and, slowly but surely, *Nordic Princess* turned in virtually her own length.

Three-quarters through the turn, Jack brought the wheel amidships and, as they steadied on homeward heading, Frank Brooker arrived back in the wheelhouse bearing two mugs of tea. Jack suspected he might just have been hovering there all along, and was thankful he hadn't disgraced himself.

'Nicely done, Jack.'

'It's certainly very satisfying.' Jack eased the throttle back up to cruising revs and soon they were parting the waters once more as they journeyed homeward.

'Well, relax now and enjoy your tea.' Frank put his own down on top of the instrument panel and once more took the helm. They were a quarter way back up the broad before he turned to the ranger and asked, 'So, how do you like working part-time?'

'It's okay. Lets me get a few jobs done at home…' Jack took a welcome swig of tea, '… but I'm not sure if that's a good thing or not.'

'I know what you mean.' Frank was long-divorced, no doubt a result, Jack suspected, of an undisguised preference for being in his yard rather than pottering at home. 'You're not ready for pipe and slippers yet, Jack, anymore than I am.' He was right there, but the ranger was still totally unprepared for Frank Brooker's next words. 'How would you feel about doing a bit of skippering on *Princess*?'

'Gosh.' So this was what this evening's activity had been leading up to. Frank had been casting his bait and Jack had well and truly taken the hook. But there were practicalities still to be considered, one being that skippering passenger boats required a Boatmaster Licence, something he had never needed in his

Navigation Ranger duties. 'It's a lovely idea, Frank, but I haven't got a ticket.'

'With your experience, we'd have you trained and qualified in no time.' Frank had obviously thought through this obstacle. 'A Merchant Navy medical, oral and practical test with the MCA and you'd be away. You'd also need a first-aid certificate, but I'm sure you've got that already.'

He had indeed; it was a requirement for all rangers on the Broads. But why was Frank asking him anyway? 'I thought skippering this boat was your whole life, Frank? You only run a couple of trips a week, so surely you can handle those?'

'I can, but I'd like to run more. And you're right, Jack, I do need to spend some time and effort on the hire fleet. The bank would certainly like to see those boats out earning cash again, but they need a lot of work first. If I had you skippering *Princess*, it would give me time to do just that.' Frank shrugged broad shoulders. 'There's not many I'd trust the old girl to, Jack, but I know you'd do a good job. I wouldn't be able to pay you much, but I think you'd find the work rewarding enough.'

'I wouldn't expect much if you accepted the cost of my training.' Jack glanced around *Nordic Princess*'s ample lines. 'A boat like this costs a lot to run, Frank.'

'Yep, but seeing how you handled her tonight, a few hours would be enough to get you ready.'

'Glad you think so…' Jack nodded in the direction of the passenger deck, '… but let me talk it over with Audrey first, and then get back to you.'

'When can you let me know?' Frank Brooker seemed anxious to know the way ahead.

Jack rubbed his forehead thoughtfully for a moment. 'I'll go and join Audrey now, talk to her over the rest of the weekend, and then call in on Monday and let you know.' He gave a reassuring smile. 'Can't think there'll be any objection.'

'Great.'

Yes, it certainly could be, thought Jack as he exited the wheelhouse and went in search of his wife.

* * *

He found her on the main deck talking to Rebecca Smith, now with time to socialise after her evening's narration and obviously happy to talk.

'Jack...' Audrey sounded pleased to have her husband join them, '… do you remember Rebecca?'

'Vaguely, but I can't remember where. The face is familiar, but...'

'... not the name.' The narrator smiled. 'You knew me as Beki Smith.'

'Of course!' exclaimed Jack, all the jigsaw pieces now slotting into place. 'You were Amy's best friend at university. We met you once when we came to visit Amy one weekend. That must have been about twelve years ago,' recalled Jack and how pleased they'd been that their youngest daughter had formed a friendship with this bright and confident extrovert. 'But why the name change?'

'Well when I took up acting, I thought that Rebecca Smith sounded better.'

'I can see that, but I hope you don't mind if I carry on calling you Beki,' said Audrey. 'We'd love to hear what you've been up to since you and Amy shared a room, wouldn't we, Jack? I sometimes wondered how you both found time to study English, what with Amy playing the drums in the jazz band and you so involved with the theatrical society.'

'So much so, that I let my studies slip and, much to my parents' annoyance decided to make acting my career. But, what of Amy? She was becoming a teacher, wasn't she?'

'Yes, and that's what she is,' answered Audrey with undisguised motherly pride. 'After her training, she managed to get a post in a London comprehensive and hopes she might soon be head of her year.'

'Good for her.' Beki seemed genuinely pleased for her old friend. 'I'm just sorry I lost touch with her. I expect she's married with her own family now?'

'No, still single,' answered Audrey with a slight downturn of her mouth. 'I don't think she ever quite trusted men again after university. She's had a few boyfriends, but nothing serious.'

'I don't blame her,' said Beki, attempting to put a more positive slant on that particular aspect. 'I'm still fancy-free myself.'

'But now a star of stage and screen?' asked Jack just little mischievously.

'I wish, but no fame or fortune yet, I'm afraid.' Beki shrugged. 'But I do belong to a small theatre group in Norwich and we rehearse and perform about five plays each year.' She glanced down at the microphone still in her hand. 'Narrating for Frank, together with serving in a small bistro, helps to pay the rent.'

'You certainly tell those ghost stories with great credibility. I suppose it's all to do with your training?'

Beki smiled. 'You're right, Jack. Of course most of my narration content is pure myth and legend, but I do have an interest in certain aspects of the spiritual world.'

'My goodness…' Audrey was a little taken aback at this revelation, '… you mean ghost-hunting and the like?'

'No, just a little semi-scientific aspect I dabble in for a hobby… but, acting is still my first love.' Beki obviously felt it was best not to dwell on her rather mysterious beliefs, and asked, 'Do you like the theatre, Audrey?'

'I used to, but we haven't been to a show for ages.'

'Then you must come and see one of our plays sometime.' Beki smiled and took a card from her shirt pocket. 'Check my website and both of you choose one you'd enjoy.'

'That would be lovely… we'd love to.' Audrey secretly hoped they'd be Jack's cup of tea, as he could be uncharacteristically caustic about some modern productions.

Beki looked around at other passengers, obviously wanting to chat with her. 'Oh well, I suppose I'd better go and do my PR bit.'

Audrey nodded. 'Of course, and I'll give Amy your love. I'll be phoning her tomorrow for our Sunday evening chat.'

'Better than that,' said Beki, nodding towards the card in Audrey's hand, 'give her my number and ask if she'd give me a ring. It would be nice to find out about the rest of our old gang. In fact,' she continued rather regretfully, 'we always said we'd have a reunion after ten years, but never did.'

'Sometimes I think the past is best left there,' cautioned Jack, knowing that not all Amy's memories of university days were happy ones. 'A lot's happened since you were students and people change over the years, and not always for the best.'

'Perhaps you're right, but I'd love to talk to Amy about old times.' Beki held out her hand. 'Lovely meeting you both again… Jack… Audrey… hope to see you again soon.'

And then Beki Smith was gone to meet the rest of her captivated audience.

* * *

Chapter Three

'You know, it's ages since we've been to the theatre. I'd love to go and see one of Beki's plays.' Audrey turned to her husband as he drove them home. 'And there's no need to pull a face like that; you might even enjoy it.'

Jack settled a little lower into his driving seat. 'I'm all for a bit of drama, Audrey, especially if it's a good mystery, but there's so much rubbish that critics seem to rave on about these days. It's all lost on me.'

'I agree,' conceded Audrey, ' but there is more to life than just crime-dramas.'

'Not love-in-a-mist, if that's what you're thinking,' grumbled Jack, searching for any good reason to avoid a wasted evening, 'because you won't find me at one of those.'

'In which case, I just might go on my own. And anyway, it would be more to support Beki. Like you said when we hired that boat from Frank Brooker, we need to help those who are struggling a bit.'

'Ah, well, I'm glad you mentioned that,' said Jack, welcoming this perfect lead for him to broach the yard-owner's idea, 'because we might be able to help Frank a little more than we thought. In fact, he wants me to start skippering for him.' Jack explained the proposal.

Audrey couldn't help an audible groan. 'So after all these years of working every day God gives, just as we start to have a little spare time together, you find another part-time job.' She turned her face to the outside. 'I can't believe you'd even consider it, Jack.'

'Yes you can, because you know me.' Jack gave his wife a sideways glance. 'This is such a great opportunity, Aud. I'd be doing something I'd enjoy and be keeping out from under your feet at the same time.'

'You mean it will keep you out of doing all those jobs I've got lined up for you around the house.' Audrey turned to look at her husband and gave a half-smile. 'All right, Jack, if it's something you really want to do, but just promise you won't be doing too many hours.'

'I'll have to clear it with the Authority anyway, first thing Monday before I see Frank to give him my answer.' Jack had never really doubted his wife's support. Audrey usually put up an initial token resistance to his schemes, but he knew that was only from her concern that he didn't overdo things. Now it was time to make concessions of his own. 'And I'll come with you to one of Beki's plays if that's what you'd like.'

'Thanks, Jack. A night out in Norwich will make a welcome change.'

'It'll certainly be a change,' agreed Jack with an inward groan, 'but I still can't get my head round a level-headed girl like Beki throwing up a university education to go on the stage. It seems such a waste.'

'Education is never wasted, Jack, and many really successful actors and comedians are graduates. She still seems a lovely girl, and I'm sure Amy will be delighted to make contact with her again. In fact,' said Audrey, fishing the mobile phone from her bag, 'I'll send her a text now with Beki's number so she can call her before our chat tomorrow.'

Jack gave his wife a wry smile, knowing full well that she'd want to hear all about the conversation between the two girls when she rang Amy on Sunday. And perhaps Audrey was right: making contact with her old friend again might just do Amy good. The fact was, he'd become increasingly concerned about his youngest daughter's well-being and wished she'd found someone special to share her life with, instead of devoting all her energy to work.

'There, I think she'll be glad to get that,' said Audrey as she pressed SEND.

Jack wasn't quite so sure, but didn't say. Besides, they were home now and Spike would be wanting his walk.

* * *

Amy Fellows was just finishing marking some pupil essays when she received her mother's text. It was unusual for her to be working on a Saturday evening, but it was that time in the school year when report writing and parents' evenings took over her life. The ring-tone from her mobile was a welcome distraction, but when she opened her mum's message she found it rather unsettling to read of her parents' meeting with her old friend. On the one hand, she felt it would be great to make contact with Beki again, as they really had hit it off and were pretty inseparable during their years at university; on the other, she worried that rekindling their friendship could well open old wounds that had taken many years to heal.

Amy sent a brief thanks to her mum, went into the small kitchen of her flat, and wondered what she should do next. As the coffee percolated, she weighed up her options. Beki had been a great support when she'd needed it and Amy had often felt guilty at not having kept in touch with her old room-mate. With her sister, Jo, a mother now and most of her friends and colleagues happily married with family ties, it would be good to spend time with someone who, she gathered from her mum's text, was similarly unattached. Her social life these days had all but dried up and, sad as it sounded, being asked out was usually an invitation to baby-sit. She certainly needed to get out of her present rut and renewing her friendship with Beki could help do just that. Perhaps it was time to put recriminations and bitterness behind her and move on.

Amy took her coffee back into the lounge and rang Beki Smith's number.

* * *

It was Sunday evening and Jack had just returned from walking Spike when he heard Audrey on the phone.

'… ah, here's your dad now… you can ask him yourself… Jack… Amy would like a word.'

Leaving their border collie in the kitchen, Jack joined his wife in the hall where she was just cupping her hands over the mouthpiece. 'She wants to ask you something.'

'Hi love, how you doing?'

'Fine thanks Dad.' Amy sounded bubbly. 'What a coincidence, you meeting Beki like that. I've already been in touch and we want to get together again.'

'That's great. When?'

'Soon. In fact, we're going to organise the reunion of all our old gang, just as we'd planned to do when we graduated.'

'What, all of them?'

Yes, Dad… all of them.'

'What, including Alistair?'

'Yes, including Alistair.'

'After what he did to you?' Amy was in her thirties now, but Jack still felt protective of his younger daughter and the last thing he wanted was to see her hurt again. 'Won't a reunion be a bit… well, awkward?'

But surprisingly, his daughter seemed quite reconciled to the prospect of moving forward and putting the past behind her. 'Oh, Dad, there comes a time when you have to let things go, and us all meeting up again could be the time to do just that…' she paused slightly before adding, '… and Beki thinks so too.'

'Yes, but surely Alistair will want to bring Clarissa with him.'

'Probably, but there'll be the rest of the gang, which will kind of water down any lingering emotions.'

'Okay, if you're happy, Amy, go for it.' Jack knew that when his daughter's mind was made up, then all he could do was try and support her decision. That just left the logistics to be decided on. 'So, where are you planning to hold this reunion?'

'Well… that's what I wanted to talk to you about, Dad. Beki and I both agree it should be something completely different from the usual old pub-and-nightclub thing, so, as she now lives close to you, we thought, how about a week afloat on the Broads?'

'On a boat… all of you in close confines for seven days… is that wise, love?'

'I can't see why not, Dad. At least we'll have other things to occupy us besides the past, and if I'm going to drive out old demons, then it'll certainly be a case of kill-or-cure.'

Hopefully not the former, thought Jack before voicing other practicalities. 'The thing is, Amy, as you know only too well, once the schools break up, all the hire fleets will be totally booked up. You'll be lucky to find a boat.'

'Ah, well, I thought that's where you might help, Dad. You know the yards and perhaps one might have a boat free to hire to a group of six reasonably responsible adults.'

Even as she said it, Jack was turning over an idea. 'I might, but can't promise. When do you need to know?'

'As soon as you can, Dad. We need to get contacting the other four, but not before we have something firm to offer.'

'Okay, leave it with me and I'll see what I can do. I'll call you tomorrow.'

'Thanks, Dad… you're a gem.'

An idiot, more like, thought Jack, as he rejoined Audrey in the kitchen.

She paused from laying the evening meal. 'Well, do you think you can help her?'

'Possibly, but I'm not convinced the whole thing is such a good idea. I'm surprised Amy sounds so upbeat at the prospect. I just hope she's thought it through and it doesn't all end in tears.'

'So do I.' Fate can often lead in strange directions, thought Audrey. Sometimes you had to follow to find out where.

*   *   *

Chapter Four

The sun was well up next morning by the time Jack eased his patrol launch into Brookerboats' basin. There was no space to moor but Frank, seeing the launch gliding in, emerged from his workshop and secured it alongside one of the sailing boats. Jack climbed across and joined the yard-owner on the jetty. Frank seemed glad to see him.

'Thanks for coming, Jack. Time for coffee, so come and have a chat.'

'Sounds good.'

Jack followed the owner into the wooden shed that comprised the entire yard's working space. Most was open workshop leading down to a slipway but, apart from some stored dinghies looking as rundown as the rest of Frank's fleet, and a miscellany of boat gear, it was virtually empty. Jack was steered to a partitioned-off cubbyhole that obviously served as kitchen-cum-messroom. There was a sink, refrigerator and, atop a sideboard, an electric kettle and some coffee-stained mugs.

'Not exactly the Ritz I'm afraid,' apologised Frank as he flicked on the kettle and hastily rinsed a couple of mugs under the tap.

'I like things simple.' While the kettle was building a head of steam, Jack eased himself onto a rough wooden bench along one side and stretched out his legs. 'First things first, Frank. I've discussed your proposal with Audrey and also had a chat with the chief ranger this morning, and the result is, I'd like to go ahead and accept.'

'That's great, Jack. Just what I hoped you'd say.' Frank left his coffee-making to shake the ranger's hand with obvious gratitude. 'When do you want to start training?'

'I'm on duty until Thursday; how about we get cracking then?'

'Suits me.' Frank pointed out his idle hire fleet in the basin. 'Doesn't look as though I'll be working on them just yet.'

'Ah, well, that's something else I wanted to ask you, Frank.' Jack explained daughter Amy's call of the previous night and her wanting to hire a six-berth cruiser for the last week in July. 'How about one of yours, Frank?'

Frank Brooker, scratched his head. 'I'd love to, Jack, but getting one ready would be the problem. The only six-berther I've got is *Brookside*, and she needs a good few week's work to bring her up to scratch. What with maintaining and operating *Princess*, plus getting you trained up, I just wouldn't have the time.'

'What does she need?' asked Jack, disappointed at his idea falling at the first hurdle. 'I'll still be patrolling three days a week, but if it's just a bit of cleaning and varnish work, I could come and put in a couple of extra days.'

'Good of you to offer,' said Frank, shaking his head, 'but, besides getting the boat half-decent, there's the engine to reassemble.' He nodded to a workshop bench where a large marine diesel lay in confusing disarray. 'I've done the overhaul, but never had time to get it together and back in. If you reckon you could do that...'

He was stopped by Jack's upheld hand. 'Sorry, but that's way out of my league. Is there no-one else who could do the work, Frank? Surely the money you'll get for the week's hire would enable you to pay for some temporary help *and* you'd be left with at least one hire-boat smartened up and available for the rest of the season. It's a time when holidaymakers are looking for late deals and, with most boatyards fully booked, you could be quite busy... and it might keep the bank off your back as well.'

'Yes, I know...' the yard owner seemed genuinely regretful, '... but the really busy period starts in a week or so and all the yards are crying out for good hands...' he glanced again at his rundown premises, '... and they can offer a season's employment, which is more than I can do right now.'

'Well, think about it and if you can find a way...' Jack glanced at his watch. 'Time for me to get going and have that chat with the owner of *Fisher of Men*. In the meantime, Frank, have you anything I can be reading up for my ticket?'

'I'll have a look. It won't take long to get you trained, so get your medical done and then bang in your application for the test.' Frank glanced towards the other small shack that served as his office. 'I've got the forms there somewhere, but it'll take me a while to ferret them out.'

'That's all right. I'll call back on my return run.' Jack swigged back the dregs of his coffee and put his mug in the sink. 'Thanks for the coffee, Frank, and don't come out; I can get myself away.'

Five minutes and he was back onto the main river, disappointed his meeting hadn't sorted Amy a boat and Brookerboats some much-needed income. Jack looked back towards the yard, where the dilapidated shed stood as disconsolate as the weatherworn boats outside. If things didn't change soon, Frank wouldn't have a fleet to worry about anyway.

*   *   *

Fisher of Men still lay where Jack had last seen her, but this time Harold Searby was topsides, his gaunt figure bent over a mop as he washed down the cabin roof. Realising the ranger's launch was coming alongside, he came down to deck level, caught the thrown lines and secured them to his own well-worn cleats. Jack quickly followed.

'Good morning, Mr Searby.' Even as he made his greeting, Jack was glancing about *Fisher of Men* and finding her surprisingly well cared for. The boat was obviously old and much used, but fresh paint, coiled ropes and clean decks spoke of an owner who took pride in his craft, if not in himself. He stood before Jack now, his gangling frame and slightly stooped body as tired-looking as the clothes hanging from it. Was it a look of fear or suspicion that seemed to flicker across his gaunt face as the ranger held out a hand? 'Jack Fellows… Broads Authority.'

'Harold… Harold Searby.' The voice carried just a hint of Norfolk accent and an indefinable refinement at odds with the rough-skinned hand being offered back. 'I guess you're here to tell me to move on.'

'If you can.' Jack sensed this man was not one to loiter in any place for long. 'Is there a problem?'

'I'm afraid there is.' He nodded down to the machinery space hidden below the aft deck they were standing on. 'Water in the gearbox. I moored here, intending it to be for just one night, but when I did my routine checks the next morning, the dipstick came up grey. I think the tube stack's corroded and leaking water. I'd probably ruin the complete box if I tried to run her.'

'Hmm, bad news.' Jack paused while a cruiser went churning past, its wash cascading against *Fisher of Men*'s yellow hull while the lines to the rhond anchors slackened and tightened with the resulting pitch and roll. 'Can I tow you somewhere to get it fixed?'

'Where?' There was an edge of despair in Harold Searby's voice, as he held out his hands in a gesture of hopelessness. 'I'd only be stuck wherever you took me. I've no money to pay for any permanent mooring or the parts to repair the box.'

'So, what do you plan to do?'

'I'm not sure.'

Jack looked again at the despondent figure before him. 'When did you last eat?'

'A couple of days ago. Boat supplies ran out and with no tender to fetch or cash to pay anyway, I…'

Jack stopped him there. 'Harold, I've got some lunch and a flask of coffee on the launch. If I bring them onboard, will you share them with me? My wife always packs far too much for just one.'

'You sure? That would be really kind of you, Mr Fellows.' There was a glint of hope in his eyes now. 'God bless you.'

Jack smiled to himself, feeling pleased that this simple gesture was so gratefully received. 'You go down and I'll get the grub.'

Harold Searby was laying plates and mugs on a varnished wooden table when the ranger joined him in the saloon. There were fitted couches either side of the table, decorated with embroidered cushions and covered by colourful throws. Harold slid easily onto one couch while Jack squeezed somewhat more tightly onto the other before opening his lunch box and placing it between them. 'Help yourself, old chap. I've a medical coming up and I need to lose a few pounds, so you'll be doing me a favour.'

Hungry as he was, Harold Searby paused for a second to give a brief prayer of thanks, before tucking into this manna from heaven with the eagerness of a man unfed for days, and with little breath for talk to its provider opposite. Jack didn't mind, it gave him time to take in the character of this singularly unique craft and the clues it gave of her equally unusual owner.

Fisher of Men's interior was largely open-plan. Right for'ard was a pair of vee-berths with a folded sleeping bag on the one that was obviously Harold's. Only some open bookshelves separated this from the rest of the living area where the unlit potbelly stove filled most of the remaining space. Along one side, the galley comprised cupboards, a sink and a small hob. Hanging from the deckhead above it were pots and pans, all as spotless as the rest of the beautifully varnished, wood-lined interior.

'You keep a smart boat, Harold.'

The owner nodded between mouthfuls. 'She's all I've got, so I have to look after her.'

Jack poured coffee into the two mugs. 'But any boat costs money to run. You must have some income?'

'I have a small monthly allowance and the public are also very kind.' He took a sip of coffee and gave an appreciative sigh. 'I hold gatherings around the Broads and invite an offertory afterwards.'

'Yes, I've heard you're something of an evangelist along these waterways.' Jack had been scanning the contents of Harold's bookcase where well-thumbed copies of 'Practical Boatbuilding' and 'Marine Diesel Maintenance' rubbed shoulders with 'Christian Environmental Ethics' and 'The Perception of Worship'.

'Yes, I try and spread the Lord's word.' Harold put down his mug and smiled for the first time, an expression warm and sincere. 'Giving thanks for creation is an easy thing to do in such a beautiful setting, Mr Fellows.' He glanced outside to where the morning sun glinted off the water, now rippling in the freshening breeze. 'If I'm to cruise around these blessed waters, then preaching and spreading God's word as I go, gives purpose to my life.'

'But you must get a bit of agro from some?' sympathised Jack.

'A little, but you have to learn to be thick-skinned. On Sunday evenings, I always stop at busy moorings and hold a small service with plenty of singing with actions for the youngsters, and usually a short Bible story with a prayer to finish. It's surprising how many holidaymakers get drawn in and end up feeling a sense of spirituality. It's not hard to convince folk of the wonders of creation when you're in the beautiful unspoilt surroundings of Broadland.'

Jack smiled and nodded to the guitar lying on the spare berth. 'Which is where that comes in?'

'Yes, and many other people bring out instruments once we get singing.'

Jack poured another coffee for himself. 'And how long have you been living this life, Harold?'

'Ten years… I think. Perhaps longer, but I had an accident, bashed my head and lost my memory.'

'What… all of it?'

'Completely. When I came round, I couldn't remember a single thing, and still can't. My former life's a complete mystery to me and I have a strong inner feeling it's best I leave it that way.'

'That's awful.' Jack looked keenly into this extraordinary man's honest eyes. 'Aren't you in contact with anyone from your past life?'

Harold shook his head. 'No-one at all, sadly.'

'You say you have a small monthly allowance,' probed Jack, increasingly intrigued by this strange tale. 'Has that been given to you since you lost your memory?'

'Yes, that's the strange thing. A largish sum was deposited into an account in my name soon after I regained consciousness, and a certain amount is transferred from it into my current account each month by banker's order.'

'So, who put it there and arranged the monthly payments?'

'The bank doesn't seem to know from their records,' replied Harold, 'and I'm loathe to look into the source too deeply in case it throws up any skeletons from my past.'

'I know it's none of my business, but don't you wonder who this apparent benefactor was?' probed Jack. 'Could it be an anonymous donation towards your evangelical work?'

Harold pushed away his empty plate. 'Of course I've been curious. I only take a few pounds in my collection and some kind souls sometimes make a more-generous offering… someone even gave me this,' he said, fingering the gold crucifix that hung on a chain around his neck, 'but nothing like that.'

Jack raised questioning eyebrows. 'If you don't mind me asking, was it a lot of money?'

'Yes.' Harold Searby shrugged thin shoulders. 'The initial deposit was twenty-five thousand pounds. When interest rates were reasonable, that managed to sustain monthly payments of two hundred. That's still what's transferred, but over the years the capital has dwindled to almost nothing.' He shrugged again. 'As you can see, I live pretty frugally and with no debts, but a technical disaster with the boat like now, leaves me pretty destitute.'

'Hmm. Do you know if you were involved with the church before you lost your memory, Harold?'

'I don't know, but one evening I happened to be walking past a church and heard such joyful singing coming from inside that I felt an overwhelming urge to take part in the service. It was the moment that changed my life.'

'And now here you are, a committed Christian spreading the Word, but living on a shoestring. I can certainly sympathise with your plight.' Jack paused. 'Just out of interest, how old are you, Harold?'

'Forty-five.'

'You look younger.' In spite of Harold's lifeworn appearance, Jack would have put him at nearer mid-thirties but, whatever his age, here he was, trying to make his own way in the world, and finding himself in a situation in which he could see no solution. But perhaps there was one, be it only temporary. 'It's obvious that you know a thing or two about boats, Harold. I don't suppose you'd consider doing some temporary work in a boatyard and earning some cash that way?'

'I'd be happy to, but the yards these days have to be careful who they employ.' Harold glanced down at his tattered shirt and stained corduroy trousers and stroked his ungroomed beard. 'Let's face it, Mr Fellows, I look a tramp, have no insurance card, work documents or any tax history. What yard would touch a vagrant like me?'

'Well, there might be just one,' said Jack, pausing to tip out the few remaining titbits from his lunch box. 'Sorry that there's not more to leave you, but I'll come back tomorrow and tow you in.'

'Where?'

'Not far,' said Jack without disclosing the idea fast-forming in his head, 'but hopefully we might solve a problem for more than just you and your boat.'

*　　*　　*

'Take him on as a yardhand?' Frank Brooker took off his well-oiled cap and scratched the back of his head. 'I'm not sure about that, Jack. From what you say, this bloke Searby sounds a bit of a nutter. I know I need some help in the yard, but having some religious fanatic is going a bit far.'

'Believe me, beneath that rough-looking exterior, he's a decent chap.' They were standing by *Nordic Princess* on which Frank had been working until the ranger motored back into the basin. Jack could understand his reticence: Norfolk boatyard owners were more suspicious than police when it came to folks outside the norm. 'I'm sure he won't push religion at you and…' Jack indicated Frank's paint-stained overalls and oily hands, '… since when have posh clothes been a priority in Broadland boatyards anyway?'

Frank smiled. 'True, but I could only pay him peanuts until some cash starts to flow again.'

'That'll be fine. Make room for him to have a free mooring here in the basin and use him to work on *Brookside* so you can hire her out to Amy and her gang and then, in his spare time, he can work on his own gearbox problem.' Jack nodded towards the boatshed. 'I'm sure in that heap of junk you call a store, there must be the parts he needs. Let him have them in lieu of proper wages.'

Frank nodded vague agreement. 'Put like that, it does make sense, Jack. And some cash coming in from the hire-fleet would certainly help keep the bank off my back.'

'You might even be able to start paying off that overdraft if Harold stays on to work on your other boats and gets them earning their keep as well,' suggested Jack cementing his argument. 'A chap like him won't be here for ever but, by that time, I should be skippering *Princess* and you'll then have the time to take over the work yourself.'

'Right…' Frank Brooker had made his decision, '… if you vouch for him, Jack, I'll give it a try.'

'Great, I'll tow him in tomorrow.' A few problems solved and now Jack glanced towards the shed. 'You said you'd find those forms for me, Frank.'

'Yep, let's get them. I have a few manuals you might find helpful as well.'

He led the way to the office, a shed within the shed, and somehow typical of his yard. It contained just one desk, two chairs and a battered filing cabinet from which Frank removed the promised forms. Jack could understand why it had taken the morning to find them. Strewn over every surface lay discarded letters, uncompleted returns and other tedious paperwork long unfiled. From the stained wooden partition walls, faded photos of the yard's old fleet looked down with seeming distaste. 'I saw those manuals the other day,' said Frank, thumbing through a pile of old books on the floor. While he searched, Jack's attention wandered to the office ceiling from which hung the models of two aircraft. One was of an old First World War biplane and the other, a gull-winged fighter of the Second.

'Did you make these?' asked Jack, gently touching the tail of the one nearest to him.

Frank looked up from his book-search and laughed. 'Oh them… yes. They're about the nearest I come to aircraft these days, but they do remind me of that other part of my life.'

'You mean you were in aviation at some time?'

Frank stood up and threw a couple of dog-eared manuals onto the desk. 'Yep, Fleet Air Arm. As a boy I grew up in this yard, but was always fascinated by anything that flew. Dad wanted me to come into the business, of course,' Frank briefly scanned the dereliction that was Brookerboats, 'but I was dead keen to be near aircraft so, much against his wishes, as soon as I left school I went into the navy and trained as an aircraft fitter.' He gave a resigned sigh. 'In some ways, they were the best days of my life.'

'So, why did you leave?'

'For Mum actually. Dad died suddenly and she needed me back here to take over, and here I've stayed, through marriage, family, and divorce while I struggled to keep the place going.'

'There are worse lives, Frank,' said Jack, wishing to bring the conversation back onto a more positive note.

But, Frank wasn't to be so easily appeased. 'I guess, but I could still lose it all yet.'

'Not if we turn your fortunes around by getting that fleet out on hire again.'

'All we can do is try. With your backing and encouragement, the future does seem a little more hopeful.' Frank forced a smile, picked up some manuals and handed them across. 'Here you are, Jack... something to study for your test.'

Jack looked down at the works on marine legislation and regulation. 'Not my first choice of bedtime reading, but I'll get my head down.'

'Good. Make sure you know your lights and collision regulations; the MCA examiner is hot on those.'

'Right.' Jack took a final look at the models. 'Who knows, Frank, get you back into the black with the bank and you could have your own aircraft flying one day.'

'We're more likely to see pigs flying first.' The yard owner shook his head. 'As things stand, I'll just be glad to keep what I've got.'

*   *   *

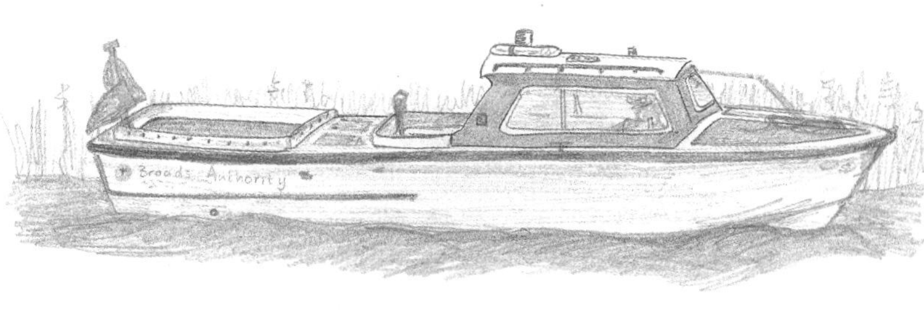

Chapter Five

'Well, is she happy now?' Jack closed the manual he'd been studying and thankfully transferred attention to his wife who'd just come off the phone after a good thirty-minute session with Amy.

'Yes, delighted, especially as Frank is going to give them a special rate for the week.'

'Which is more than I would have done,' admitted Jack with a grunt. 'I know Amy and Beki don't have a lot of cash to throw about, but I bet those lads are all pretty flush now. There's that Oliver Stanhope. Isn't he an MP?'

'Yes, and Spencer Ovington, the one who studied aeronautics, is now an airline captain who, according to Beki, lives on a barge and sails in his spare time.'

'Good, so he'll be a useful hand on *Brookside*,' said Jack, '... assuming it's ready for them, that is.'

'I thought it was all sorted now, with Harold Searby working for the yard.' Audrey was a little dismayed that there could still be doubts in this well-laid plan. 'It will *have* to be ready, Jack. We don't want Amy and her friends let down.'

'I'm sure it will be,' reassured her husband. 'I towed *Fisher of Men* into Brookerboats this morning.' He gave a little chuckle. 'You should have seen Frank's face when that scarecrow jumped ashore, but he soon warmed to him after Harold straightway wirespliced a new shroud onto one of the half-deckers. Searby knows his boats and I left him and Frank going over the work needing to be done on *Brookside*. Don't worry, Aud, she'll be ready.'

'I hope so.' Audrey sank onto the sofa beside her husband. 'You say that's the only six-berth boat Frank's got?'

Jack nodded. 'Yep, which should be perfect. Amy says there'll be six of them, assuming everyone comes.'

'That's right. She's going to telephone Spencer and Beki will call Oliver.'

'So who will call Alistair Hepscott?' asked Jack, raising a question he knew his wife had been diplomatically avoiding. 'Surely Amy won't want to.'

'She won't have to Jack, and as Beki doesn't really want to speak to him either, she's going to ask Oliver to do the dreaded deed.'

'Why have Hepscott along anyway if no-one really wants to see him?'

'Because that's the idea of reunions, Jack. To bury old hatchets and reminisce about the good times. Amy's been carrying this particular baggage for too long now and she's hoping that seeing him again will finally bring closure.'

'... or open up old wounds. And presumably, they're going to invite that wife of his, Clarissa, as well?'

'Of course. She *was* one of the gang, Jack, but I'm certain we're worrying unnecessarily. She's probably got more children by now, and she won't want to come away without them so, hopefully, Alistair will have the sense to make an excuse to back out as well,' persisted Audrey, well aware this was all a sore subject with her husband. 'You can't expect a man to leave his wife at home.'

'I'd leave them both at home,' replied Jack, with feeling. 'Clarissa knew how much Amy loved Alistair, but that didn't stop her seducing him away at the first opportunity.'

'They were all just young, Jack. Young love always comes with its share of pain.'

And it *was* all twelve years ago, conceded Jack to himself. Was he being unreasonably harsh? He threw the manual onto the coffee table. 'Let me get this right, Aud. Our Amy and this economics student Alistair Hepscott were in love and, from the way I understood it, about to get engaged. Then comes the time for final exams and both decide not to see each other while they hit the books. Very wise, except Alistair is studying figures other than the ones in his textbooks.'

Audrey flinched a little at her husband's recall. 'That's one way of putting it, Jack, but do you have to be so blunt?'

'Yes, if it makes things clear. And it all came to light because Beki Smith, who wasn't too bothered about her own revision, went to a nightclub and caught two-timing Alistair with fellow-student Clarissa.'

'... being somewhat intimate,' agreed Audrey.

'*Extremely* intimate,' Jack emphasised. 'So intimate, in fact, that he got Clarissa pregnant.'

'Well, obviously they didn't know that then,' pointed out Audrey. 'That only came out later.'

'... after Beki had finally had the courage to tell Amy what she'd seen.' Jack shook his head. 'Thank goodness she waited until after the exams. At least Amy came out of all this with a good degree...'

'... but also a broken heart,' completed Audrey sadly. 'It was a terrible shock for her, Jack, and it wouldn't have been so bad if Alistair hadn't denied everything and pleaded with her to give him another chance.'

'I'm glad she didn't, although at the time, I was disappointed it didn't work out.' Jack sat back into the sofa. 'Until then, I actually liked Alistair. He certainly had charm and manners.'

'As you'd expect, being the son of a lord.' It was Audrey's turn to sigh. 'I had great dreams of our Amy eventually being Lady Hepscott.'

'She never would have been though.' It was time for Jack to make a small confession. 'I did run a check when Amy started to get serious. Lord and Lady Hepscott never had any children of their own and adopted Alistair when he was just a baby.'

'Well, well, you kept that under your hat, Jack. I presume that means he hasn't inherited the title,' deduced Audrey with just a little humph of satisfaction, before turning sharply to her husband. 'Did you run a check on all of your daughters' boyfriends?'

'Only those who seemed a bit too good to be true,' Jack admitted with a shrug of his shoulders. 'But anyway, Amy didn't have another serious boyfriend after that.'

'Poor girl. She just didn't want to be hurt again,' admitted Audrey regretfully.

'Presumably, Alistair checked the child really was his?' asked the always-sceptical Jack, who'd disliked Clarissa even before her deceit against Amy.

Audrey nodded. 'Oh yes. Apparently Lord Hepscott insisted on DNA checks and they confirmed it. Alistair admitted that to Amy... said he still didn't want to marry Clarissa, but that the family put pressure on him to avoid any scandal.'

'Serves him right,' said Jack unsympathetically. 'But Clarissa certainly did all right for herself, didn't she, getting a husband with an up-and-coming career in his father's bank. Bankers, I wouldn't trust one of them, the greedy...'

'... we won't go into that, Jack,' interrupted Audrey, 'and from what I've heard since, Alistair's rise in the bank has been purely on his own exceptional ability. According to the papers, when Lord Hepscott died year ago, Alistair was actually tipped to become chief executive.'

'... with Clarissa enjoying everything that money can buy, while our Amy lives alone in a one-bedroom flat.'

'Now, don't be bitter, Jack. We mustn't begrudge others their happiness. Who knows? Amy may have had a lucky escape.' Audrey glanced at the clock. 'How about an apple with some cheese and biscuits before we go to bed? It'll help us unwind.'

'Great, but just the apple for me, love.'

Audrey looked taken aback. 'Are you sure?'

'Absolutely. I've got a medical next week for my ticket. I rang the surgery this afternoon.' Jack patted his increasing girth. 'Seven days to get fit.'

It'll take a bit longer than that, thought Audrey with a smile as she headed for the kitchen.

* * *

'Who was that?'

In her Kensington town-house, Clarissa Hepscott looked up from the pages of a society magazine, shifted her ample weight just slightly, and contemplated her husband over designer reading glasses. She'd assumed it must be another call from their legal advisor and, these days, any such conversation usually left Alistair distracted and unapproachable. But this time he'd returned from his study looking more sanguine than she'd seen him for weeks.

'It was someone I haven't spoken to for years: Oliver… Oliver Stanhope.'

'What, that bore in our year at university, who was always going on about putting the world to rights.' Clarissa made a point of going back to her magazine and merely muttered as an aside, 'He's an MP now isn't he?'

'Yes…' Alistair sat down in his chair to one side of the marble fireplace, '… politics always was his thing.' He glanced across to his wife. 'At least he did *something* with his education.'

But Clarissa missed the jibe completely. 'So, what did he want? Doubtless a contribution to one of his lame causes.'

Alistair smiled. ''No, actually it was to ask us to go on holiday with him.'

Clarissa looked up and lowered the glasses to the end of her nose. Alistair was sure she'd been born with a sneer, and the glare over the top of them was anything but benevolent. 'He wants… what?'

'For us to attend a reunion, a get-together with our old gang from uni. It's being organised by Amy Fellows and Beki Smith.'

'Good Lord…' Clarissa gave a contemptuous little laugh, '… and where are they going to have this happy little gathering?'

Alistair ignored the sarcasm and explained.

‘A boat… six of us… all sharing! My God!’ Clarissa threw the magazine onto the coffee table between them. ‘You said “no”, of course.’

‘No, I said we’d come… or, at least I would.’ Alistair sighed. ‘Why not? I’ve got the time now and an escape to the Norfolk Broads will at least put me out of arms-reach of lawyers and auditors.’

‘Well, that’s your own stupid problem, Alistair. If you were so keen to escape afloat, you should never have sold our cruiser.’

‘That gin-palace,’ responded her husband scornfully. ‘A million pound’s worth of bling and gloss that we seldom used. No, it’ll be nice to spend some time on a *real* boat again.’

‘Well, if you think I’m going to leave the comfort of my home to endure a week cramped on an old wooden hire cruiser with people I don’t like, then you can think again.’ Clarissa folded tanned arms. ‘If you’re so desperate for a holiday, then why don’t we go to our flat in Saint Tropez?’

‘Because we don’t *have* a “flat in St Tropez” anymore. Didn’t I tell you? The bank’s sold it.’

‘It’s what? It can’t.’ Clarissa was upright now. ‘That was ours.’

‘No it wasn’t, the bank put up the money… remember?’ Alistair was dismayed to find that he was almost enjoying shocking his wife. ‘And before you start complaining about leaving “my home”, you’d better get used to it.’ He waved his hand over the opulence of their London pad. ‘This is going on the market as well… and probably a good thing. It’s way too big for us anyway…’ He paused before giving the knife another twist, ‘… it’s not as though we have any children.’

Clarissa swallowed back the nearest she ever came to a tear. ‘So… what about the cottage in the Cotswolds?’

‘That too.’

‘And you’re just going to sit back and let it happen, Alistair?’ The shock of these revelations had dented even Clarissa’s abundant self-possession. ‘Surely you could do a deal, where you surrender your golden handshake in exchange for my… our homes?’

‘There won’t be any “golden handshake”, Clarissa.’ Alistair kept his eyes fixed on his wife’s. He wanted there to be no misunderstanding here. ‘After what’s happened and all the other furore over bankers’ bonuses, there’ll be nothing for me except…’ he lowered his eyes to fingers he noticed were just very slightly trembling, ‘… a possible gaol sentence.’ But this was not the time to show weakness in front of his wife. Alistair shook away the thought and made an effort to brighten. 'So, it's off to Norfolk. It'll be good to see the old gang again and talk about something other than money.'

'I expect it will… like that Amy Fellows.' Clarissa's eyes had hardened again. 'And don't try to pretend that you don't still carry a flame for her. I know how close you two were.'

'Until you wrecked it!' Alistair was half out of his chair before getting a grip on his emotions. He sank back, deflated by the pain of memories he could never quite put behind him. 'And don't be ridiculous, it's twelve years since I last saw Amy.'

'So you tell me.' Clarissa picked up her magazine again in a show of contempt. 'And don't look forward to enjoying taking up where you left off either, Alistair, because, against my better judgement, I shall be coming too, just to keep an eye on you.' She pushed her glasses back up. 'It's probably the last holiday we'll have together for a long time anyway.'

It certainly will, thought Alistair, leaving the room and all the tension close contact with Clarissa always engendered. She was right about one thing though: he *was* looking forward with all his heart to seeing Amy Fellows again.

*   *   *

Spencer Ovington was deep into the theoretical intricacies of CFM 56-5C turbofan engines when his mobile rang.

'Spencer… it's Amy Fellows here… do you remember me?'

He did indeed, and with that recognition went any irritation at having his studies interrupted.

'Amy… good grief… of course I do… what a surprise after… what… twelve years?'

'Yes, too long, but it's good to talk to you again, Spencer. I hope I'm not interrupting anything?'

'Not at all, Amy. I'm glad of a break from what I'm doing. I've got a technical exam in a few days and was just swatting up on the manuals.'

'Yes, Beki told me you were an airline pilot now. Sounds the perfect job for you, Spencer. I remember how flying in the University Air Squadron was your first love when we were students, so it's great you managed to make it your career.' Already Amy was finding this catching up an intriguing business. 'Is this exam something you have to do regularly?'

'No, thank goodness. Up until now I've been flying Airbus A320s, but I got my captaincy about three years ago, and now the company has selected me to upgrade to A340-300s… if any of that means anything to you,' he finished off with a chuckle.

'Not really,' admitted Amy. 'They're all just planes to me that other people go on holiday in.'

'I suppose it's "horses for courses", Amy. Weren't you going to be a teacher?'

'Yes, and now I'm hoping to be made head of year at the London comprehensive I'm teaching at.'

'You've done well then.' Spencer pushed his manual even further away. 'We ought to catch up properly some time.'

'Ah, well, that's why I'm ringing.' Amy went on to explain the plans for a reunion.

'Sounds a great idea,' enthused Spencer. 'I'd certainly love to see you again, and… I suppose… the others. When are you planning this for?'

Amy gave the dates and immediately Spencer was flicking through his crew roster. 'Should be okay. I'll have my training completed by then, before I start flying these big beasts on the line, so a week's break in between would probably do me good.'

'What a life,' laughed Amy. 'It must be wonderful flying around the world at someone else's expense. Do you go far?'

'Australia, Hong Kong, Singapore and the like which is pretty "far", I guess.'

'That's about as far as you *can* go! The tube into The City once a month is as adventurous as I get these days,' Amy admitted. 'Compared to your globetrotting, Spencer, wandering around the Broads for a week is going to seem a pretty mild adventure.'

'Not at all,' assured the pilot. 'In fact, I've always wanted to visit the area to look up something for myself.'

'Oh, what's that?' asked Amy, intrigued.

'Just a bit of family history, but I'll tell you more when I see you.' There was certainly a note of enthusiasm in Spencer's voice. 'What sort of boat are we going to be in? Sail or motor?'

'A very old motor one,' confessed Amy, afraid her description so far hadn't done much to inspire confidence, and knowing Spencer must be used to far greater luxury than he'd find on this trip. 'You actually live on a boat, don't you?'

'Yes, an old Dutch barge so, you see Amy, I'm all for traditional boats.'

'Well, this is traditional alright,' she chortled. 'From what Dad says, I reckon Noah must have got his hand in on this before building the Ark.'

Spencer laughed. Amy had always been able to do that: make him laugh and take life a little less seriously. She'd also been one of the few to realise that, when it came to girls, his confident exterior was cloaked by the curse of shyness. Otherwise, he might have asked… Spencer steeled himself to confront an issue often clouding his memories of those bittersweet days. 'But how about you Amy? You must be married by now. Who's the lucky man?'

'There isn't one. I'm still on my own.'

'Really…' Spencer sounded pleased, '… like me.'

'… and Oliver,' continued Amy. 'He's coming too.'

'Great!' Spencer had liked this other member of their gang, who shared many of his interests, if not his lack of interest in politics, '… though, I'm surprised he can get away from constituency matters.'

It was Amy's turn to laugh. 'The House of Commons will be in their summer recess by then,' she explained. 'Beki managed to catch him tonight between late-sittings.'

'Beki Smith? She was a good friend to you, wasn't she? Your best, in fact, apart from…'

'… Alistair Hepscott. It's all right, Spencer,' soothed Amy. 'I can say his name now without getting upset.'

'Ah, that's good. I'm glad you've got over him.' The pilot paused. 'Presumably *he* won't be at the reunion?'

'He will, actually,' admitted Amy. 'Beki just forwarded me a text from Oliver to say Alistair sounded surprisingly keen on the idea.'

'Oh… pity.' Spencer had never been good at hiding disappointment.

But Amy was quick to put his mind at ease. 'Don't worry, Spencer, I'm over him now… and, anyway, having you and Oliver there will keep things light-hearted.'

'We'll try… if Oliver hasn't got us into World War Three by then,' replied Spencer light-heartedly. 'He always said he was going to be Prime Minister. I wonder how far he's got?'

*   *   *

On the backbenches of the House of Commons, Oliver Stanhope struggled to stay awake. Late-night sittings were mercifully rare in these enlightened times, but the second reading of this Bill had been circulated as a three-line whip, making his attendance virtually mandatory. So, here he was, with the debates droning on and divisions still some way off, thinking more and more of bed in his small flat in Victoria… that and the communications he'd had earlier in the evening.

For good or bad, smartphones were allowed in the Commons now. Oliver had never been one who liked these intrusions into the sanctity of the chamber, but his constituency manager insisted on keeping in constant touch and so, much against his better judgement, he kept his iPhone on.

Tonight though, his irritation when a message came through, had changed to excited anticipation when he saw who it was from: Beki Smith, a girl he'd known at university and someone for whom he'd always had something of a soft-spot. She'd asked him to call and he'd straightway crept out from another interminable speech and done just that.

It was good to hear Beki's voice again, especially as she was inviting him to join the old gang for a week's reunion on the Norfolk Broads. It wasn't something he would have normally chosen to do, but she'd asked him to contact their other old chum, Alistair Hepscott.

He and Alistair had never been bosom pals, but Oliver had certainly been aware of his steady rise in the world of finance and of how, when he was first elected, the banker had called to congratulate him and offer a very lucrative deal. He'd been pleased to take advantage of it and content to leave his money in Alistair's competent hands. Now, that arrangement could well provide the solution to a crisis all set to ruin him. It was something too delicate to talk about on the phone, but this reunion could well be the perfect opportunity for a one-to-one discussion. So Oliver had been more than willing to call immediately and pass on the invitation, even though he was extremely doubtful if such a high-flying executive would have the time for frivolous days afloat.

But to his amazement, despite sounding quite subdued when he first answered the call, Alistair had shown real enthusiasm for the whole idea and gave a firm directive to "count him in". Oliver came off the phone with renewed hope that removed any doubts he might have felt about the ethics of asking a banker for help.

For, politically, Oliver despised banks and all they stood for. He had little doubt their executives were to blame for all the country's current financial problems and, if he'd followed his conscience, would have led a more aggressive challenge of their high salaries and ludicrous bonuses.

That would have certainly gone down well with his constituents in the midlands, where unemployment and financial hardship were already beginning to bite. Instead, he'd done nothing, kept his silence and suffered the guilt of knowing he was the last man in the House of Commons right now who should have the nerve to question others' financial ethics. Why? Because…

He was brought out of his musings by the Speaker's call for divisions to vote on the Bill. Filing out to be counted by the whips, Oliver found himself thinking again of Alistair Hepscott and how ironic it might be that a banker's help could now be the saving of his parliamentary career. For there was much he still wanted to achieve in his term of office, and getting the current crisis behind him would be the new start he needed. It was an anxiety that had been hanging over him for almost a year now, suddenly brought to immediate recall by the presence at his shoulder of the last man he wanted to encounter this evening.

'Ah, Stanhope. Managed to sort out your little problem with IPSA yet?'

The speaker was an MP from the other side of the House, a particularly belligerent politician whose policies Oliver disliked as much as the man himself and which he'd opposed for as long as he'd been in parliament. The Independent Parliamentary Standards Authority had taken over MP's finances in the wake of the expenses debacle and, as far as Oliver was concerned, were about as loved as the KGB. One aspect of their new domain was a total transparency in which claims, payments… and irregularities… were exposed for all to see.

'No…' Oliver shuffled slightly, '… but, I will.'

'Well, I'd make it sooner than later if I were you, old chap.' Oliver's opponent was making a poor effort to disguise his smugness. 'They're looking for someone to make an example of right now, and you could fit the bill nicely.'

The bell sounded to file back in to hear the result. An hour ago, Oliver would have been quite depressed at this last exchange, but now he was feeling more upbeat than he'd done for a long time, and all thanks to this upcoming reunion on the Broads. Just getting away from the madhouse of Parliament would be a relief in itself, but all the more so when it held the solution to his predicament.

And how good it would be to see Beki Smith again.

Back in the chamber, Oliver made his way along the green leather benches and took his usual seat, buoyed by a renewed sense of optimism. Strange how everything could suddenly be seen in a different light. Once again he felt a surge of pride at being part of such a venerable institution.

Get his own house in order, and he could once again make his mark in this one.

*   *   *

Chapter Six

'Right, Jack, see if you can bring her alongside.'

A week had gone by, and the ranger was having his second session of handling *Nordic Princess*. By now he was getting the measure of the old boat, her stopping distance, turning radius and how she responded to wind at slow speed. That was certainly going to be a factor today as he tried a first attempt at docking.

With the tide ebbing, he was now turning her back upriver to stem the flow as they came in, the moderate breeze blowing them off the quay and making that turn just a little trickier. 'She's got a right-handed prop,' explained Frank as Jack backed-and-filled to get her round in a river width not much greater than the boat's length, 'so coming starboard-side-to is always best. That way the paddle-wheel effect of the prop reversing will pull your stern in as you approach the quay… and also have her pointing the right way for your next trip,' he added as he moved out onto the wheelhouse wing, leaving Jack to sort things out very much for himself.

They were pointing into the quay now at just about the optimum thirty-degree angle, the forward movement opposed by the flowing tide, combining to edge *Nordic Princess* towards her berth in a slow, but controlled, crab. From the corner of his eye, Jack could see Harold Searby making his way from shed to quay to receive their lines. Already having an extra hand in the yard was proving an advantage. Jack pulled the engine control back to STOP, while leaving the boat to continue her way ever closer. Engine now to SLOW ASTERN, more to have the reverse gear engaged and ready than to have any noticeable check on their speed. Out on the wing, Frank Brooker was glancing ever more frequently into the wheelhouse, but Jack was determined not to bring the wheel over before he felt it just right.

Just feet to go now, and he wound the big wheel hard over and increased the astern revs to HALF. With a slight judder, *Princess* started to slow while the churning prop swung her stern steadily in towards the quay. 'Ready with the backspring, Frank?' Jack checked. She was almost stationary now and, even before they were parallel, Jack brought the engine back to STOP and watched with satisfaction as the momentum carried the stern those last few degrees and *Nordic Princess* snug into her berth. 'Secure back spring.'

As ordered, Frank heaved the coiled line down to Harold on the quay who quickly dropped its eye over the big bollard just aft of their midships. Once again Jack went SLOW AHEAD on the engine which, with the wheel still hard over and the backspring taught, effectively held the boat hard against her fenders. 'Make fast, fore and aft,' he ordered. More lines went curling quaywards to be secured by Harold.

'All stop,' said Jack to himself, pulling back the engine control. The backspring slackened and the head rope tightened as he joined Frank out on the wing to check the lines.

'Perfect, skipper.' Frank nodded back to the wheelhouse. 'Finished with engines.'

'Aye aye.' Jack went back in and shut down the big diesel.

Frank leant over the guardrail and lit a cigarette. 'You're ready for your test now, Jack. Have you done your medical yet?'

'Tomorrow.'

'Good. When that's done I suggest you bang in your papers and get a test date. Then just come in the day before and take her yourself for a last practice.'

'Sounds good. I'm happy if you are, Frank.'

'I'll be even happier when I've had a cup of tea,' laughed the owner, as he jumped down to join Harold on the quay. Jack grabbed his coat and joined them.

'Good trip, Mr Fellows?' Harold, looking the part in a pair of light-blue overalls, was cheesing down the ropes and checking their tension with his foot.

'Yes thanks, Harold… and the name's Jack.' The ranger paused to look around the yard. 'You seem to be settling in here very well.'

Where piles of scrap timber once lay against the shed side, there was now clear space while just beyond, a bonfire smoked its last flicker. The quay-heading had been scrubbed of a year's accumulated filth while even the boatyard sign shone with renewed cleansing. Atop the previously naked flagpole, a houseflag now cracked in the afternoon breeze. 'I found that stuffed under a workbench,' explained Harold. 'Thought, with the yard cleared up a bit, we ought to give the old flag a flutter.' He turned to Frank. 'That engine's all together again now, boss. If you're feeling strong, we could get it in tomorrow.'

'Great, let's have a look at it.'

It was hard to miss *Fisher of Men* as they made their way to the shed. Now moored in the basin, her yellow hull stood out like a banana in an apple-barrel and looking all the smarter for a good wash and clean. 'Having Harold sleeping here is good for security too,' commented Frank with a backward nod as they entered the shed.

In the workshop, the diesel engine, newly assembled, now swung from a small gantry, its brass ancillaries shining, the block and cylinder-head smart in fresh black paint.

'If she runs as well as she looks, I'll be a happy man,' said Frank with a smile. 'You've done a good job, Harold.' He gave his new yardhand a slap on the back. 'This calls for that cup of tea.'

'No sugar in mine,' shouted Jack after him as the yard owner disappeared into the messroom. He turned to the bearded figure wiping his hands on some cotton waste. 'You seem to have fitted in here just right.'

Harold Searby nodded. 'I like to be busy and there's a lot here to do.' He glanced around the squalor of Frank's workshop and nodded to the pile of scrap parts that now lay in somewhat better order. 'But, I did find the parts I need for my gearbox amongst that heap. Frank says I can have them and use the shop to do the job.'

'Good.' Jack scanned his face: a little less sallow with eyes not quite so dark. 'And, you're eating okay now?'

Harold nodded. 'Yep, the boss brings me some groceries and says he'll even try to pay me a bit when the cash starts coming in.'

'How about *Brookside*?' asked Jack, glancing in the direction of the cruiser, which had now been hauled closer to the shed. 'Do you still think you can have her ready in a week?'

'I hope so, if that engine runs okay. I've already cleaned and polished her insides and put a coat of paint on the hull.'

'Yes, I thought she was a different boat when I saw her this morning.' Jack paused, uncertain how to broach a subject that was still bothering him. 'Harold, this loss of memory thing... would you like me to make some enquiries... try and get you your identity back... I do have contacts...'

'That's kind of you, Jack, and I'm really grateful for all the help you've given so far, but...' he looked down at his oil-stained shoes, '... sometimes I think a man's better off not knowing his past. Sometimes there may be things he'd rather not know.'

'Such as having a criminal record?' It was a time to be blunt.

Harold Searby looked up and smiled very slightly. 'I've found a good life in the service of The Lord, Jack. Something tells me I haven't always been so blessed. I think I'd rather know me as I am than what I might have been.'

'I'm sure that what you *were* wasn't that bad.' said Jack, sympathetically. Frank was still making the tea and now the yard phone had rung as well so they had a few extra minutes before he returned. 'Harold, you say your last memory is waking up from your accident; where exactly were you when you came round?'

'On a boat… some boat.'

'Your boat… you mean *Fisher of Men*?'

Harold shook his head. 'No, some other boat, but I don't know which. I have vague recollections, after a few days, of being transferred to *Fisher*, but everything is pretty hazy.'

'And were you alone or was someone actually caring for you?'

'A woman…' Harold pushed back his long hair as if to clear his thoughts with it, '… some woman was caring for me.'

'Who? Do you have a name?'

'Yes… it was Mary.'

'Just Mary? No surname?'

'No… she never told me… and as soon as I could look after myself, she was gone.' Harold shook his head. 'I'm sorry, Jack, but so much of it is still a blur. It's a bit like you trying to remember the first days of your own life.'

'Yes, I can see that, but one more question you might be able to answer. The church or chapel where you say you found new spiritual strength; can you remember where that was?'

'Oh yes, I'll never forget it…' Harold smiled with happy recollection, pleased to be finally able to contribute something, '… it was the United Reform Church in Beccles.'

'Have you been back since?'

'Only a few times, but on Sundays I'm usually holding my own gatherings elsewhere.'

'Didn't anyone there give you a clue to your earlier life?'

'I never asked.'

'Mind if I do?'

'I'm not sure, Jack. Do you really feel it's that important?'

'It might be.' The ranger looked him in the eye. 'I can understand why you're wary of delving into the past, Harold, but old skeletons have a habit of crawling out of the cupboard and experience has taught me that it's always better to face your demons than to try and bury them. My advice is to let me find out what I can, keep any findings strictly between us and face the facts as we find them.'

Harold took a deep intake of breath and made his decision. 'Okay. I trust you Jack. If you think that's best, go ahead.'

'Good man.' Jack gave him a slap on the back, but further discussion was ended by the rattle of tea mugs as Frank returned.

The yard owner seemed a little cheerier than of late. 'Got a small hire tomorrow, Jack.' Frank, opened a packet of biscuits. 'Only one of the sailing boats but, apparently, word is already getting around that our boats are being cared for again…' he glanced towards the yardhand contentedly sipping his tea, '… thanks to Harold here.'

'Good. Get me doing some extra trips on *Princess* for you, and the cash'll be rolling in…' Jack shook his head as Frank offered a biscuit, '… assuming I pass my medical tomorrow.'

* * *

'Good, that's it.' The doctor smiled and wrote some final figures onto the form before him. 'A little weight loss might not do any harm but, for a man your age Jack, you're in remarkably good health. He scribbled his signature on the bottom and added the practice stamp. 'I'll get this posted off.'

'Phew, thank goodness for that.' Jack pulled his shirt back on and breathed again. He avoided visits to the surgery if ever possible, but Doctor Reynolds had been a naval surgeon early in his career and continued to have that down-to-earth attitude of anyone associated with the sea. So much so, that Jack felt he could squeeze just a little more information from this consultation. He finished buttoning up his shirt and asked, 'Have you time to answer one medical question, doc?'

'Why not, you're paying for it Jack. That's a hundred and fifty quid, by the way… to the receptionist on the way out.'

Jack gulped slightly, remembering that medicals such as this did not come under the NHS. 'Right… well this doesn't concern *me*… just someone I recently met.'

'Go on.'

'He's a man who reckons he suffered total loss of memory from a head injury… but can it really be that serious and long-lasting?'

‘It depends on a lot of factors.’ The doctor wrinkled his nose slightly and sat back in his chair. ‘How long has… this person… been without memory?’

‘Ten years.’

Doctor Reynolds frowned slightly. ‘That’s an exceptionally long time, Jack. You say this was caused by an injury… what sort of injury?’

‘I don’t know. Does it matter?’

‘It could do. Temporary loss of memory is just one of the symptoms of traumatic brain injury. Depression or a complete change in social behaviour are some of the others. But, sometimes, if there’s been no actual intracranial injury, then just the trauma itself can cause the amnesia.’

‘You mean the brain blots out things it doesn’t want to remember?’

‘Exactly.’

‘But surely that would only apply to the bad memories. This chap’s got no recall, whatsoever, of anything before his accident. Is that possible?’

‘Sometimes, in serious cases, especially if he didn’t receive correct treatment at the time.’ Doctor Reynolds shook his head. ‘Even something as simple as lack of vitamins could delay his recovery. Where was he treated for this head injury?’

‘I don’t know.’

‘But he’s a local man?’

‘He has a slight local accent, but whether that’s only post-traumatic is anyone’s guess.’

‘Well I can check if you like,’ offered the doctor. ‘Give me his name.’

‘Harold Searby.’

The doctor jotted the name onto his pad. ‘I won’t be able to discuss medical details with you, Jack, but I imagine you’d just like to know what happened.’

‘That would be great.’

‘Right, give me a few days…’ he stood up and shook the ranger’s hand, ‘… and good luck with your skippering.’

* * *

‘Two white lights above a green on the left and a red on the right.’

Audrey sat across the kitchen table from her husband, the Admiralty Book of Lights, propped up against the tea pot. Jack paused from buttering another scone.

'er… large ship coming towards you.'

'How large?'

'I'd don't know, do I… I can't see the thing.'

'No need to get tetchy, Jack. Remember, I'm just trying to help and you should know from the lights.' Audrey had known it was a mistake agreeing to Jack's request for some testing, but getting the medical out of the way had obviously inspired this fresh attack on the theory… and her scones. 'And just because you've been found fit doesn't mean you can now binge.'

'When you've been eating like a rabbit for the past week, it does.' Jack poured another cup of tea. 'All right, give me the answer.'

'It means the vessel is over fifty metres long. Ships less than that carry only one steaming light.'

'Okay… give me another.'

'Right… an all-round white and an all-round red above the same navigation lights?'

'A ship unable to manoeuvre?'

'No.'

'Trawlers with their nets out?'

'No.'

'I used to know all this when I was in Thames Division,' mourned Jack. 'I'm too old now to be learning all this stuff again.' He held up his hands in submission. 'Go on… tell me.'

'A pilot vessel on duty.'

'Strewth… are you sure?'

'Of course… look!' Audrey thrust the page in front of her husband's nose. 'You're not too old, Jack, but you do need to get your head down pretty seriously if you're going to pass that test.'

'Don't I know it.' Jack pushed the manual away. 'The trouble is, I've got this mystery of Harold Searby on my mind as well.'

'But you've got him a job and mooring for his boat, Jack,' pointed out Audrey. 'Why worry where he comes from when even he doesn't seem bothered?'

'You know me, Audrey; I can't stand loose ends.' He indicated the manual. 'The trouble is, getting ready for the test doesn't give me the time I need to follow up some leads.'

'What leads?'

Jack shrugged. 'Just one actually. Harold told me the church that helped him find his way again. I was wondering if they'd known him before. I was going to ring them, but…'

'… could *I* do it for you?' Audrey gave a little roll of her eyes. 'I suppose I could, but why I should get involved in one of your investigations, Jack Fellows, goodness knows.'

'Thanks love. You'll be that much better at talking to some church ladies than I'd ever be.'

'That's all right,' said Audrey with artificial acquiescence. 'At least now you can get back to your studies without other worries.'

'I suppose so,' groaned Jack as he once again started to pour over the pages. It was only minutes though before he was distracted again by the ring of the telephone. 'I'll get it.' He was half out of his chair, glad of any excuse to avoid the bookwork, but still too slow for the likes of Audrey.

'No you don't. You keep learning those lights, Jack.'

She was gone almost thirty minutes, which meant it was probably one of their daughters, and he could guess which one.

'Amy?'

'Yes, and sounding pretty chirpy,' confirmed Audrey, settling back into her chair. 'They break up on Friday and the reunion's all arranged with all six of them coming.'

Jack closed his manual again. 'Hmm, I was hoping the Hepscotts would do the decent thing and give it a miss.'

'Well, they *are* coming, so that's that,' said Audrey, bringing the matter to a close, 'and Amy will be here this weekend. She thought the extra week before they go would give her time to get reacquainted with Beki and sort out provisions for the holiday.'

'It'll be lovely to have her around,' reflected Jack with a smile, 'and good for her to get to know her old chum again.'

'Also,' said Audrey slowly, as though testing the waters before the next request, 'it's been a long time since she was on a boat with us and she was hoping you might be able to get her a bit of handling practice before they all arrive.'

'I'm all for training,' agreed Jack, 'but surely some of the lads have handled a boat before?'

'Obviously Spencer Ovington has and I saw a photo once of Alistair Hepscott at the wheel of some flash cruiser he owned, but I can see what Amy's thinking,

Jack. The whole thing was her idea, and she doesn't want to make a fool of herself in front of the men.'

'Especially, Alistair Hepscott.' Jack pursed his lips. 'All right, love, I'll see what I can do. In the meantime, I need to get some practise in myself on these accursed rules and regulations.'

'You certainly do. Let's see how much you learned while I was on the phone.' She reopened the manual. 'Right, how often do you have to sound your whistle in fog?'

'We never do on the Broads,' responded Jack, defensively.

'That's not the point; how often?'

'I can't remember.'

'Well, it's one long blast every two minutes.'

'Perhaps I ought to be sounding a whistle right now,' grumbled Jack with increasing dismay. 'All this marine law stuff is a complete fog to me.'

'Never mind,' countered Audrey, 'come the weekend, you'll have your daughter to test you.'

* * *

'Are you sure this will be okay, Dad, my coming on the launch with you?'

'Of course it will.' It was Monday morning, and dawn not long past as Jack drove in to work with Amy beside him. After enjoying a weekend together at home, despite a little teacher/pupil tension on the revision front, it was back to ranger duties on the river and the opportunity to get his daughter afloat. 'You won't be able to handle the boat, of course, but it'll be good for you to get used to a bit of deckwork again.'

'I used to enjoy leaping ashore with the ropes.' Amy hadn't actually rejoiced at rising before dawn on the first day of her school holidays, but was well-aware her father couldn't be late for work. Driving through the Norfolk countryside with its occasional glimpses of river and marsh, brought back such happy memories of school holidays spent afloat with her parents and older sister. But those were many years ago. 'I don't think I can remember the knots anymore, Dad,' she confessed with a smile.

'It won't take long to show you the few you'll need,' he reassured her. They were pulling into the field office carpark, the offices and maintenance sheds still damp with early-morning dew. A uniformed figure ahead of them was just entering the wooden building. Jack led his daughter over a small bridge to where the launches lay ready in their own basin.

'Morning, Jack.' An upright figure in overalls sporting a Broads Authority logo, came out of the shed to greet them.

'Ted, just the man I want to see. Amy, this is Ted Chapman, a ranger like me for many years before coming ashore to maintain the launches instead.' Amy and the engineer shook hands, but it was something else that Jack wanted to discuss with him. 'This chap Harold Searby we were talking about last week, Ted… you were on the southern rivers for years, so you must have known him quite well?'

'We all did,' acknowledged the engineer. 'He was quite a popular character with a kind heart. Bit eccentric, of course, but the boaters seemed to enjoy that and his Sunday evening sing-a-longs.'

'When did all that start?'

Ted scratched his head. 'About ten years ago, I guess.'

'But what about before he became a regular figure seen on the southern rivers; did anyone know anything of his previous life, Ted: where he worked, where he came from?'

'No,' said the engineer, shaking his head. 'He just seemed to appear one day, living on that boat of his, wandering from place to place spreading the good word. But what he did before then is a complete mystery.'

'To him too, it seems.' Jack picked up his bag. 'Thanks, anyway, Ted; it was worth a try.'

'Sorry I couldn't help more.' Ted Chapman indicated the ranger's launch. 'She's all set for you.'

'Thanks.' Jack turned to his daughter. 'Come on Amy, let's get you afloat.'

* * *

It was the most delightful of days to be back on the river: clear skies, warm sun and just the lightest of breezes to keep temperatures moderate. Although still early morning, boats were already on their way, up and down-river to destinations that even their crews were probably as yet unaware. Most waved as they passed the ranger's launch and Amy joined her dad in returning the greetings.

'Gosh, this brings back lovely memories.' She paused to watch a sailing cruiser, huge gaff sail sheeted wide to the following wind, come sluicing past, winches purring as the crew goosewinged the jib. Amy sighed. 'Can't wait to get going ourselves on Saturday. I think what appeals to me most is not knowing where you're going to end up each night.'

'Yep, that's the glory of the gypsy life,' agreed her father with a laugh. '"Unsure of station or intention", as they used to say.'

Talk of water-gypsies reminded Amy of something. 'That chap you were talking to the engineer about… sounds as if he's something of an enigma.'

'He certainly is.' Jack explained the story of Harold Searby and how it was thanks to his work that she'd have a boat at all on Saturday. 'You'll be meeting him yourself soon,' he concluded. 'We'll call in and check on progress.'

'Great.' Amy was more excited than she cared to admit, at seeing the boat they'd be staying on, and her thoughts were well into the following week when she was brought back to the present by the ringing of her dad's mobile phone.

'Fellows.'

'Jack, Doctor Reynolds here. You asked me to check on one Harold Searby. Well, no joy, I'm afraid. They've done a complete run of health records for the area, and no Harold Searby was ever registered with any doctor we know of.'

'Really? Well thanks for trying anyway, doc. I much appreciate your trouble.'

'Bad news, Dad?' asked Amy, seeing her father's disappointed expression as he came off the phone.

'No, not really,' Jack slipped the phone back into his pocket. 'Just another avenue closing and a mystery getting just a little deeper.'

* * *

'That's good, Amy… once around the cleat and then two figures of eight.' They were in Brookerboats' basin now and Jack was refreshing his daughter's memory on how to secure the lines.

'… and finish off with a hitch,' confirmed Amy, making the underhand loop and pulling it tight. Her dad had been pleased to see a vacant mooring when they'd entered the basin. It meant one of the boats was out on hire. Now he was striding down the wood-slatted quay-heading to where the cruiser… *her* cruiser… lay. She quickly followed.

From her dad's description, she knew *Brookside* was old and wooden but now, as Amy took in the long white hull, straight stem and varnished topsides with their little brass portholes, she wouldn't have wanted any other boat.

She was big and sturdy too but, right now, overshadowed by a large mobile crane that bore the name of another boatyard. From its outstretched boom, a weighty engine swung precariously in the light breeze. *Brookside*'s centre wheelhouse had been folded down and the engine was suspended directly over the open void. One man stood on the cruiser's side deck directing the crane-driver, while another rather lean-looking character with a beard was waiting in the boat to receive it. He smiled up at Amy as they approached.

'You're getting there, Frank,' said her dad to the man on the sidedeck, whom she realised must be the yard owner, Frank Brooker.

'Yep, a couple of hours should see it in and ready to run.' He raised his brows. 'That's when the fun will really start.'

'It'll run all right,' reassured the man who had been guiding the engine into position, and was now climbing out to join Amy on the quay. She didn't need her dad's introduction to know who this was.

'Harold Searby.' He looked at his oily hand, smiled and decided not to take Amy's. 'Good to meet you.'

Amy smiled back to both men. 'Thank you for all you've done to get this boat ready for us.'

'Thank *you* for hiring it.' Frank Brooker nodded towards *Brookside*'s interior. 'Bit of a mess right now, but come back later and you can have a look round.'

'I'd love to. I can't wait for Saturday and the chance to handle her.'

'But before then, I've got a bit of excitement of my own,' said Jack, taking a letter from his pocket. 'This came from the MCA over the weekend. I've got my test on Friday.'

'Great!' exclaimed Frank.

'If I'm ready,' added Jack.

'You will be. Come in on Thursday and take *Princess* out for a bit of practice.'

'Yes, that'll be good.' Jack indicated his daughter. 'Okay if I bring Amy? She's been helping me with the theory revision.'

'Of course.' Frank glanced towards the engine. 'Best get on.'

As Jack and Amy wandered back to the launch, they paused to look at Harold's unique-looking boat.

'My goodness; the Yellow Peril,' laughed Amy. 'Harold has obviously modified the boat to his own needs, but what was it before?'

'Goodness knows…' admitted her dad, '… but that's a good question, Amy, and you've got me thinking.' Once again, the ranger made a note of *Fisher of Men*'s registration number, before leading them back to the launch.

Minutes later, they were back on the river.

*   *   *

'Henry, Jack Fellows again.' As they purred along the river Jack was back on his mobile calling Dragonfly House, the Broads Authority's Norwich headquarters, and specifically, Henry Mayhew, his friend there who looked after boat registration. 'It's about *Fisher of Men* again, that cruiser registered to Harold Searby.' The ranger confirmed the Broads registration number. 'I need a little more on that boat's history, Henry… like the name of the registered owner prior to Searby… thanks, Henry… look forward to hearing from you.'

'Still trying to find out more, Dad?' Amy was just finishing her packed lunch, but her father hadn't even touched his yet. Give him a mystery, and he was like a dog with a bone. She couldn't imagine him ever changing.

Not that it would have occurred to Jack to even try. 'Yep. If I can find the man who sold Harold the boat, it might be a clue to his past. It would have been under a different name back then, but the registration number won't have changed.'

'Ever thought that Harold might not want to know his past, Dad?' Amy didn't want to put a wet blanket on her dad's endeavours, but she knew her mum dearly wanted him to stop becoming involved in other people's lives.

'Actually, he doesn't,' acknowledged Jack, 'and I have a feeling it's his own in-built defence mechanism that's blocking his recall.'

'It must have been something pretty horrible that caused his accident then.' Amy gave her father a questioning look. 'So, why drag it all up if he doesn't want to know?'

'It's me that wants to know,' admitted Jack, 'because there are so many unknowns in Harold's story: a mysterious accident, a boat he owns but doesn't recollect buying and a monthly allowance from a mysterious benefactor.' He turned to his daughter with a resigned look. 'I'm afraid the old instincts are demanding answers to at least some of those questions.'

Amy was all set to pursue a counter-argument when her own mobile rang. 'Hello… lovely to hear from you… yes, that would be great… see you there, then.' She switched off and turned to her dad. 'That was Beki… wants us to meet up in Norwich tomorrow.'

'That'll be nice.' Jack was glad to change the subject too: his daughter could be as dogged as her mum when it came to seeing other people's points of view. 'We'll call and have another look at *Brookside* on the way home, and then you'll really have something to tell her.'

After twelve years, we're going to have plenty to talk about, don't you worry, thought Amy with a smile. But it would be good to look round the boat. She hoped the engine thing had all worked okay.

* * *

The sound of a running diesel came to Jack and Amy's ears long before they reached Brookerboats' yard. It was almost five o'clock now, a time when river traffic quietened and any sound was amplified in the early evening stillness. Engine noise should have been an intrusion in this tranquil environment but, knowing it probably spelled success on the engineering front, both Jack and Amy were glad to hear it.

More pleasing yet, was the sight of a healthy flow of cooling water flowing from *Brookside*'s exhaust as they glided into the basin. Harold came to take their lines as they nudged alongside, giving Jack a thumbs-up as he did so. 'She's running like a Swiss watch, Jack.'

'So I hear.' Jack shut down his own engine and listened to the throaty rumble of the engine at high-idle. 'Any trouble starting?'

'No, fired on the third go.' Harold was obviously justly proud of his project. 'Lots of smoke, but she's settled down nicely.'

Frank joined them and looked towards the cruiser. 'Everything's pretty much shipshape now, Amy, so go and take a look at your boat.'

'Right.' She scampered off down the quay.

'A final clean-up in the engine bay tomorrow, and then I'll give the whole wheelhouse a re-varnish.' Harold indicated some cushions that had been airing in the day's sun. 'Get them back in and she'll be ready to go.'

'And then we can start on the next one,' stated Frank, although Jack noticed the half-questioning glance he gave Harold as he said it. 'Already I'm having calls about *Brookside* for the rest of the season and… ah, your Amy's got a question,' he broke off, and went to answer her.

'Frank's obviously well-pleased with your work, Harold,' commented Jack in the few minutes they were alone, 'but don't let him keep you here longer than you want.'

'I won't.' Harold nodded to *Fisher of Men* lying at her own mooring beside them. 'I need to get her fixed first anyway but, you're right, I am getting itchy feet.'

'I can understand that, and Frank's going to have more time to work in the yard himself if I get my ticket on Friday.' Jack said no more because Frank and Amy were coming back up the quay.

Amy was obviously well pleased with her boat. 'She's great Dad. Oodles of room with three double cabins which will work out just right.'

'Ah, meant to tell you about the bedding,' admitted Frank. 'So long since we did any hiring, that we haven't got any.'

'No problem; I'll tell all the gang to bring sleeping bags,' replied Amy. 'I'm sure we'll be really comfortable. The boat's got such a lovely stable feel to her. She doesn't even tip as you step aboard.'

'That's the glory of these old wooden cruisers,' agreed Frank, obviously proud of his boat's resurrection. 'And you'll find she handles sweetly as well.'

'Hmm, she'll need to,' sighed Amy, 'because I really haven't had much experience.'

'Don't worry, your Mr Hepscott has,' reassured Frank, 'and you'll soon pick it up again yourself.'

'And I'll get you to put the launch alongside when we get back to base,' said Jack, checking his watch, '*and* you can come along when I have my final practice on Thursday… if that's okay, Frank?'

'Of course, Jack. You'll need a deckhand anyway.' Frank nodded towards the *Princess*. 'Another week and you'll be skippering her on your first charter.'

'If all goes well on Friday,' agreed Jack, hoping the others couldn't see his fingers well and truly crossed.

*   *   *

Chapter Seven

'My goodness, it's just like some Shakespearean playhouse.' Amy stood on the open stage of the Maddermarket Theatre, looking up from the auditorium to the public galleries running along each side.

'Yes, that was the idea when it was designed and converted from an old Catholic school in 1921.' Beki led them to the front of the stage. 'As you can see, it's quite small really,' she went on, 'but that's its charm and why the public love it.'

Amy looked out over the rows of seats and could imagine them full of theatre-goers. 'Small it may be, but I wouldn't want to stand here in front of three-hundred or so people trying to remember my lines.'

'Yes, nerves are something you have to live with in this game,' agreed Beki, taking them to one side as some theatre hands started manoeuvring large pieces of scenery onto the stage, 'especially first nights.'

'Looks as if you have one soon,' observed Amy, as the stage gradually took on the appearance of the living room of a country house.

'Yes, tomorrow. We're putting on an Agatha Christie.'

'And have you got a good part?' Amy could well imagine the nervous tension involved in such a production.

'Yes, quite a long one,' explained Beki. 'I play the niece of the victim and end up being one of the suspects.'

'And did you do it?' asked Amy.

Beki shook her head, smiling. 'Ah, that would be telling. You'll have to come and see for yourself. In fact,' she continued as a thought struck her, 'why don't you bring your mum and dad on Friday as my guests.'

'That would be wonderful…' but then Amy remembered her father's other commitment that day, '…except Dad's taking his test to skipper your trip boat, on Friday.'

'All the better,' stated Beki, triumphantly, obviously not to be put off that easily. 'Knowing your dad, he'll pass with flying colours and an evening here will be the perfect way to celebrate… and your mum will enjoy it too,' she added for good measure.

'She certainly would,' agreed Amy. 'Thanks, Beki. Count us in.'

'Good.' Beki Smith rubbed her stomach. 'I don't know about you, but I'm feeling pretty peckish. Let's go and get some lunch.'

* * *

'You're making a good job of that, Harold.'

Frank Brooker looked down into *Brookside*'s wheelhouse area to where his temporary yardhand was applying the last coat of varnish. Now, the wooden internal structure, wheel, instrument panel and panelling, shone with a glistening freshness.

'Thanks. Glad you're pleased.' Harold pointed to the chrome throttle lever and trim around the wheel. 'Soon as this varnish has set a bit, I'll give that a final polish and she'll be ready to go.'

'Great.' Frank put his hand in his back pocket and brought out five ten-pound notes. 'You've worked hard on this boat, and I want you to take this.' He passed them down.

But Harold didn't immediately accept. 'I can't take that, Frank.' He indicated over to where *Fisher of Men* still lay at her mooring. 'You letting me have a berth here and the parts for my gearbox will be payment enough. That was the deal.'

'I know, but things are a bit healthier on the cash front right now, and you'll need to buy some more food and top up your fuel.' Before Harold could protest further, Frank thrust the money into his hands. 'Here, take it… you've earned it.' Then he nodded back towards *Nordic Princess*. 'The old girl's alternator's been tripping out recently, so I'm off to buy her a new one. If you finish here before I get back, could you start taking the old one off for me?'

'Be glad to, and thank you for this,' said Harold, slipping the notes into his overall pocket. Minutes later Frank was departing in the battered old yard van, leaving Harold Searby putting finishing touches to *Brookside*'s varnish and touched by his boss's generosity.

* * *

'You must enjoy working here, Beki.' It occurred to Amy that, like the theatre, this bistro was also small in size but big on atmosphere.

'Yes, and strangely enough, I love to eat here as well, when I get the chance.' Beki poured them both a glass of wine as they waited for their meal.

'I can understand that.' Amy took in the wicker tables and chairs and the African prints on the walls which gave the place a distinct ethnic feel. Not unlike the café they used to escape to together in their student days. 'This is quite like old times.'

'Yes, isn't it just. I remember how we used to sit over our hot chocolate making big plans for the future.'

'Which have pretty well panned out,' said Amy, taking a sip of her wine. 'You work in a theatre and I'm teaching.'

'In some ways I envy you,' confessed Beki. 'Half a day a week I work with youth classes at the theatre. It's great fun and very rewarding.'

'Not too late for you to train for teaching. I'm sure you'd be a natural at it.'

'… if I didn't still have stars in my eyes.' Beki gave a reflective sigh. 'You probably remember my hopes for a career in TV drama. They didn't quite work out, but I still have the dream.'

'And you must never let go of your dreams.' For just a second, Amy found herself contemplating her own words, before brightening and saying, 'But you obviously love the theatre work you are doing, and working for Frank Brooker on *Nordic Princess* must be great fun.'

'Yeah, you're right, and I'm really looking forward to having your dad as skipper.'

'Bless him, he's so keen to get started. I just hope he passes the test. He's brilliant at boat handling, but he's been a real pain at home trying to learn the theory. Now I know what *they* had to put up with when I did my A-levels.'

'I'm sure he'll pass with no problems.' Beki was sure Amy was worrying unnecessarily. 'Anyway, we certainly owe him an evening out for organising our boat for next week. I'd have never even thought of using one of Frank's; they're in such a rundown state.'

'Thank goodness Dad found that Harold chap to work on *Brookside*,' said Amy. 'He's made such a lovely job of her. I hope the rest of the gang are pleased.'

'They will be.' Beki raised her glass. 'Here's to a great week.'

'A great week.' They clinked glasses.

Beki sat back and surveyed her friend with a satisfied look. ' It's good to see you again, Amy…' her smile hardened only a little, '… and looking happier than the last time.'

'Ah yes, our graduation.' Amy lowered her head slightly. 'Not all our memories of those days are happy ones are they?'

'No.' Beki paused, before pressing on. 'Amy, are you sure about next week… spending a whole seven days with Alistair and the dreaded Clarissa?'

Amy shrugged. 'You can't let the past rule you forever. Some things you never forget, but you do come to terms with them.'

'I still can't believe he's had the gall to accept the invitation. None of the gang ever forgave him for hurting you like that.' Beki gave a little frown. 'Telling you he was busy cramming for finals when, all the time, he was out having a good time with Clarissa…' She shook her head. 'Goodness knows how he could afford the time; he never was that bright a student as it was.'

'I know,' agreed Amy. 'He seemed to really struggle with his assignments and was always asking me to help him, so no-one was more amazed than me when he came out with a First. And he didn't even want to be there. It was his dad, Lord Hepscott, who pushed him into it. Anyway, it all came right for him in the end,' she added, not wanting to sound sour, 'because he's done really well in his banking career since.'

'Only because his dad was Chief Executive,' answered Beki, rather unkindly.

'But, from what I've read in the financial press, he's built himself a reputation for brilliance as an investment banker,' persisted Amy.

'At others' expense, and not without the odd hiccup in his early days,' cautioned Beki, before admitting, 'but, yes, he has done well and certainly better than with his marriage to Clarissa which, from what I've heard, has been pretty crap.'

'Really?' Amy was genuinely surprised to hear this. 'You said they were all over each other at the nightclub. Mind you, I was surprised as well as hurt that Alistair fancied her, as we all thought she was a hard-nosed cow. I can't imagine their marriage being a bundle of fun but, presumably, they have at least one child to keep them together.'

'But, they haven't.' Beki leaned a little closer. 'You probably never heard, but the baby was still-born.'

'Oh, that's sad,' said Amy. 'And they never tried for another?'

Beki shook her head. 'Apparently not. I think Alistair felt he'd been manipulated into a loveless marriage for nothing and, by all accounts, since the tragedy they've lived together in name only.'

'If it's that bad, I'm surprised Clarissa even wants to come to our reunion.'

'I can't believe she does,' stated Beki. 'Clarissa was never the rough-it sort and there's probably only one reason she would put up with a week on an old wooden boat.'

'Which is?'

'You.'

'Me?' Amy wasn't sure how to take this conjecture and, anyway, their meals had just arrived.

Beki waited until the waitress was well clear, before continuing. 'Yes, *you*. You remember how Alistair pleaded with you to give him another chance when I caught them out… swore he still loved you.' Perhaps it was Beki's sense of drama that made her pause before continuing, 'Well, my guess is that he never stopped loving you, which is why his marriage has been a sham and why he was so dead keen to attend our little get-together. I'm not surprised Clarissa's coming, just to keep tabs on the poor bloke.'

'Crikey, I didn't give that a moment's thought.' Amy picked up her drink and swirled the wine around in the glass before taking a lingering sip. 'The last thing I want is to be a source of friction between a married couple.'

'I wouldn't worry about it.' Beki poured them both another glass. 'I suggest we just concentrate on having a good time with the other lads and let the Hepscotts sort out their own problems.' She leaned closer again, keen to lift the mood. 'I'm really looking forward to this week, Amy, and we mustn't let anything spoil it. The break will do us both good. I don't know about you, but having three jobs doesn't allow me much time for recreation.'

'Teaching's a bit the same,' empathised Amy. 'It takes over your life, leaving precious little free-time.'

'So, do you find time to play the drums these days?' asked Beki, smiling with the recollection of her friend's obsession with Karen Carpenter.

'No, not since I played in the band.' She looked enquiringly at her friend. 'Besides the theatre, do you have any other outside interests?'

'Just one.' Beki gave a slight shrug. 'Perhaps I'll tell you about it next week.'

Amy wanted to ask more, but didn't. Somehow she found the secrecy of her friend's hobby as vaguely disturbing as the thought of her old flame still harbouring feelings.

*   *   *

Jack found Harold at work in *Nordic Princess*'s engine room when he and Amy arrived for his final practice on the Thursday. Not having located Frank in the yard, he'd boarded the trip boat where the sound of tools on metal deck-plates led him down the vertical ladder to the machinery space.

'Almost done, Jack.' Harold looked up and indicated a gleaming new alternator. 'Apparently she's been a bit sluggish starting lately, so Frank's told me to change it. Last thing you want for your test is a non-starting engine.'

'Yeah, it'll be stressful enough without something like that.' Jack leaned over the main engine to examine the work. Like everything on *Princess*, the alternator was big and this new one, obviously expensive. 'That must have made a bit of a dent in poor Frank's bank balance. I hope he can afford it.'

'Apparently he can,' said Harold, gathering his tools. 'In fact money doesn't seem to be too much of a problem at present. He's gone off again today to buy some new batteries for the other cruiser, *Brookland*.'

'Really?' Jack knew Amy had paid a deposit for the week's hire, but that wouldn't even scratch the surface of Frank's sudden spending spree. 'Perhaps this new energy in the yard has inspired the bank to be more understanding.'

'I wouldn't know what banks think,' commented Harold, wiping a rag over the already gleaming engine. 'My financial concerns are usually only limited to whether I have enough cash or not, but I'm all for doing up boats.' He glanced around at the brass telegraph, valves and ancillaries, all shining in the engine-room lights. 'If we can get the rest of the fleet looking as good as this, it will be money well spent.' He pulled a voltmeter from his toolbag. 'I've already checked the filters and oil for you, Jack, so go and start her up, and I'll just check the output.'

Back in the wheelhouse, Jack soon had the diesel rumbling on tick-over, the momentary belch of exhaust from the funnel dissipating in the westerly breeze. 'I hope the weather's as good as this for the test tomorrow,' he said to Amy, who had just joined him from her own tour of the boat.

'You'll do fine, whatever, Dad,' she reassured him. 'Tomorrow night you'll be looking forward to a good whodunit at the theatre to celebrate.'

'I hope.' Jack had been relieved that the play had been an Agatha Christie and was grateful to Beki for giving them all complimentary tickets, but knew he wouldn't be getting too enthusiastic until his test was passed.

Harold joining them interrupted further thoughts. 'Yep, fourteen volts. She's ready when you are, Jack.' He wiped his hands and nodded down to the mooring ropes. 'Shall I look after the lines for you?'

Jack shook his head. 'Thanks anyway, but I'll get Amy to handle them. It'll be good experience.' He indicated the engine-temperature gauge on the panel and turned to his daughter. 'While it's warming I'll brief you on what to do. If you just standby on the quay to help as needed, Harold, we should be just fine.'

Ten minutes later, and *Nordic Princess* was once again making her stately way downriver, Amy coiling ropes on the foredeck and Jack too preoccupied with his first solo command to even consider why Frank Brooker suddenly had money to spend.

* * *

'Right, captain, let's see if you can moor up to a buoy.'

Jack wasn't sure if the MCA examiner calling him "captain" was a good sign or not. All he did know was that he had to keep his concentration going for a little while yet.

After a morning of answering questions on dozens of different light combinations, rights-of-way and boat documentation, it was a relief to be out on the water in an environment he was familiar with. Now they were at the far end of the broad and the examiner had spotted a free buoy on which to test his handling skills. Jack brought the engine to DEAD SLOW and edged in towards the allotted spot, positioning to bring the boat dead to wind in the last few yards of run-in.

The problem he knew he would be encountering was that *Nordic Princess*'s bow was high and totally obscured the buoy in those last few yards. But, thankfully, he'd practised this very manoeuvre yesterday, with Amy in the bow signalling how much further to run once that happened. The buoy was quite close now and the boat creeping ever closer. Jack went SLOW ASTERN to slow them yet further, wanting, at all costs, to avoid the disgrace of "running down the mooring". *Princess* continued in and now the buoy was disappearing under the bow. HALF ASTERN and he was looking out of the side-window for some reference as to when the boat had stopped altogether. When he judged it had, he brought the engine to STOP and turned his attention to the examiner.

'Right, captain, let's go and see how you did.'

Together they left the wheelhouse and headed for the foredeck, Jack collecting the boathook as they went. Would the buoy be too far away to hook on or, worse still, out of sight below *Princess*'s black hull? They reached the stemhead and looked down.

The buoy sat directly below them in a perfect position for pickup.

'Good,' praised the examiner and indicated the boathook, 'and you won't need that; we won't be picking up.' He nodded back up the broad. 'Let's go home.'

As they cruised back to the yard, Jack knew he'd done well enough so far. There was still the critical bit of coming alongside and the wind today was quite fresh but, barring unforeseen disasters, he knew he should handle it satisfactorily.

As it was, using all his concentration, the landing was the smoothest he'd yet achieved in *Princess* and, with the lines ashore to Harold's waiting hands, he relaxed for the first time in hours.

Had he passed? The examiner had given no indication so far, but now he was working his way through his checklist, ticking off all the evolutions and questions he had wanted to cover. But there was one item left unticked.

'Ah, captain… one more question I should have asked you earlier…'

Jack waited. So, the ordeal wasn't over yet. This could yet be the one he couldn't answer.

*   *   *

Chapter Eight

'"How often do you sound the whistle in fog?" You're kidding.' Audrey took the Pimms and lemonade from Jack and gave him a beaming smile, as relieved as he was that he'd obtained his "ticket".

'Thank goodness you'd quizzed me on that one, Aud, or I might have blown it at the last hurdle.' He turned to his daughter, as overjoyed as the rest at her dad's success. 'And thanks to you too, Amy, for all those hours of going over marine law and the like. I'm just glad it paid off.'

Jack sat down on a garden chair with a well-earned beer and let out a long, contented sigh.

'I bet Frank's as pleased as you are,' said Amy, handing round some crisps.

'He would be if he knew.' Jack stretched forward to pick up Spike's ball and threw it to the far end of the lawn. 'Actually, Frank hasn't been in the yard all day.'

'Strange. I would have thought today of all days he would want to be there, if only to offer moral support.'

'In fact, he hasn't been around much all week,' continued Jack. He turned to his daughter. 'I know you left a cheque for Frank for your hire next week. How much, exactly?'

'Only a hundred pounds deposit. I couldn't afford more until the rest of the gang pay their share on Saturday. Then we'll give him the full amount, as agreed. Why do you ask, Dad?'

'Oh, just that Frank seems to have become suddenly flush with cash at the same time as he's spending time away from the yard.' Jack frowned. 'So, none of the others have paid him yet?'

'No.'

Audrey felt it was time to curb her husband's curiosity. 'He's probably doing some outside boat job for a customer, Jack. With Harold in the yard now, he can afford to be away from Brookerboats for a bit.' Mention of the yardhand's name reminded Audrey of something she'd forgotten in all the excitement. 'Oh, by the way, Jack, I managed to talk to someone at the church Harold went to. A very pleasant-sounding lady who remembered him well.'

'Good…' Jack looked up expectantly, his hand still gripping the ball firmly clenched in Spike's mouth, '… and?'

'And nothing, I'm afraid. No-one there had ever met Harold before the day he came to that service.'

'Oh,' Jack shrugged away his disappointment, 'no link there then.' After some playful growling, Spike had relinquished the ball and sidled up to Amy, in the hope of scrounging a crisp. 'We seem to be finding nothing but dead ends as far as Harold is concerned.'

'Does it matter, and is it any of our business anyway?' questioned Audrey. 'The poor man's finally making a bit of money, which is just what you wanted, and what do you do? Become suspicious… and don't make yourself too comfortable, Jack. Remember we're off in less than an hour.'

'Is it that time already?' Jack checked his watch. 'I'd better get a move on.'

Audrey gathered up the glasses and put them on a tray. 'I'm really looking forward to this. It's ages since I went to a play.'

'And save your deductions for tonight, Dad,' Amy called after her father as he stepped into the conservatory. 'Sussing a stage whodunit is about as much detection as you need to do these days.'

Jack turned and gave his daughter a long-suffering look before going off to shave and shower. He knew his family was right. He couldn't even start to explain that old familiar feeling of unease. Something wasn't quite right, but he couldn't think what.

* * *

'Here's to Jack Fellows and his future skippering.' Beki Smith raised her glass to her host. 'Well done for today, Jack. I knew you'd do it.'

'Just the same, I'm glad to have it behind me,' acknowledged Jack with a smile, 'and I can't think of a nicer way to celebrate than being with you all here tonight.'

After the enjoyment of the theatre, they were relaxing with Beki in the agreeable atmosphere of a Tombland restaurant. Soft music played in the background, the meals were ordered and Jack felt the contentment of a challenge met and the company of his nearest and dearest. He was also grateful to Beki for coming up with this most perfect of evenings. He raised his own glass back to her.

‘And congratulations to you too, Beki, for such a great performance.’

‘Yes, it was wonderful; I loved every minute of it,’ agreed Audrey, enthusiastically. ‘I just don’t know how you remember all those lines.’

‘Sometimes we don’t,’ confessed Beki with a laugh, ‘but I’m just glad you all enjoyed it.’

‘We did indeed,’ replied Amy, ‘and I was guessing to the end who did it and, even then, I got it wrong.’ She took another sip of her orange juice: it was her dad’s night out and she’d be driving them all home, including Beki, who was spending the night at the Fellows’ and who now turned to her father.

‘How about you Jack? I’m sure you had it sussed pretty quickly.’

‘I had my suspicions pretty early on, but not through any great detective work,’ Jack admitted.

Beki looked surprised. ‘After all your years at Scotland Yard, I’d have thought this would have been a doddle.’

‘Not really. Real-life crime, especially murder, never quite slots into place as neatly as it does in fiction. In the real world, the villain is usually doing his or her best to fool the police and the police are doing their best to see through it. With a story, it’s simply the writer trying to fool the reader. So, in my own investigations, I was always after the most likely suspect and I was usually right. In fiction, I’m usually putting my money on the *least* likely suspect and, like tonight, that’s how it was.’ Their meals arrived and all eagerly tucked in. Jack ordered another bottle of wine. It was a jovial gathering, though the chat seemed to revolve around law-breaking. ‘The fact is, Beki, most crime these days is solved in the laboratory rather than by good old-fashioned sleuthing.’

‘And yet you still have perfect crimes.’ Beki gladly accepted a top up of her glass. ‘I can think of a few cases where no-one was ever brought to trial.’

‘Too many,’ agreed Jack, ‘but they’re not your “perfect crime”… usually just a case of insufficient evidence. The real “perfect murder” is where no-one even suspects a murder has been committed. There must be hundreds of those that we’ll never even be aware of…’

‘… and, therefore are never publicised,’ finished off Beki. She thought for a moment. ‘I guess the ones that really do fascinate us, are when it’s so obviously murder and the police are sure of the culprits, but can never prove their guilt beyond reasonable doubt.’

‘Like the Wallace case in Liverpool or Lizzie Borden in Fall River USA,’ pointed out Jack. 'But, those were all a long time ago, Beki. With modern forensics, even Jack the Ripper would probably be behind bars eventually.'

'But surely, forensics will only work if the police connect you to the crime in the first place,' joined in Amy. Being so young, she had never discussed her father's work while he was in the police but, after tonight's play, she was finding this discussion surprisingly fascinating.

'In a way. If you're not already on police files and they don't suspect you initially, then you've certainly increased your chances of getting away with it.'

'Like, if a murder was committed and the person who did it could prove they were many miles from the scene at the time?' asked Beki.

'By using a false alibi, you mean?' queried Jack.

'No, by actually *being* miles from the murder scene.'

'But that's impossible.'

'Nothing's impossible, Jack.' Even as she said it, Beki sensed a darkening of the atmosphere around the table. It was time to change the subject. 'But, tomorrow, Amy and I set sail on our little adventure, so here's to fair winds and blue skies.' She raised her glass once more.

'Yes, here's to you both,' said Audrey, thankful that this line of conversation had now been dropped. 'Hopefully, cruising along the quiet, unspoilt waters of Broadland, you'll be far from crime and be chilling out in the company of old friends.'

Jack raised his glass also, but said nothing. This celebratory evening was not the time for cynical thoughts.

* * *

'*One* suitcase… I told you, Clarissa, just *one* case!'

Alistair Hepscott finished throwing some casual clothes into his waterproof kitbag and looked with dismay at the piles of totally unsuitable garments his wife had selected from her dressing room.

'You must be joking.' Clarissa threw to one side the silk kimono she'd failed to cram into the third of her set of matching luggage. 'How could I possibly get a week's outfits into one measly case?'

'For goodness sake, all you need to take are casual clothes and trainers. We're going on a Broads cruiser, Clarissa, not the *Queen Mary*. You'll be snacking in the cabin, not dining at the captain's table.'

'More's the pity,' grumbled his wife. 'And anyway, I used to pack these clothes when we went away on *our* boat.'

'That's because it was *only* us on board. This time, we're sharing a much smaller cruiser with four others.'

'God, what a thought! A week making small-talk to people I have nothing in common with,' sneered Clarissa as she kicked one of the suitcases under the bed. 'And did I hear right? We're having to take sleeping bags? You know full well I haven't slept in a bloody sleeping bag since that disastrous night on safari.'

'Well, I can assure you, Clarissa, there are *no* tarantulas in Norfolk and as for the company, just cast your mind back to our student days before you got so high-and-mighty. You looked up to these people and were so desperate to fit in and be part of their group, so don't you dare look down your nose at them now,' retaliated Alistair with barely suppressed anger. 'For just once in your life, try and rough it a bit with the rest. The other girls will be casually dressed, so why can't you be?'

'Yes, I'm sure you're really looking forward to seeing Amy Fellows, no doubt still looking good in tight jeans, aren't you?'

'Don't be ridiculous.' Alistair was well aware of his wife's jealous nature. 'If you're going to be like this all week, I'd rather you didn't come.'

Clarissa's hard eyes narrowed. 'I *bet* you would. Well, if you think I'm going to sit at home taking flack from all and sundry while you escape to the wilds of Broadland, you've got another think coming. This week's been hell with you being away on business.' She pointed an accusing finger. 'The sooner you sort out this whole mess, Alistair, the better.... which reminds me, your solicitor rang yesterday before you got back.'

'Now you tell me.' Alistair flopped on to the bed. 'What did he want this time?'

'It's the bank. They wanted you to come in for another meeting next week. I told the solicitor we were off on some mad nautical jaunt, so he's going to put them off until the week following.' Clarissa smiled a mirthless smile. 'So, you'd better make the most of your week's freedom, because it might be the last you'll have for a while.'

Certainly with you, thought Alistair, as he stood up and carried his kit downstairs.

'And don't forget to bring plenty of cash,' shouted his wife after him. 'At least then we can jump ship whenever possible and eat out, rather than sharing unpalatable food and company on board.'

Alistair threw an oilskin on top of his bag. Life was bad enough without the likes of Clarissa. Well, thankfully, it wouldn't be for much longer.

* * *

'… and then the captain said, "the Thames, I thought this was the Humber".' Beki and Amy had a good chuckle at this, another of Jack's anecdotes of life on Thames Division police launches.

Audrey had heard the story many times before, but still managed a polite smile. Beki, though, had thoroughly enjoyed the repertoire and, wiping laughter-tears from her eyes, said, 'It's amazing, isn't it, how everything seems that much more melodramatic when you're afloat.'

'Well, I certainly hope you don't have too many dramas to tell us about when you get home,' laughed Audrey.

'Don't worry, Mum, it's going to be just great,' Amy replied.

'The only drama we're likely to have is when Clarissa can't find the dishwasher,' joked Beki, grinning broadly.

'Oh dear, I hope she doesn't cause problems for you all.' From Amy's accounts of their time at university, Audrey was well aware of this young woman's shortcomings. 'It only takes one bad apple to spoil the barrel.'

'She can spoil it for Alistair, if she likes, but she won't for us,' answered Beki, resolutely. 'We're going to give them the for'ard cabin and we'll all keep our distance in the stern.'

'We'll just tell her that's First Class and she'll be happy,' added Amy with a good chuckle.

Jack was pouring after-dinner coffees. 'From what you've said, I should think Alistair'll be glad to get back to his desk in the city after a week with you lot.'

'I'm not so sure.' Beki handed round some mints. 'Any City bank must be a pretty stressful place to work in these days.'

'Yes, if you're wondering how much longer you've got a job,' said Jack, cynically, 'but the likes of Alistair are probably too busy counting their bonuses to worry about such things.'

'I'm not so sure.' Beki placed her cup back on its saucer and looked up to see curious expressions on everyone's face. 'One of our repertory players worked at Alistair's bank and told me of all the trouble they had some years ago.'

Jack's eyebrows raised just a little. 'Really? What trouble?'

'Apparently, a large sum of money went adrift. "Unauthorised speculation",

I think he called it. Whatever, Alistair came in for a lot of suspicion at the time until they found the real culprit.'

'Who was…?'

'A chap called…' Beki searched her own memory bank for the name, '… Matson… that's right… Jacob Matson. Apparently, he'd been siphoning off funds and it only came to light when the bank did a surprise audit.'

'How much are we talking about?'

'Over three million pounds.'

'Phew! And, presumably, this Matson got a long jail sentence?'

'He would have if they'd caught him,' explained Beki. 'Unfortunately, just as the enquiry began, he did a bunk.'

'Scarpered?' Jack leaned forward. 'You mean, totally disappeared?'

Beki nodded. 'Yes, never to be found… or the money either,' she added, taking another sip of her coffee. 'But papers left behind in his office clearly pointed to his guilt which let Alistair off the hook.'

'When did all this happen?' asked Jack.

Beki thought for a second. 'Oh, about ten years ago, I suppose. Only a couple of years after Alistair started working there.'

'So, how come we never heard of it at the time?'

'Because the bank managed to keep it all in-house. Presumably a scandal like that would have lost them customer confidence. In those days we trusted banks,' said Beki with a shrug, 'and Lord Hepscott was still in the chair. I guess the fact that it all took place within his son's department made him all the more determined that it should never become public.'

'I bet. So, in spite of that hiccup, Alistair's career went on from strength to strength.' Jack sat back in his seat. 'Lucky old Alistair.'

'Well, at least he's not too proud to come and share a week roughing it with his old gang,' said Amy, still quick to speak up for her old flame.

'Jack, it's nearly eleven,' realised Audrey, looking at her watch, 'and these girls probably still have some packing to do.'

'Right, you all go and get the car and I'll settle up.' He tossed the keys to Amy.

It had been a great evening, made all the more intriguing to Jack by unexpected revelations that had managed to surface. He gave his bankcard to the waitress and watched while she tapped keys on a computer to finalise the amount owing. Just like police work, everything was that much more hi-tech these days, he thought to himself.

But, as Beki had said, perfect crimes still happened, and banks could be cheated out of millions.

*   *   *

Chapter Nine

Saturday morning, the first day of their cruise, dawned bright and sunny. After early breakfasts, Jack and Audrey drove Amy and Beki out to Brookerboats' yard.

Amy knew she was keyed up, not at the prospect of taking a boat out, but in the knowledge that this same morning she would be meeting Alistair again for the first time in twelve years. How should she be with him and, more importantly, how would he be with her? Their last parting had been anything but harmonious, both of them distraught at the thought of ending a very loving relationship. Perhaps it was just as well that Clarissa would be blessing them with her all-controlling company. That, at least, would preclude any inappropriate stirrings.

One thing that immediately eased tensions as they drove into the yard, was the sight of Oliver Stanhope. The MP came straight over and big hugs all round immediately bridged the years apart.

'My goodness, Oliver, you must be keen.' Amy stood back to survey this old chum. He was still as attractive as ever, though his eyes had lost the sense of fun and purpose she'd remembered from their student days.

'Drove up yesterday and spent the night at a local B&B.' He cocked his head back in the direction of London. Couldn't wait to get away from the madhouse of Westminster and see you two again.'

Amy wondered if it was her imagination or did his eyes linger fractionally on Beki as he said that? Whatever, the girl herself seemed just as moved by the reunion.

'I can't wait to hear all the government gossip,' Beki laughed, giving the MP another big hug.

'What, so you can go repeating it to all your theatrical friends? I'm not that daft,' he ruffled her hair, 'but it will be great to have some down-to-earth chats again, away from press intrusion and political angst.'

'I'll leave you lot to catch up,' said Jack, excusing himself and heading off to find Frank. He found him on board *Brookside*, warming the engine.

''Morning, Jack. Congratulations on the ticket.'

'Thanks, Frank.' Jack climbed down into the boat to join him. 'Now I'm looking forward to putting it to use.'

'How about tonight's trip… care to do that?'

'I'd love to, Frank, but I'm a bit loathe to leave Audrey alone. After having Amy with us for a week, the house will feel a bit empty.'

'Ah, well, I might have the solution to that because, as you know, Beki will be off cruising, so Jenny the stewardess is going to have a go at the commentary. It'll be good experience for her, but will leave me short-handed on the hostess front, so I was just wondering if Audrey…'

'… could come and give a hand.' Jack indicated to where his wife was chatting with the youngsters. 'I'll ask her for you, but I'm sure it'll be okay.'

'Thanks, Jack.' Frank blew out his cheeks. 'I'm going to need all the help I can get this coming week. Things have suddenly got very hectic.'

'Yes, you've been pretty illusive these last few days,' commented Jack, curious to know the reason for this sudden burst of effort.

'Oh… you know… the odd job here and there,' explained Frank, with obvious reluctance to go into any further detail. 'Having Harold in the yard now has let me get away to do some outside jobs I've been promising for ages.'

You'd have been better working on your own boats, thought Jack, but didn't say, especially as Harold had just joined them with some freshly-washed curtains.

'I'll just get these up for you,' he explained, coming on board and making his way to the aft cabin.

'Thanks, Harold, and then would you top up the fresh water tank,' requested Frank, shutting down the engine.

'I'll leave you to it and get back to the family.' Jack made his way back down the jetty in time to see a smart estate car pull into the yard and a tall blond-haired man get out. Although they had never met before, there was something about his bearing that spoke of reliability, responsibility and an air of command. Jack went over to him. 'You must be Spencer Ovington.' He held out his hand and the airline pilot shook it back.

'That's right, and you must be Amy's dad…'

'… Jack. Good to meet you.'

By this time, the girls and Oliver had rushed over to join them with another round of hugs and the shaking of hands.

'This is all a bit luvvy for me,' said Jack with a smile as he rejoined Audrey on the quay.

'That's the way they are now, Jack, but it's just nice to see them all enjoying themselves. I'll miss those girls tonight.'

‘Ah… well… that’s something I want to mention,’ Jack started to say, but got no further because their attention was suddenly drawn to a gleaming Daimler, just ghosting into the yard. ‘Uh, oh… is this who I think it is?’

‘I’m afraid it is.’ Audrey felt as nervous as the rest at this long-dreaded encounter with the Hepscotts.

Amy’s knees weakened at the sight of the car, and all her resolve left her. She tried to remember some advice her dad had given when she’d mentioned, over breakfast, just how nervous she felt. ‘Just think how he’ll be feeling, Amy. Don’t forget you were the innocent party.’ So, she took a deep breath, and with an outward air of confidence she didn’t feel, walked towards the car as Alistair was just stepping out. He was still slim, she was glad to note, though there were some premature signs of grey peppering his otherwise dark hair. But when he saw her, his smile was just as entrancing as ever.

‘Hello, Amy.’

‘Hello, Alistair… long time.’

Their hands touched and he kissed her gently on the cheek.

The moment Amy had been dreading had passed more painlessly than she had dared to imagine. It was good to feel his touch again and she would have prolonged the moment if a pair of hard eyes hadn’t been scrutinising their every move from the passenger seat. Sensing his wife’s displeasure, Alistair opened her door and a rather large woman in a linen suit and straw hat emerged blinking into the sunlight.

‘Clarissa.’

‘Amy.’ As Clarissa nodded back, her only other gesture was to pull down large sunglasses from the brim of her hat.

Just as well, thought Amy. She had no wish to meet this woman’s eyes.

‘Is that our boat?’ asked Alistair, sensing the tension and indicating the only cruiser looking smart amongst the dilapidated fleet. ‘Let’s have a look.’

He led them along the jetty to where the rest of the gang were already inspecting *Brookside*. Jack and Audrey stood to one side and noticed the muted greetings from the others. It was Alistair, however, who made a sincere effort to lighten the mood when he said brightly, ‘She looks great, Frank.’ He turned to his wife who had followed apathetically behind. ‘This’ll be perfect, won’t it Clarissa?’

If this gesture of bringing his wife into the circle was meant to improve her mood, it failed miserably. Clarissa merely looked over the top of her sunglasses and said disapprovingly, ‘Is this *it*?’

It was Spencer Ovington who attempted to bring her round. 'This is how Broads cruisers used to be, Clarissa… far more atmosphere than your modern fibreglass gin palaces.'

On reflection it, perhaps, wasn't the most diplomatic of openings.

'Really?' Clarissa removed her sunglasses altogether so that Spencer could take in the full effect of her stare. 'Well, all I can say is that *our*… "gin palace"… was twice as big as this, and…' she transferred her glare to *Brookside*, '… infinitely more comfortable.'

The pilot glanced quickly to Alistair who gave an almost indiscernible shake of the head, but further conversation was interrupted by Amy bringing her parents to the fore.

'Mum… Dad… you've met Alistair before, haven't you?' There was a slight edge of nervousness in Amy's voice as she remade the introductions.

'Yes.' Jack's voice was as natural as he could manage.

But, once again, it was Alistair who saved the moment. He held out a firm hand, met Jack's eyes with obvious sincerity and said, 'Good to meet you again, Jack.'

Another milestone passed, thought Amy but, just the same, she was glad that Frank Brooker seemed keen to move things on.

'Right, I expect you'd like to have a look around her and then get your things onboard.' Frank nodded to the men in the party. 'But first I'll get Harold here to show you the engine routines.'

Harold had just emerged from the aft cabin and was already raising the engine covers in the wheelhouse. He nodded greetings to the men. 'Just a few things you'll need to do each day.' In his Brookerboats' overalls, he was now looking far more respectable, and the men listened courteously as he went through the routines of checking oil level and weed filters.

Spencer and Oliver listened intently, but not so the third man in their party. It was only momentary, but Jack had noticed a flicker of unease pass across Alistair Hepscott's face at his first glance of the yardhand. Now, as Harold gave the short briefing, the banker seemed oddly distracted. It wasn't something the others would even notice, but Jack knew all too well the significance of the forced smiles and nervous laugh. Then the engine covers were replaced, Frank was climbing on board to join them and Alistair had regained his composure.

Jack and Audrey remained on the quay while *Brookside* was introduced to her new crew. There was general admiration when they all re-emerged… except from Clarissa who was the last. 'God, you call that a bathroom… I could hardly squeeze in.'

'Not surprising,' whispered Oliver, just loud enough for everyone to hear.

Clarissa shot him a withering glance before further complaining, 'And you didn't show us the shower.'

'Yes he did,' intervened Beki, 'it was in the same loo you couldn't get in.'

'Lord save me,' muttered Clarissa, before adding, 'the next thing you'll tell me is that there's nowhere for me to plug in my hair-dryer.'

'Ah… funny you should say that…' started Frank, but he was spared more revelations by Spencer.

'What would be great, would be if we could do a bit of sailing.' He looked towards the half-deckers moored around the basin. 'Frank, would we be able to take one of these as well?'

'I'm sure we've got one free for the week, but I'd better go and check.'

'Great and, of course, I'll willingly pay the extra. In fact, I'd like to pay the whole balance for the week.' He held up his hand at the protests from the rest of the gang, '… no… my treat. Why don't you lot start getting your kit on board and I'll go with Frank and check if we can have a sailboat.'

So, while bags were transferred from cars to boat, Jack joined owner and pilot in the yard office.

Frank scanned the week's pages of the bookings diary. Most were still empty. 'Yep, looks like *Babbling Brook* is free for you.' He wrote some figures onto a scrap of paper. 'So, adding that to the balance, that's the total.'

'Fine.' Spencer brought out a handful of cash and handed it over to a grateful Frank who somehow found the receipt book amongst the debris on his desk and started to write one out. But it was the aircraft models on the ceiling that had caught Spencer's professional eye.

'A Sopwith Pup and a Corsair.'

'That's right.' Frank handed over the receipt. 'You seem to know a bit about aircraft as well as boats, Mr Ovington.'

'I learned to fly while at university and now I'm an airline pilot. Just an airborne bus-driver, I'm afraid, but I know that's a Pup because my grandfather flew in the Royal Naval Air Service in World War One… quite near here actually.'

'What, Yarmouth air station?' Spencer had certainly got Frank's attention.

'Yes, Curtis flying boats off South Denes.'

‘That must have been incredibly demanding,’ said Jack, well imagining the challenge of operating early flimsy aircraft off the hostile North Sea in winter.

‘Pretty hairy, according to Grandad,’ agreed Spencer, ‘which is why they sent him to survey the broad near here as an alternative.’

‘The broad!’ The thought of one of his favourite locations being used as a flying boat base was a surprise to Jack.

‘Grandad told me what a beautiful place it was,’ continued Spencer. ‘He never went into details, but I got the distinct impression he was so entranced by the place that he gave an unfavourable report to ensure it was never used.’

‘Good for him,’ said Jack.

‘And Yarmouth’s only a few miles from here,’ added Frank.

‘I know. I’ve always wanted to see where Grandad flew from, which is why I jumped at the chance of Amy’s reunion.’ Spencer’s thoughts were already ranging ahead. ‘And perhaps sail on the broad too?’

‘You certainly will.’ Frank thumbed in the direction of the quay. ‘Go and tell Harold to put *Babbling Brook* alongside.’

Spencer went off to load his kit on *Brookside*.

‘Well, there’s one satisfied customer,’ remarked Jack.

‘Let’s hope so.’ Frank Brooker shrugged his shoulders. ‘We need as many of them as we can.’

‘What up, mate?’ Jack had caught the edge in Frank’s voice.

‘Just that I got this in the morning’s post.’ He passed across an official looking letter.

It was from HM Revenue and Customs with a final demand for unpaid tax. Jack stared at the figure. ‘Phew, over ten thousand quid. I wouldn’t have thought you’d earned enough for that sort of tax, Frank.’

‘It goes back a long way, Jack. That’s why they’re running out of patience.’

‘Ten grand is a lot of money.’

‘It is when you haven’t got it.’

‘But, you seem to have had a bit of spare cash lately, Frank.’

‘Which has all gone on parts for the boats.’

There was no explanation of where that cash had come from and Jack didn’t ask. Instead, he suggested, ‘Can’t you offer to pay them by instalments?’

‘I’ve tried that,’ said Frank, glumly ‘but I reckon the government’s as hard up as the rest of us right now, and they want their money.’

‘Yes, hard times,’ agreed Jack before giving the yard-owner a friendly pat on the back. 'I'd help you myself, Frank, but a police pension and ranger's pay doesn't exactly put me in the surtax bracket.'

Frank shook his head. 'Don't worry, Jack. I'll think of something.'

Further discussion was ended by Audrey's appearance in the office. 'They're all set to depart, Jack, so let's wave them off.'

*　　*　　*

Out on the jetty, *Brookside*'s engine was running once more with the sailing boat, *Babbling Brook*, already breasted alongside.

'She's a bit rough, but I'm sure she'll give you a good sail,' Harold was saying to Spencer. 'I wish I'd had time to give her a once-over, because that main halyard is showing a bit of fraying at the yard. Keep an eye on it and give us a call if it starts to look seriously dodgy.'

'I certainly will,' promised Spencer, climbing back on board the cruiser and preparing to take first trick at the wheel. He looked around him. 'Where's Alistair?'

'He just popped back to leave his car keys with Frank,' said Beki from the foredeck. 'Oh good, here he comes now.'

'Right… sorted,' said Alistair, jogging back up to the boat.

'Good… you look after the stern-line,' ordered Spencer, '… and you, Oliver, the bow.'

As the two men let go their lines and prepared to cast off, it was time for Amy to make her farewells to her parents. 'Bye, Mum. You can enjoy some peacc and quiet again tonight.'

'Nice thought, except your dad's volunteered me for crew duties with him on *Princess*,' grumbled Audrey, relaying the news only just broken to her by her husband as they'd made their way from shed to quay. But her protest was only tongue-in-cheek. She smiled and wrinkled her nose. 'Actually, it'll be nice to have something to occupy me.' She gave her daughter a big hug. 'Take care, love, and don't do anything silly.'

'And get straight in touch if you need any help,' said Jack with a big hug of his own.

'I will, Dad.' And then Amy was hopping on board followed by Alistair and Oliver with their lines. There was an increase in *Brookside*'s revs as Spencer eased the two boats away from the quay, out into the basin and onto the main river. On the foredeck, Beki gave an enthusiastic wave while, from the wheelhouse, Amy blew a kiss. The only one not topsides was Clarissa, still where last glimpsed, reclined on her bunk and absorbed in a magazine.

Best place for her, thought Jack. Then he went back to the shed to talk to Frank about the evening's trip.

*   *   *

He found the yard-owner just hanging the keys to Alistair's Daimler on a hook behind the office door. Frank hadn't joined them in the wave-off and now looked a little bit distracted.

'Cheer up, mate.' Jack felt he should say something positive. 'And don't let things get you down. I'm sure we'll find some way to keep the tax-man off your back.'

'Oh that.' Frank seemed almost dismissive. 'That will get sorted somehow.'

'Good. So, what's the problem, then?' Jack glanced outside to the now-vacated berths. 'Your first hire of the season's underway and there'll surely be more to come.'

Frank seemed to make an effort to shake himself out of black thoughts. 'You're right, Jack. Sometimes you have to stop trying to control your life and let it control you.' He glanced at his watch. 'You know, I can't remember the last time I had a Saturday evening off. Just for once, I think I'll treat myself to a night out. I could do with a drink while I think things over.'

'That's more like it.' Jack gave him a reassuring slap on the back. 'Leave *Princess* to us, and go and take your mind off whatever's bothering you.'

As he made his way to the trip boat to prepare her for the evening's cruise, Jack felt concerned about Frank's state-of-mind. At the same time, he was glad he hadn't mentioned an earlier happening that had made him just a little bit curious.

*   *   *

Chapter Ten

'I just hope the gang are all still talking to each other and having fun.' Audrey had taken just a short break from her stewarding duties to join Jack in *Princess*'s wheelhouse.

'They'll be fine.' They were on the main broad now and this was the first time Jack had relaxed since getting underway. He nodded down to the far end. 'With a bit of luck, we might even see them.'

Like anyone new to a job, he'd been more than determined that all should go well and, so far, it had. He cast his wife an admiring glance in her white shirt and black skirt. 'You seem to be handling that bar like an old hand.'

'I wouldn't say that.' Audrey's mouth did an affected downturn. 'I've done a lot of things in my time, Jack Fellows, but this is my first time as a barmaid.'

'… and a deckhand too, but you and Jenny did a really expert job with the lines on departure.'

Audrey gave a little sniff. 'A pity Frank wasn't there to see us off, especially as this was your first trip.'

'He's taking a night off,' explained Jack. 'He seemed to have something on his mind and felt the need of a break.'

'I don't blame him really,' sympathised Audrey. 'He's probably just a bit anxious that all goes well for *Brookside*'s hire.'

'Yeah, you're probably right.' Jack turned and gave his wife a loving wink, 'and, anyway, we did okay without him, didn't we?'

Audrey nodded. 'And Jenny's doing a great job with the commentary, considering it's her first time.'

This evening's trip wasn't a ghost cruise, so Jenny had only had to describe the passing scene as they made their way down river and broad. After a slightly nervous start, she'd soon got the measure of her new role and now seemed to be actually enjoying it as much as the passengers. 'First time for all of us really,' said Jack. 'Lucky for me I've got such a great crew.'

'We try to please…' Audrey gave a mock curtsy before glancing out of the wheelhouse and at the several empty glasses needing to be cleared, '… which I won't be doing much longer if I don't get back to my duty station.'

'Just wait 'til we've turned round.' They were at the end of the broad now, and Jack was slowing, close by the moorings of the nearby inn. Right at the entrance to this dyke he spotted the two boats, side by side. 'And there they are.'

'Oh good, they've found a perfect spot.' Audrey pointed to *Babbling Brook*'s lugsail, now out of its cover. 'Looks as if they've had a sail already, but I can't see any of them now.'

'That's because they're all in the pub putting away some grub and booze,' laughed Jack.

Audrey smiled back. 'Well, as long as they're all enjoying themselves, that's the main thing.'

* * *

They were indeed. Seated in the pub and tucking into hearty meals, the gang had so far put old differences behind them and were enjoying the simple pleasure of renewed friendship. Around them, other holidaymakers also relaxed in the congenial ambience of soft music and happy chat within walls lined with faded photos of century-old boating scenes and glass-encased stuffed pike. Outside, a dozen-or-so boats lay at their moorings, seemingly resting from the day's endeavour in preparation for the next. In this cordial atmosphere, even Clarissa was making an effort to come up with something positive.

'I must say,' she mumbled between mouthfuls of curried chicken, 'this is almost as good as we'd get in London.'

'Why shouldn't it be? Norfolk isn't completely in the stone-age, you know.' Beki had been born and bred in the county.

'And they can certainly build boats,' said Spencer, keen to diffuse any latent discord. 'That lugger we brought, sails like a dream.'

'As long as it holds together,' laughed Oliver. He'd joined the rest in a brief afternoon sail with Spencer soon after arrival at the broad. 'I don't know much about boats, I admit, but surely a lick of paint wouldn't do it any harm.'

'It's the main halyard that worries me more,' replied Spencer, frowning slightly. 'Harold was right: it needs renewing. We'll have to keep checking it doesn't fray any more.'

'Whether it does or not, you won't get me into that tippy thing.' Clarissa was the only one who hadn't joined them for the lively thrash in *Babbling Brook*.

'You don't know what you're missing, Clarissa,' said Amy, still savouring the thrill of churning up and down the broad under Spencer's very competent hand. If this holiday was meant to provide a change from work with fresh air, mild adventure and good company, so far it had been a total success.

But Clarissa was not one to miss the chance of a jibe. 'I'm completely aware of what I'm missing, Amy. Are you?'

Amy felt the sting in that remark's tail, but even before she could think of a reply, Alistair broke in with a laugh. 'I think the only things we'll miss tonight are our beds.' He glanced around the others. 'Are your bunks as hard as ours?'

'Yes, pretty firm,' agreed Oliver who was sharing his cabin with Spencer, 'but I guess that's what roughing it's all about.'

'If "roughing it" is what you like,' grumbled Clarissa. 'On our own cruiser…'

'… the berths were so soft you had backache for weeks,' interrupted Alistair, ignoring the glare he received from his wife. 'I'm all for a firm bunk.'

'What sort of cruiser did you have?' Once again, Spencer was diverting an awkward situation.

'Oh, a big steel forty-five foot sea-going job.' Alistair waved a dismissive hand. 'So plush you didn't know you were on a boat and burning enough diesel each trip to run a car for a year. No wonder we hardly ever took it out for our own enjoyment.'

'Well, *I* liked it,' pouted Clarissa. 'At least we could invite your banking friends on board to enjoy the sort of luxury they were accustomed to. The catering firm always provided top-notch food and everyone just loved coming, didn't they, darling?'

'Of course they did, but for all the wrong reasons,' replied Alistair. 'I couldn't stand half the people we felt we had to invite, with their name-dropping and misplaced arrogance.' He gave a wry smile and just the briefest of glances towards Amy. 'Can't you see that it's all so superficial, Clarissa? It's where you are and who you're with that's important.'

'I agree,' nodded Oliver. 'I feel better already. This place feels a million miles from Westminster.'

Spencer topped up his cabin-mate's wine. 'So, how are things in the seat of power?'

Oliver shook his head. 'Pretty fraught at present. That banking crisis really threw a spanner into party finances…'

'... not to mention, the MP's expenses scandal,' interrupted Clarissa, scathingly. Loyalty to her husband's career had never been her strong suit, but she was damned if she'd listen to his profession being slanged by this jumped-up politician. 'No doubt you'll be claiming this holiday as some sort of fact-finding expedition?'

'Of course not,' mumbled Oliver, without looking up.

'I think these past couple of years have been pretty crap generally,' said Spencer, turning to Alistair beside him. 'They can't have been easy for you.'

'You can say that again.' The banker looked into his empty glass. 'In fact...'

'... Alistair's thinking of taking early retirement,' broke in Clarissa. She pushed her own glass towards Spencer for a refill and asked, 'So, where are we bound tomorrow?'

There was a collective shrugging of shoulders around the table.

'I'm easy,' said Oliver.

'So am I,' reiterated Amy.

'Perhaps another sail here in the morning,' suggested Spencer, 'and then on to another broad.' He turned to Beki. 'Any suggestions?'

'If we're not leaving here until midday, we want somewhere reasonably close. Ranworth might be a good option. The moorings there are pretty popular and usually full, but there's a dinghy dyke so we can anchor *Brookside* on the broad and go ashore in *Babbling Brook.*'

'Sounds good to me,' agreed Alistair and there was general nodding from the rest, followed by a yawn from Oliver.

'Sorry everyone, but it's been a long day.'

'For all of us,' replied Spencer. 'I think we're all ready for a bit of kip.'

'Good idea.'

The bill was paid and all wandered out save Clarissa and Oliver who weren't going to miss the chance of a real loo before retiring.

Outside, the clear sky and full moon cast spectral shadows across the moorings. There was a slight nip in the air and Spencer and Beki wasted no time in forging ahead to *Brookside* and climbing aboard. Soon, cabin lights showed behind the curtains, but Alistair seemed to be holding back and it was obvious to Amy he wanted to talk. Even as she was considering the wisdom of this move, he stopped completely just beyond the pub and turned towards her. 'Amy... we may not get another opportunity to talk, but I just wanted... well, I just wanted to say I'm sorry.'

She tried to brush it off. 'Oh, Alistair, that's all in the past. Let's leave it there.'

'I wish I could.' He drew just a little closer. 'Believe me, Amy, there hasn't been a day in all those years since, when I haven't thought of you and what might have been. If I could only have explained at the time… that it was you I wanted to marry all along, but…'

'Alistair… stop!' Amy ran a hand through her hair. 'This isn't going to help either of us. What's done is done and it's no good regretting it now. We can't change anything, so what's the use.'

'But things can be changed, Amy. That's what I wanted to tell you…'

'Thank you for waiting for me, Alistair.' The voice was Clarissa's, emerging out of the blue and full of sarcasm.

Amy was relieved that the situation was taken out of her hands. 'Just marvelling at the reflection of the moonlight on the water, Clarissa. Isn't it just breathtaking?'

Any response Clarissa intended was thwarted now by Oliver joining them. 'Alistair, I wanted to catch you before we got on board. Can we just have a quick chat?' He turned to Amy and Clarissa. 'Sorry, ladies… you don't mind do you?'

'No of course not.' Amy took the banker's wife by the arm. 'Come on, Clarissa, let's get into our cosy bunks.'

Alistair watched them depart with very mixed emotions. He turned to Oliver. 'Does this have to be now, Oliver? Can't it wait until tomorrow?'

'It really is quite urgent…' there was an edge of desperation in the MP's voice, '… and only you can help.'

'In what way?'

Oliver explained his plight. 'The solution really is quite simple, Alistair, but time's the factor.'

'Otherwise?'

'It's the end of my parliamentary career.'

Alistair hesitated. 'All right, Oliver, give me the details and I'll try and sort it.'

'When, Alistair?'

'First thing Monday.'

'Thanks, so much. I really am grateful.' He patted the banker's shoulder and walked on ahead.

Alistair watched him go, took a packet of miniature cigars from his pocket and lit one up. He certainly felt no immediate desire to join Clarissa in their cabin. Instead, he strolled to the end of the moorings and stood looking out across the moonlit broad, trying to somehow let the peace of this scene soothe his troubled mind. Strange, how water always had this calming effect on him.

Only he knew Oliver's cause was doomed from the start. Just one more worry to add to the rest. He threw his cigar into the black water.

This holiday would soon provide the solution to them all.

*   *   *

The next morning found Jack back on the river wearing his ranger's hat, covering for a colleague who was due a Sunday off.

He didn't mind. It was a sunny day with a cool freshening breeze and he found patrolling in his launch almost relaxing after his first trip on *Princess* the evening before.

The breeze had brought out the weekend sailing cruisers, presenting a challenge for novice holidaymakers on their first full-day afloat. "Always pass astern of a sailing boat" *The Broadcaster* advised, but even so, on a narrow stretch of river, passing a tacking craft churning across your bow with lee-rail under water was always a nerve-wracking business. Nevertheless, with give-and-take from all sides and an understanding from most sailors that it was not always easy to keep out of their way, the morning proved uneventful. Everyone seemed good-humoured and, except for holding out a SLOW DOWN sign occasionally, Jack enjoyed a pleasant few hours.

Just ahead of him now was a busy staithe where he would stop for lunch. He regularly chose this spot in order to deter passing boats from speeding. Cooking and eating while being tossed around by wash wasn't easy, and lack of consideration for other river-users was one of Jack's pet hates. But, as he ghosted in, he espied a boat he recognised with BROADS CHAPLAIN on canvas dodgers along the side. Just the man, he said to himself and, instead of taking up one of the public mooring spaces, he breasted up alongside the chaplain's boat.

The Reverend Bill McGlyn was not on board when the ranger climbed over his floating office to the bank, but talking to the crew of a large cruiser further down the quay. Jack always enjoyed a chat with this intelligent man who combined a deep-rooted love of boats with his sincere conviction that, in these magical waterways, nature and spirituality came easily together.

'Hi Jack, good to see you.' He joined the ranger on a seat just back from the water's edge. 'How's life treating you?'

‘Just fine thanks, but there is something I’d like your help with.’ Jack told the chaplain of Harold Searby’s situation and his own, so far, futile attempts to find out the man’s history. ‘How about you, Bill? I was hoping you might know something.’

‘Yes, I’ve heard of his work, but only met him the odd time. Until now, he seems to have kept to the southern rivers, but I’m glad he’s decided to venture into our neck of the woods.’ The chaplain shook his head. ‘But as to his background, I’m afraid I’m as ignorant as you.’

‘He told me he became a Christian *after* losing his memory,’ said Jack, ‘and, through Audrey, I’ve made enquiries at the church he said he attended for a short while, but no-one there seemed to know anything about his past. Congregations can be like that, can’t they?’ The ranger sighed. ‘I must admit I know very little about the personal lives of people at our church, and I’ve been going for years! But, I can’t help feeling he may have been a churchgoer *somewhere* before his accident.’

‘Apparently not, otherwise I’m sure someone would have stepped in to help him after his accident.’ The chaplain raised questioning eyes. ‘Are you absolutely certain he can’t remember *anything* about his previous life, Jack?’

‘Not a thing, but I get the impression that he’s worried his past might not have been as virtuous as it should have been.’

‘Which is why you’re pursuing his case,’ said the reverend with a knowing smile.

Jack returned it. ‘Just like to tick all the boxes, padre.’

The chaplain twiddled his thumbs. ‘You say he’s working for Brookerboats at present; I’ll try and call in there and have a chat.’

‘I’m sure he’d like that. Everyone seems to know *of* him but, beyond that, the man’s life’s a complete mystery.’

‘Perhaps we should let sleeping dogs lie, Jack. The chap seems to have found peace in an otherwise chaotic world. Is it up to us to interfere?’

‘I’m all for peace,’ agreed Jack, noticing a dayboat churning towards them with throaty exhaust and churning bow-wave, ‘… which is more than this boat’ll give us if I don’t slow him down.’

He jumped back onto the launch for his speed sign and loudhailer.

*   *   *

Speed certainly wasn’t a problem for the crew of *Brookside*. After a good sail on the broad and a very tight, piloted bridge passage, it was late afternoon before they turned into the dyke leading to Malthouse Broad and the village of Ranworth. As predicted, the public moorings were full, with several more boats lying at anchor on the broad itself.

'That looks a good place over there,' said Alistair, steering the cruiser towards a sheltered, secluded spot at the far end. 'Well out of the way with plenty of room to swing.' A wide lazy turn brought *Brookside* into the diminishing wind while Spencer went for'ard to handle the mudweight.

As they neared the anchorage, Alistair brought the engine to neutral. 'Anchor aweigh!'

Spencer lowered the heavy mudweight until it was kissing the surface of the broad. The engine was running astern now with *Brookside* slowing further, finally stopping and then gathering a little sternway. Once again, Alistair brought the engine to neutral. 'Let go!'

The mudweight sank to the bottom of the broad and slowly the anchor rope paid out until it became taught, held and then slackened once more. Alistair turned off the engine and suddenly peace descended upon them.

Standing on the sidedeck, Amy took in the tranquillity of their surroundings. She had really enjoyed their casual passage down the river, even though the freshening breeze had caused more than one interesting encounter with tacking yachts. But that, surely, was all part of the fun, and even Clarissa had managed to chill out slightly, face-down on a large towel on the cabin top. Alistair too, with his wife relatively content, had also relaxed, entering into the spirit of the reunion with no attempt to repeat his entreaties of the night before. Amy hoped it stayed that way and that they could just enjoy the peace of this delightful setting. She picked up the binoculars she'd brought from below and scanned the scene in closer detail.

At the public moorings she saw some shops and, beyond them, on the other side of a road, an attractive-looking pub, *The Maltsers*. Doubtless, that would be visited in due course. They'd passed a conservation centre on entering the broad, something else to explore. Most imposing of all though, and dominating the skyline was the imposing tower of a church. Amy checked the guide she'd been studying. Saint Helen's of Ranworth and known as "The Cathedral of the Broads". It wasn't really a cathedral, but certainly worthy of a closer look when they ran ashore.

'Cup of tea anyone?' Down in the galley, Beki was already filling the kettle.

'G&T for me,' answered Clarissa from atop the cabin, making only a half-hearted effort to rise.

'Okay, I'll get that,' offered Alistair, well aware that no-one else was going to act as steward to his wife.

Certainly not Beki. In spite of her previous reservations for a man who'd hurt her best friend, she found herself actually warming to Alistair. Or was it only pity for his being married to such an awful woman? Seeing Amy, still with a youthful spirit and figure, he surely must be bitterly regretting the indiscretion that had forced him into the arms of another.

'… and get my fleece while you're at it,' further ordered Clarissa. 'I'm starting to get a little chilly up here.'

'Come down then.' Clearly there were limits to even Alistair's patience, but everyone on board preferred Clarissa's absence to her presence, so Beki was quick to throw up a blanket in an effort to head off her possible descent.

'It's such a beautiful evening. How about a sail?' suggested Oliver. He was another one Beki felt sorry for, but for some other, indefinable, reason. He was trying so hard to relax and fit in with the rest, but beneath his cheerful exterior, she was sure there lurked some deep personal problem.

'Good idea, but let me check that main halyard first,' cautioned Spencer. 'My guess is it won't take another thrashing.' He jumped down onto the centre thwart. The rigging was still lowered from their bridge passage with the mast lying in a crutch, its head up by the half-decker's transom. Spencer took the section of bad cordage and examined it closely. He was soon shaking his head. 'No, as I thought: frayed almost to nothing.'

'Can't you just cut out the bad bit and tie a knot in it?' suggested Oliver, looking down from *Brookside*'s side-deck.

'Not really. It needs to run freely through the block at the masthead and a knot would prevent that.' Spencer ran a hand through his hair. 'If it were rope, I'd cut and splice, but this is halyard and needs an expert.' He looked up, sadly. 'Sorry, folks, but no more sailing today.'

'We need to ring the yard and get one of them to come out,' said Amy, cradling her mug of tea. 'I know Frank won't mind.'

'I'm sure he won't, but I don't think it's much use calling him this late in the day,' joined in Alistair en route to his wife with drinks and fleece. 'First thing tomorrow morning will be fine.'

'And we can still use *Babbling Brook* to row ashore in,' pointed out Beki. 'We've been on the boat for several hours now and a good walk will do us good.'

'A stiff drink, more like, after going ashore in that,' mumbled a voice from up top.

'Well, you can always stay here on harbour watch,' called up Alistair with only the slightest of smirks to the others.

'I wish,' muttered Spencer under his breath, as he climbed back on board. He too was torn between dislike and pity for the man who could have had the best girl in the world.

One thing had surprised Spencer though: from the way he'd brought *Brookside* up to her anchor, Alistair Hepscott certainly knew how to handle a boat.

*   *   *

'Ummm, That was scrummy.' Beki pushed away her plate. 'You're a good cook, Amy.'

'I think anything would taste nice after a day on the river and a long walk.' Amy gathered up the empty plates and piled them by the sink. After an enjoyable ramble ashore, they'd all agreed a meal afloat would work best, anchored as they were, out on the broad. She enjoyed cooking, and so was happy to volunteer to do this evening's honours. Spencer, Oliver and Beki had been willing galley slaves, peeling the vegetables and washing the utensils as she finished with them. The result had certainly been worth the effort, and now they all sat back around *Brookside*'s polished table with cleared plates and satisfied appetites.

'We might make you ship's cook permanently,' joked Spencer, topping up their wine-glasses, 'but not the washer-up. That's a job for us galley slaves.'

'Pity the boat doesn't have a dishwasher?' grumbled Clarissa, pushing forward her glass for a refill.

'But it does,' laughed Spencer with a nod towards the Hepscotts. '*You*!'

'Fair enough,' acknowledged Alistair. 'You lot prepared it, so we can do our bit, can't we, Clarissa?'

'If you say so, Alistair.' Clarissa took a long quaff of her wine.

'… but not for a while yet,' suggested Amy, loathe to see their congenial setting disturbed. Outside, the evening twilight was turning to night, the waters of the broad flat calm in the moonlight with only the occasional thud of oars in rowlocks, breaking the peace of this idyllic setting. There were half-a-dozen other boats lying at anchor and, as people retired down below, lights started to appear behind closed curtains. Amy struck a match and lit the candles they had placed in the empty wine bottles on the table, and soon flickering shadows played across the panelled bulkheads and deckhead above.

'I wonder if there's a ghost boat on this broad?' said Oliver, half-joking, but sensing the ethereal atmosphere that moon and candlelight had produced.

'Don't be ridiculous,' scoffed Clarissa.

'Only one sort of spirit you believe in, eh, Mrs Hepscott?' Spencer gave Amy a wink across the table, and there were grins all round at Clarissa's childish pout.

Beki, though, was slowly turning her wine-glass before the candle, its flame glowing like a wavering phantom through the translucent, rose-coloured liquid. 'Actually, there is supposed to be a ghost here, a twelve-century monk who's often seen rowing himself and his dog across the broad in the early morning mist.'

'What, poppycock!' Clarissa gave her a pitiful look. 'Don't tell us that when you narrate those spooky stories on the passenger cruises, you actually believe them?'

'Most stories are pure legend, I agree,' defended Beki, 'but some have a core of truth behind them.'

Oliver sat back with a quizzical grin. 'So, Beki, have you actually *seen* a ghost?'

'No, I never have, but that doesn't mean I don't find the subject fascinating. In fact,' said Beki, her tongue loosened by the effect of the wine, 'supernatural research is something I do.'

'You mean ghost-*hunting*?' Amy remembered Beki's hesitancy in explaining her hobby but, faced with a cabin-full of slightly inebriated sceptics, she had clearly lost that inhibition.

'No, something I can actually practise myself, on my own.'

'What, for goodness sakes?' Even Spencer was being drawn into the intrigue of this conversation.

'Astral projection.'

'Astral… what?'

'Projection.' Beki sat back and folded her arms. 'Basically, it means exercising deep meditation to the extent that you can project yourself into another dimension.'

Alistair leaned forward. 'To where, exactly?'

'To anywhere you want to go.'

'But, surely, that's just exercising your imagination isn't it?' questioned Oliver with a frown. 'I mean, I can sit back and imagine myself in all sorts of exotic spots, but I haven't actually *been* there.'

Beki nodded. 'But what if someone actually *saw* you in the location to which you'd projected yourself?'

'You've actually done that…' Alistair's wide eyes were fixed on Beki's, '… actually appeared in another location while not actually leaving your room?'

Beki shook her head reluctantly. 'No, not yet, I'm afraid, but I know people who have. It's just a matter of training yourself to rise to that higher plane.'

'Well, the only plane I want to rise on is one that will fly me to some nice place abroad,' ridiculed Clarissa, helping herself to more wine and casting a pitying look towards Beki. 'I've never heard such a load of bunkum.'

'I don't know, there are times when I wish I could project myself to anywhere but where I am.' Speaking the words, almost to himself, Alistair was suddenly aware he was baring a little too much soul. Quickly replacing sobriety with a smile, he added, 'Sounds a useful skill to me, Beki. You'll have to teach me how to do it.'

'… but, in the meantime, let's all have some coffee,' said Amy with a little shudder, as she rose and put on the kettle.

Somehow, she'd found that last conversation a little disturbing, especially those last words of Alistair's. He'd laughed at the time, but Amy was conscious of a world of emotion behind them. Was life with Clarissa really that intolerable, or was there yet more troubling this seemingly successful man?

*　　*　　*

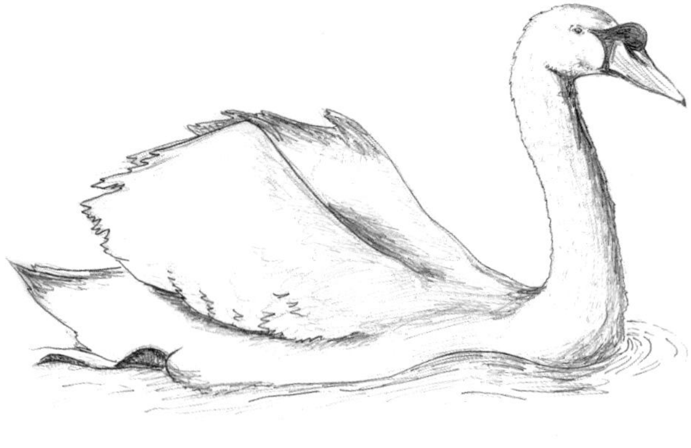

Chapter Eleven

It was eight o'clock on Monday morning and, in Brookerboats' yard, Harold was just preparing one of the other half-deckers for a day's let when Frank came scurrying along the quay.

'Harold, I've just had Spencer from *Brookside* on the phone. They're at Ranworth and the main halyard on *Babbling Brook* is shot and needs replacing. They don't want to risk sailing again until it's fixed.'

'I knew it would,' answered the yard-hand. 'I'd have liked to replace it before they left, but everything was a bit last-minute.'

'Yeah, I know and, unfortunately, I'll need the van for another job this morning. I told them it would be afternoon before I could get you over there.'

'Where are you going?' asked Harold.

'Just to Norwich.'

'Then, why not drop me on the way.' Harold indicated a car just pulling into the yard. 'Here come our customers. Ten minutes will have them away and then I'll be ready.'

'You'll be stuck in Ranworth for a few hours before I can pick you up again,' Frank pointed out.

'No problem; it's one of my favourite places to visit and there's plenty to do.' Harold thought for a second. 'We ought to let them know I'll be there this morning.'

Frank shook his head. 'No need. *Babbling Brook* will more than likely be left in the dinghy-dyke and it'll be a nice surprise if you turn up early. You may even get it fixed before they return to the staithe.' He gave his yard-hand a slap on the back. 'Get your gear and I'll go and sort you a new halyard.'

Frank returned to his shed, happy to have at least one problem resolved.

* * *

'He says it'll be afternoon before Harold can get here,' reported Spencer, switching off his mobile. He glanced across the broad where the ripples of the day's breeze were already glistening in the morning sunshine. 'Pity, it would have been perfect for a sail.'

All except Clarissa had risen early, tempted out of their cosy sleeping bags by the early rays of sun reflecting dancing water patterns on the deckhead above them and promising a glorious day ahead. The men had enjoyed a row around the broad, sighting no ghost monk, but greeting other early-risers, until the aroma of bacon and eggs frying in the galley enticed them back on board. Sitting in the open-wheelhouse, they'd chatted amiably until eight o'clock when Spencer had called the yard. The result was not quite what they'd hoped for.

'Well let's go for another walk this morning instead,' proposed Amy, laying aside her breakfast plate. 'I'm sure it won't take long for Harold to fix it, and then we can still have our sail later in the afternoon.'

'And we'll probably feel more like it after a bit of exercise.' Oliver glanced towards Alistair. 'Some of us need to make some calls anyway, and the rest of you won't want to listen to boring business conversations on the boat.'

Beki frowned. 'You lot ought to try and forget work for a few days and just enjoy the beauty of the real world around you.'

'You're a one to lecture on the "real world" after what you told us last night,' laughed Spencer. 'I'm surprised you're not already "projecting" yourself to the shop for some fresh milk.' He stared distastefully into his mug of black coffee. 'We could certainly do with some and a few other goodies too.'

'Perhaps you chaps can decide what we need while you're doing the washing up,' suggested Amy with a grin.

'Try not to wake Clarissa,' pleaded Alistair as the men tumbled below with clattering plates and cutlery. 'She didn't sleep too well last night.'

Probably because she was snoozing all through the day, thought Amy, but didn't say. In all honesty, she would have been happy for Clarissa to sleep away the whole holiday.

* * *

While the gang was preparing to go ashore, Jack was already back patrolling the river. It was one of those idyllic Broadland mornings and few boats were underway at this time, their occupants content to have a lazy start. The only intrusion into this timeless scene was the purr of the launch's engine and the ring of his mobile phone.

'Jack… Henry Mayhew here. Sorry to be so long getting back to you, but you wanted the history of *Fisher of Men*.'

‘Yes please, Henry.’

‘Right, well it was sold to the present owner, Harold Searby, ten years ago by a boatyard on the southern rivers… J F Hendricks & Sons.’

‘And are they still operating?’

‘Yep, but not a hire fleet anymore. These days they just concentrate on third-party maintenance and sales.’

‘Okay…’ Jack fished out his notebook, ‘… give me their address, please, Henry.’

He jotted down the details, thanked his colleague and switched off.

He’d be taking a little trip to the southern rivers as soon as he could. Perhaps there lay some clues as to who Harold Searby really was.

* * *

‘Isn’t this just beautiful?’ Amy had paused to admire the unspoilt countryside, stretching away on either side of the narrow lane along which they were ambling. Through a gap in the hedgerow, beyond fields of barley, she could see a distant cluster of houses nestling in a hollow, with the tower of the village church rising in medieval grandeur amidst the parish it served.

They all gathered to look at the view, Alistair standing just a little too close to Amy for comfort. He inhaled deeply, breathing in the sweet smelling, unpolluted air and said wistfully, ‘Yes, so good for the soul. This really is a world away from the sights and sounds of London. I wish my wife were here to see this. A bit of rural exposure might do her good.’

‘It might even help to restore her life’s values,’ said Beki, who made no secret of her contempt for Clarissa, ‘but I doubt it.’

They could talk freely, because the lady in question was the only one not joining the walk. She’d come ashore with them but, after doing the shopping, planned to have a leisurely sit with a coffee and scone at the quayside café before crossing the road for something stronger. ‘I’ll be in *The Maltsters* by the time you get back,’ she’d told them, and then gone her own way. Everyone seemed much more relaxed without this member of the party and there probably wasn’t one of them, including her husband, who wouldn’t have minded if she’d taken the next bus homeward-bound.

‘I’d forgotten how invigorating fresh air could be.’ Oliver, took a great lungful as though it were nectar. ‘If you could bottle this, it’d fetch a fortune in London.’

'I thought you City types loved the stench of car exhausts and sweating bodies,' joked Spencer as they moved off once more.

'Not me.' The MP looked around him. 'Compared to this, life in London is like being set on "fast forward".'

Alistair nodded. 'Which would be okay if you could just rewind in the same way.' He gave Amy a knowing glance.

She chose to ignore it. This was too lovely a day to be blemished by regret. Besides, the roads they were following looped back to the village via the church and she wanted to explore Saint Helen's before they returned. They were just nearing its imposing splendour when Alistair's mobile phone rang.

He hung back, engrossed in a conversation obviously far from amicable. He finally switched off and caught them up by the church gate.

'Is everything all right, Alistair?' Like the rest, Spencer could tell the banker was clearly upset.

'Not really, but nothing is these days.'

'Can we help?'

Alistair shook his head. 'I don't think anyone can now.'

'We're just going into the church to look around,' said Amy, feeling at a loss as to how to help him. 'Why don't you come with us and forget work for a while.'

'Thanks, I'll just stay here, but, Oliver…' he turned to the MP, '… can I just have a word with you?'

They left them by the church wall.

* * *

'Eighty-nine steps, two ladders and a trapdoor! That'll be *some* a climb.'

Amy was reading aloud the sign at the bottom of Saint Helen's tower. They'd already spent a good half-hour trying to identify the twelve Apostles on one of the finest rood screens in the country and marvelling at the illuminated manuscript, used as a songbook in the church since before the Reformation. But no visit to this church was complete without sampling its unique view.

'I bet it's worth the effort.' Spencer went through the narrow archway at the foot of the steps. 'Come on, girls, I'll beat you to the top.'

'I'm sure you will,' said Amy as she and Beki followed him up the narrow, winding stone stairway that allowed no room for passing anyway. Lord help us if we meet someone else coming down, she thought as they climbed ever upwards, almost dizzy with the spiralling ascent. Pausing to look through the small windows on the way gave them a taste of the spectacular views they would get at the very top. Finally they emerged onto a landing where an iron ladder took them partway up through the belfry and to yet another platform. They stopped here for a moment to look at the bells which hung from a massive oak beam, their ropes disappearing down through openings in the belfry floor. Beside them was a final wooden ladder that took them up to a trapdoor and onto the viewing platform. Once again, Spencer led the way and soon they were all standing within the castellated battlements of the tower top, momentarily spellbound by the amazing vista all around them.

Spencer was the first to break the silence. 'It's going to be a good sail this afternoon,' he observed, looking at the weathervane above his head. It depicted a monk in a boat with a dog peering out from the bows.

That must be the one whose ghost haunts the broad, thought Amy, but only momentarily, because it was the view now that had caught her full attention. 'Blow your sailing, Spencer. Look at this. It's fantastic!' She was gazing out over the tower's edge. 'I can see the wind turbines on Scroby Sands. And that must be the big-dipper at the Pleasure Beach at Yarmouth!' she exclaimed, pointing out to the southeast.

'And I can see How Hill over there *and* Happisburgh lighthouse.' Beki was gazing out in a northerly direction.

'Alistair and Oliver don't seem to be having a particularly amicable chat,' said Spencer, looking down to where the two small figures still stood by the wall.

Beki joined him, gazing below. 'I wish we could hear what they're talking about.'

'Whatever it is, Oliver doesn't seem too happy. 'Amy could see the MP arm-waving and gesticulating.

'No doubt we'll find out later.' Spencer went over to the east wall and looked out across the broad. Like toys in a bathtub, there were several boats, some lying at peaceful anchor while others cut a white wash across the water's glinting surface. His attention was caught by the sight of a sailing boat creaming out from the dinghy dyke. He screwed up his eyes against the light of the sun. 'If I didn't know better, I'd say that was *Babbling Brook*… in fact…' he peered even more intently, '… it *is* her.'

'It can't be,' Amy replied. They all knew that Clarissa, of all people, would never attempt to sail a boat on her own.

‘She’s certainly never sailed before in her life and wouldn’t have a clue what to do,’ agreed Beki, anxiously.

‘I’m not so sure whoever’s at the helm has either,’ gasped Spencer. ‘Look!’ The half-decker had almost reached *Brookside* by this time, but suddenly her yard had dropped and the boat swung wildly away. There appeared to be much commotion on board and Spencer wasn’t prepared to waste another moment watching. He turned to the girls. ‘I think we should get back a.s.a.p. and see what on earth’s going on.’

As one, they ran down the stone steps of the tower, barely registering the long descent. Dashing out into the sunshine, they found MP and banker still embroiled in discussion, but it was Alistair who immediately sensed alarm.

‘What on earth’s happening?’

‘I don’t know, but we need to get back to the staithe immediately.’ Spencer was already running down the road with Beki and Alistair hard on his heels.

‘Come on, Oliver.’ The MP was hesitating to follow but, for Amy, it was simply a case of priorities. ‘You can tell me later what *your* problem is.’

‘Yes, perhaps I will.’ Oliver glanced unhappily after the departing trio. ‘I can’t think what could be worse than mine, but I suppose we’d better find out.’

They followed together at a fast run and soon they knew this was no minor incident.

Halfway down the hill they heard the sound of an emergency vehicle’s blaring siren.

* * *

Chapter Twelve

By the time they arrived at the staithe, paramedics were already stretchering a seemingly-lifeless figure into the back of their ambulance.

'My God!' Alistair sprinted the last fifty yards and, by the time Beki and Spencer caught up, he was already turning to face them, his face a mixture of anguish and relief. 'It's not Clarissa, it's Harold… he's…'

'… just unconscious, sir,' broke in the lead paramedic.

'What… happened?' gasped Spencer, still recovering his breath.

'Some boating accident, sir, but you'd best ask *her*.' The paramedic nodded towards the pathetic-looking figure of Clarissa, sitting on a low wall, huddled in a blanket and being comforted by a young couple. Alistair and Beki went off to her side just as Amy arrived.

'It's Harold,' explained Spencer.

'Are you friends?' asked the paramedic.

'Sort of. His name's Harold Searby and he works for the boatyard we hired our cruiser from.' Even as the paramedic wrote this down, Amy steeled herself to ask, 'Will he… be alright?'

'Early to tell, but I'm sure you've no cause to worry.' The paramedic climbed aboard next to his patient. 'The important thing now is to get him to A and E.'

'Which hospital?'

'James Paget, Gorleston. We happened to be close, so they sent us.' He passed down a card with telephone numbers. 'Ring in about an hour, and they should be able to tell you something.' He closed the doors, the engine started and they were speeding away, lights flashing.

Oliver finally jogged up. 'What happened?'

'We're not sure, but Clarissa will tell us.' Amy led them over to where a sobbing figure sat being comforted by her husband.

'It's all your fault… all of you…' Clarissa was still mildly hysterical, '… leaving me to deal with that incompetent yardman.'

'Alistair took the glass of brandy that someone had kindly brought from their boat. 'Here, drink this, calm down and tell us exactly what happened.'

‘I’d just come out of there,’ she spluttered between gulps and poking a finger in the direction of the shop, ‘and there he was, fiddling with the boat.’

‘Harold?…’ Alistair turned back to Spencer, ‘… I thought he wasn’t coming until this afternoon?’

It was Clarissa who answered. ‘The yard-owner… what’s his name?… Frank… managed to drop him off early. With the boat here, he got straight to work on that rope and had it mended in no time.’ Clarissa took another good swig of brandy. ‘So, as he seemed to be at a loose end, I got him to take me back to *Brookside* so I could sunbathe in peace. I pleaded with him to row, but he said it would give him a chance to check the rigging if we sailed so, against my better judgement, off we went.’

‘With, presumably, him helming,’ muttered Spencer.

‘Of course… you wouldn’t catch me trying to handle the wretched thing. That boat’s an absolute death-trap. It shouldn’t…’

‘Just tell us what went wrong,’ broke in Alistair, taking the now-empty glass from his wife’s hand.

‘Nothing at first… he pulled up the sail and seemed to be handling things well enough. It was only when we got near the cruiser that the stupid man lost control completely.’

‘How exactly?’

Clarissa ran a shaking hand through her hair. ‘I was up in the front and he just shouted something like “Standby with the headrope”, whatever that meant. I wasn’t sure which blessed bit of string he was talking about, but there was one on the mast which I undid.’

‘You unhitched the main halyard?’ asked Spencer with dismay.

‘If you spoke in English, I might know what you’re talking about,’ mumbled Clarissa. ‘Obviously that Harold chap hadn’t made himself clear and just shouted “not that one”, so I let it go and the whole sail came crashing down.’

‘And, presumably, the yard struck him on the head?’

‘The wooden pole that the sail was fixed to, if that’s what you mean.’ Clarissa nodded out across the broad. ‘So, there I was, marooned with an unconscious man at my feet. How was I expected to know what to do, for God’s sake?… I really thought the boat would go over and I’d drown.’ She paused for maximum effect.

If it was meant to evoke sympathy, it worked only with her husband. ‘All right, you’re safe now.’ Alistair cradled his wife’s head in his hands. ‘How on earth did you get back to the staithe on your own?’

'The man who takes boat trips across the broad saw what happened and came straight out to help us. He towed us back to the staithe and called for an ambulance.'

'You mean the skipper of the electric boat, *Helen of Ranworth*, which takes people too and from the Conservation Centre? We had a chat with him when we first arrived, didn't we? Well, thank goodness someone had their wits about them,' remarked Beki pointedly.

But the sarcasm was lost on Clarissa. 'Yes indeed. I was in a terrible state, but the ambulancemen barely noticed me.'

'I think we get the picture,' muttered Alistair, standing up. He turned to the others. 'First thing is to ring Frank and let him know what's happened. I'll do that.' He got out his phone. 'The signal's pretty weak just here, so I'll walk up the hill a bit and see if that helps.' He nodded to where *Babbling Brook* lay in the dinghy-dyke. 'You go and check her over, Spencer, and then we can get back to the cruiser and take it from there.'

'Sounds like a good plan. I'm sure she won't have come to much harm, but I'll give her a good look-over just in case.' He set off for the boat, and, for the sake of something to do, Amy went with him.

'Gosh, Spencer, not a good start for our week of fun. Poor Harold.'

'Don't worry.' He put his arm around her. 'I'm sure he'll be back on his feet in no time.'

Amy blinked back tears and nodded. It was good to have Spencer's arm around her, even if her predominant emotion was one of guilt. Was it really very wrong to wish it were Clarissa and not Harold, lying in hospital right now?

*　　*　　*

'According to the doctor in Casualty, there's no serious injury and he's starting to come round.' Back on *Brookside*, Alistair put his mobile back in his pocket and gratefully accepted the mug of coffee being handed to him by Amy. 'Still a bit confused apparently but, in a few hours, he should be fully conscious. They'll keep him in overnight for observation but, all being well, he should be discharged tomorrow.'

'Thank goodness for that.' Amy breathed a great sigh of relief. 'Poor Harold, he was only trying to help and ended up in hospital.' She took a welcome sip of coffee. 'We really should try and visit him tonight. Dad says he has no family.'

'Of course we must, but *you* mustn't feel guilty, Amy.' Spencer nodded to the cabin roof and Clarissa's ample form soaking up the sun. '*She* obviously doesn't.'

'Clarissa's still in mild shock, Spencer,' reproved her husband with forced loyalty. 'It was a horrible experience for her.'

'Not as horrible as for Harold,' Beki retorted. She glanced up at the blue sky and back to the shimmering waters of the broad. 'The fact is, what's happened has happened and there's nothing we can do about it, so there's no point in sitting here moping. I think we should move on.'

'You're right,' agreed Alistair. 'I think Clarissa would benefit from a change of scene; this place has such distressing memories for her now.'

'I've got an idea. If we want to visit Harold tonight, why don't we head for Great Yarmouth?' spoke up Amy. 'Then, at least, we'll be fairly close to the James Paget hospital.'

'And you can check out your grandfather's old flying ground,' perked up Beki. 'Hopefully we'll have time to fit in some estuary sailing on Breydon Water as well.'

'Sound's good to me.' Spencer reached across for the tide tables and scanned the times. 'Low water at Yarmouth is just before seventeen-hundred today.' He glanced at his watch. 'Five hours from now and, with the tide ebbing, we'll have ample time to get there.' He turned to the MP, sitting slightly morose in the corner. 'What do you think, Oliver?'

'I really don't care.' The MP shifted only slightly in his seat. He seemed to have withdrawn in mind and body alike and there was a noticeable coldness now between him and Alistair. 'One place will be much like another to me.'

'Oh, come on, Oliver, buck up,' chided Beki, giving him a gentle hug. 'Things can't be that bad. You've got air in your lungs and good company to share, so don't spoil it for the rest of us.'

'No, you're right.' Oliver made an effort to sit up and smile. He glanced towards the main river. 'A night on the tiles sounds a great idea.'

'Right, Yarmouth it is then.' Spencer jumped up and started the engine. 'About eighteen miles according to the pilot so, with the tide under us and allowing for a stop at Acle to lower *Babbling Brook*'s mast, we should be there in less than four hours.' He went for'ard to haul the mudweight. 'You take the wheel, Oliver. Something to take your mind off whatever's bothering you.'

Amy and Beki gathered up the mugs and took them down into the galley, while Alistair checked the lines holding the smaller boat alongside. Atop the cabin, Clarissa glanced briefly at the activity and then resumed sunning herself.

*   *   *

Jack was just reaching the limit of his patrol when word came through on the VHF about the incident at Ranworth. There were no specific details, but those there were, gave him an uneasy feeling that it may have involved Amy and her gang. He straightway rang her mobile.

'Oh, Dad… I'm glad you rang…' Amy gave a quick summary of all that had happened.

'Well, it's not your fault, Amy, and it could have been worse. Does Frank know?'

'Yes, Alistair called him before we set off.'

'Where are you now?'

'We've just passed Stokesby, heading for Great Yarmouth.' She explained the plan to visit Harold that evening.

'I'd like to see him myself. Ranworth isn't in my patch but, as there's injury involved, I can write up the incident report for the Broads Authority.' Jack quickly checked his watch. 'If I get back to base early, I'll come and meet you at Yarmouth Yacht Station, get Clarissa's side of the story, and then give a couple of you a lift in my car to the hospital.'

'That sounds great, Dad…' Amy paused, '… and it'll be lovely to see you anyway.'

Jack rang off, turned the launch in mid-river and headed back to base.

He could tell from her voice that his daughter was still upset by all that had happened, but she'd feel better once she'd seen that Harold was okay. Like he'd said to Amy, it could all have been much worse.

Why then, did he have that uncomfortable feeling that it still could be?

*   *   *

Chapter Thirteen

'They say he's coming round slowly and they're about to move him onto a ward.' Once again Alistair switched off his phone.

For the last few hours they'd been cruising through flat marshland, following the meandering course of the Bure as it took them ever closer to Great Yarmouth. There was a saltiness in the air now, and the lowering tide was revealing shelving mud on either side of the channel marked by posts. As they were nearing their destination, Alistair went for'ard and made yet another call to check on Harold's progress. 'He's doing fine, thank goodness, and they're moving him into a room of his own,' he explained as he joined the others in the open wheelhouse.

'I don't know why you keep ringing the hospital. Anyone would think you had a personal interest in the man,' moaned Clarissa.

'Yes, well if it hadn't been for your crass stupidity the poor chap wouldn't be in there.' He took off his sunglasses and gave his wife a hard stare. 'I really am getting to the end of my patience with you and your self-centredness. You don't give a damn for anyone else.'

'*Well…*' Clarissa threw her magazine across the wheelhouse and flounced off down below. All felt it was probably the best place for her as they were now nearing the Yacht Station.

'Not the prettiest scene so far,' remarked Amy at the wheel, steering them past broken quays and the derelict buildings of what had once been a busy marina.

'No, but at least there are some interesting boats in front of us over there.' Spencer was pointing to the west bank where a miscellany of fishing and work boats were moored beside old wooden piles.

'And here's the Yacht Station itself,' smiled Beki as, to port, dozens of pleasure craft nestled up to a much-smarter and obviously better-managed quay. There was a station office and, on the quay itself, uniformed rangers were checking moorings and generally helping the visiting boats. For most of the quay's length, boats were moored two abreast and Amy wondered if there'd be room for their large cruiser and half-decker. And why were they passing the yacht station so quickly when she had the engine throttled right back?

‘That’s the tide taking you faster,’ explained Spencer, indicating the steep harbour walls on each side. ‘It’s narrower here, so the ebb just sluices through.’

But it was an iron girder bridge right ahead of them that had captured Amy’s immediate attention. It looked very low and was getting closer at a frightening speed. ‘I think you ought to take it now, Spencer.’

‘Well I don’t; you’re doing just fine.’ He stepped a little further away. ‘Bring the engine right to stop and let her slow even more through the water… that’s right… now wheel hard over and give her some revs to help her round.’

Amy did as ordered and they turned across the river, though seemingly still crabbing towards the bridge. ‘She’s going sideways, Spencer!’

‘Don’t panic, Amy. That will stop as soon as her nose is into the tide.’ Sure enough, *Brookside* appeared to be stopping as they came around parallel to the bank. Water was still sluicing down her side but, relative to the buildings beside them, there was no motion whatsoever. ‘Now you’re stemming the tide and still have complete control,’ assured Spencer.

Amy looked across to the Yacht Station, hovering beside them. A uniformed ranger was pointing just astern of them to where a single boat lay alongside the quay. ‘I think he’s telling us we can moor there.’ Now the ranger was waving them in. ‘It’s behind us, Spencer, so I’ll have to turn us round again.’

‘No you won’t. Just ease your revs slightly and let her drift astern with the tide.’

‘If you say so.’ Amy throttled back very slightly and *Brookside* continued pointing upriver but easing ever so slightly down.

They were abeam the mooring spot now. ‘Turn her in a bit and ease up the revs again.’

Now they were crabbing towards the other moored boat and the ranger was obviously happy with progress because he gave Amy a thumbs-up and reassuring smile. By now, Alistair was up for’ard with the head-rope and Oliver was ready with the stern. When the two boats were almost bow-to-bow, Alistair heaved his line to the ranger who made it fast to a bollard. Amy brought the engine to stop and *Brookside* strained back on her head-rope. Oliver threw across his line, a few slight adjustments, and the three boats were snug beside each other and she could stop the engine completely.

‘Phew!’ In the silence that followed, Amy forced her clammy hands off the wheel, only realising now the grip she had been holding it with. ‘That was interesting.’

'You did great.' Spencer gave her a pat on the back. 'Well done, Amy.'

'Yes, with you telling me what to do.'

'Only this once. You'd know next time.'

'I hope so.' Amy looked down at the river still flowing fast alongside. 'It's a bit different here than further upriver.'

'Very much so,' agreed Spencer, 'but, in some ways, a good tide makes coming alongside even easier… as long as you do it right.' He gave her a grin and encouraging hug. 'Come on, skipper, let's go ashore and pay our dues.'

Leaving Beki to get the kettle going, they went to the office, paid the mooring fee and got assurance they would be safe moored right where they were for the next twelve hours. 'The boat inboard of you will want to be off at low-water tomorrow morning,' explained the ranger, but you probably will as well.' They were making their way back to *Brookside* when Jack appeared on the quay.

After a quick hug with Amy and a few words with his fellow-rangers, he joined the rest onboard for a welcome cuppa. Even Clarissa emerged from her self-imposed sulk.

'Do I really have to complete this?' she asked, scanning the form Jack had given her as though it were the carrier of bubonic plague.

'Yes, you were involved in an incident where there were injuries, which makes it a reportable accident,' explained Jack rather brusquely, 'so the sooner you explain what happened, the better.' He turned to the others. 'I shouldn't think the hospital will want us descending on Harold in great numbers, so I suggest I only take two of you to see him.'

'Obviously Amy should be one,' offered Alistair, 'and I'd like to be the other, seeing as it's my wife who caused the whole mess in the first place.' He glanced towards Clarissa in the corner, her hands cradling a gin and tonic.

'If that's what you'd like.' Jack would have preferred not to have to rub shoulders with the man who'd jilted his daughter, but there was logic in Alistair's suggestion. 'Finish your tea and we'll head straight off.'

After agreement for them all to meet up at nine-thirty at the Britannia Pier, the hospital visitors climbed across the inboard boat and made their way to Jack's car parked just outside the Yacht Station gates. They were soon heading for Gorleston.

* * *

'We ought to take something for him,' suggested Amy as they entered the hospital main doors. Luckily the shop was still open. 'A bunch of these will at least brighten his room,' she said, selecting the best of the day's remaining flowers.

'Here, I'll pay for those,' offered Alistair, taking out his wallet and handing over a twenty-pound note. 'None of this is your doing.'

Jack didn't argue with that or Alistair's next statement as they traversed the sterile corridors to Harold's room. 'God, I hate hospitals.'

They were words that echoed Jack's own thoughts. He'd spent enough time in them during his police years, but never lost the feeling of dread that engulfed him as he breathed in clinical smells combined with the lingering aroma of hospital food. Most hospitals these days, including this one, tried to ease the ambience with bright colours, modern design and artwork, but Jack was still feeling far from comfortable when they reached Harold's ward and checked with the duty nurse.

'How is he?'

'Doing fine. He's come round now, but's still a bit groggy so don't stay too long.'

'We won't.' Jack turned to the others. 'Perhaps I'll go in alone first.'

'Why?' Strangely, there seemed an element of concern in Alistair's voice.

'Simply because I don't want to subject him to a room full of visitors if he's not up to it.'

'Yes… of course,' agreed Alistair, forcing a smile, finding a pair of chairs and sitting down with Amy outside the room.

Jack found the patient sitting up in bed, his head swathed in bandages and, in his hospital issue nightshirt, looking as clinically clean as his room. Harold gave a smile, but it was one of gratitude for company rather than any recognition. There were some comfortable chairs around the bed and Jack settled into the nearest.

'Well, Harold, you've done it again.'

'Again?' Below the bandage, Harold squinted slightly as he tried to bring the ranger into focus, but he appeared to be very confused. 'I'm sorry… I don't… you are?'

'Jack… Jack Fellows. Don't you remember, Harold: you were knocked unconscious on a boat.'

'Yes, I remember that. On *their* boat.'

'That's right, and they've come to see you… just for a few minutes.'

Jack ushered in Amy and Alistair after a whispered, 'Still a bit confused.'

'So sorry about what happened, Harold,' sympathised Amy as she laid the flowers on the bedside table and sat down beside him. But, there was little response.

It was Alistair's turn. He leaned closer and smiled. 'At least you've got a bit of privacy in here.'

Harold blinked twice. 'Did *you* arrange that, Alistair?'

'Yes, after what happened, it was the least I could do.'

'It certainly was.' There was a glint of anger in Harold's eyes, but he blinked it away and glanced around him. 'Quite comfortable actually. I knew Tony Blair would shake up the NHS.'

Amy went to say something but was stopped short by a firm nudge from her dad, who simply said, 'The main thing is for you to get better and back to work as soon as possible, Harold.'

The patient nodded. 'Yes, the bank will wonder where I am…' he paused, obviously trying to assemble confused thoughts, '… but why do you all keep calling me "Harold"?'

'Because that's your name,' broke in Alistair.

'Why, what do *you* think your name is?' asked Jack.

But, Harold's eyes were once again half-closing.

'I think he's had enough, Jack,' stated Alistair decisively.

'Yes, let's let him rest, Dad.'

'All right.' Jack paused before giving a comforting hand. 'Take it easy, Harold, and get back to us soon.'

They all bade farewell, but the patient seemed only vaguely aware. Outside the room, Jack told the others he would meet them at the main entrance. 'I just want to have a chat with a doctor.'

'He's just with a patient at the moment, but he'll be along very shortly,' said the cheerful ward-nurse, and soon Jack was introducing himself to a young physician with a colourful shirt and friendly smile.

'We've just been visiting Harold Searby.'

'Ah yes, the gentleman with the head injury.'

'Are you aware,' asked Jack, 'that he was already suffering loss of memory from a previous head injury?'

'Really?' The doctor flicked through some notes. 'According to this, we have no previous medical records for him at all, which doesn't help, seeing as he's obviously suffering some present amnesia.'

'... but actually recalling events current at the time of his first accident. Doctor, is it possible,' asked Jack, 'for someone already suffering amnesia from one accident to have that memory restored by a second?'

'In other words, for him to think that he's here now as a result of his first head injury and everything in between to have been wiped out?'

'Exactly.'

The doctor frowned. 'Amnesia's a complicated condition and quite selective in its way. What you've just described is certainly rare, but by no means unknown.'

'How long before he's up to more intensive questioning?'

'Is this official?'

'It could be.'

'Probably twenty-four hours, but we'll see how he progresses.'

'Thanks, doc.'

Jack made his way back down, to find Alistair deep in conversation with Frank Brooker. The yard-owner had obviously just arrived.

'Jack, I've been busy on a job, but came over as soon as I could. How is he?'

'Confused. I should keep your visit short.'

'Right.' Frank wore a worried expression and looked genuinely anxious. 'Rotten luck, this happening just as we started to see a bit of light at the end of the tunnel.'

'Yep, but I think this accident might shed a bit more elsewhere.'

'In what way?'

'Can't say just yet, Frank, but I have some thoughts.' Jack turned to Alistair. 'Where's Amy?'

'Just popped to the lady's room... ah, here she is.'

Jack gave his daughter a brief smile. 'Right, let's get you back into town. It's been an eventful day to say the least, but you might still have time for a bit of fun before it's through.'

* * *

Accomplishment rather than fun was what Spencer Ovington was experiencing at this same time, sitting on the beach at South Denes. It had been a long walk from the boat and, now he was here, he felt a slight sense of anti-climax.

Granted, he was sitting very close to where his grandfather had flown on missions in the First World War, the place central to so many of the old man's stories. Making this pilgrimage of sorts, was something he'd always wanted to do, to try and sense the atmosphere of those times and the sacrifices made by so many. But now he was here, the fence of the new outer harbour prevented him from even setting foot on where the air station had been. Worse still, peering through it, it was obvious that not a single building remained of what must have once been an extensive base. Almost a century ago, inexperienced airman had launched off into the hostile North Sea in the earliest of flying boats and not a memorial or even a commemorative plaque was there to show they had even existed.

Spencer sat back and tried to imagine this location then. From what his grandfather had told him, this area was just open dunes with those early primitive flying machines operating off the denes themselves. Eventually, larger flying boats had come into service, launched into the North Sea from a slip now obviously long-absorbed into the new harbour. He could only wonder at what it had been like in those days, flying far out of sight of land with no navigation aids other than your watch and compass, enduring long patrols over an inhospitable ocean in winter searching for U-boats and other enemy naval units? And then had come the Zeppelin raids and Yarmouth itself had been the first town in the country to know the horror of aerial attack. Sopwith Pup fighters had been brought in to combat this new threat, notching up more than one victory against these sinister raiders.

Hard to imagine all that now, thought Spencer as he looked around him. To the north, the Pleasure Beach marked the start of the promenade with its plethora of entertainment, while beside him, in the new harbour, a ship was being loaded with what appeared to be parts of a huge wind turbine. Only one thing remained unchanged: the North Sea, stretching out to fill the whole eastern horizon. How calm and inoffensive it looked on this still, balmy evening, glimmering in the evening summer sun, but how quickly its mood could change to become hostile and bleak. To his grandfather, in winter, it must have been a far greater challenge than exchanging fire with the enemy.

Spencer's thoughts turned from rough, stormy seas to the sheltered inland waters of Ranworth's Malthouse Broad, and the unfortunate chain of events resulting from Clarissa's stupidity. How on earth did her husband tolerate the woman? As much as it galled Spencer to admit, Alistair came across as quite a decent type: considerate, decisive and, for someone in his position, relatively modest. But it was knowing how he had hurt Amy all those years ago that still soured Spencer's judgement of the man. He knew he was being irrational and that dwelling on the past was insane, but he seemed powerless to stem the feeling of intense jealousy that was boiling up within him. For the truth was, he knew *he* still loved Amy.

If only he'd had the courage to contact her in the years since university, to tell her how he felt. With Alistair back in the frame again, he'd probably missed his chance for a second time. He'd assumed that an attractive, vivacious girl like Amy would be married with children by now, or at least be in a stable relationship, and had been delighted to find she was still unattached. But this euphoria had soon been dampened by the realisation that she might be single because *she* still loved Alistair. Had she, in fact, arranged this holiday so they could be together? He'd caught the banker, on off-guard moments, giving Amy lingering, intimate looks and was sure it wouldn't be long before the man made a move. Spencer kicked the sand despairingly and his mind wandered back to the bravery of those airmen who were prepared to battle to the end for victory over the foe. It brought him to his senses with a jolt. No, he thought to himself, I'm damned if I'm going to sit back and watch Alistair woo Amy all over again without a fight.

He glanced at his watch. An hour yet before their meeting by the pier. Time to think of a way to win Amy's heart. He wondered, briefly, what Beki and Oliver were doing.

* * *

In fact, they were as far north of the pier as he was south, sitting on a bench-seat deep in conversation. The promenade here was much narrower, far quieter and separated from the sea by a couple of hundred yards of dunes and marram grass. Beki had sensed Oliver wanted to talk and so had steered them here and finally asked what was worrying him.

The MP had offered only token resistance to airing his problems before explaining completely. 'It's this bloody expenses thing, Beki; it could be the ruin of me.'

Beki well-remembered all the furore over the many abuses of the parliamentary expenses system, but thought this had all died down now.

'It has for most,' groaned Oliver, 'but some of us, and me in particular, still have the threat of legal action hanging over us.'

'For what, exactly?' Beki knew these were searching questions, but if Oliver wanted someone to pour his heart out to and perhaps offer help, then she needed the full facts.

'The old chestnut of claiming work done on a constituency residence I was sharing with my sister.'

'Oh dear.' Beki looked at Oliver beneath furrowed brows. 'How much?'

'Thirty-four grand.'

Beki's eyebrows rose slightly. 'Not an insignificant amount, but can't you just pay it back?'

'That's what the IPSA are demanding,' explained Oliver, 'and I would if I could, but the reality is I'm pretty strapped for cash right now.'

Cash shortage was something Beki herself had been living with most of her life, but assumed that it wasn't a problem for MPs who were all pretty well off. 'Surely you've saved something during your time in Parliament?'

'Yes, I have, but it's all tied up in investments made for me by Alistair.'

'Alistair?'

'Yes. When I first got elected, he rang me up and congratulated me on winning the seat. We had a long chat about our work and he bragged about the wonderful returns he was able to make on certain investments. I admitted being a complete clown when it came to finance, and that my life's-savings were making very little interest in a bank deposit account. He kindly offered to look after that side of things for me and assured me I'd make a killing. All I had to do was transfer my money to this special account and he would make sure it was invested wisely.'

'That was very kind of him, especially when he's, presumably, dealing with investments worth millions.'

Oliver nodded. 'That's what I thought, and I was really pleased to take him up on his offer.'

'So, how much have you invested to date, Oliver?'

'All my original savings, plus a steady monthly transfer since. It all comes to close on eighty-thousand.'

'Phew!' Beki blew out her cheeks. 'No problem paying off your expenses thing, then. Cash in the investments and you're quids-in.'

'If only it were that simple,' moaned Oliver, despair creeping back into his voice. 'After our meal on Saturday, I managed to catch Alistair and told him I needed to do just that and pretty damned quick.'

'And…?'

'… and, at first, he pretended not to even remember the arrangement.'

'Perhaps not surprising, considering,' conceded Beki. 'He's come on a long way in the last few years and, amongst the billions he's probably now handling, your little nest-egg must be pretty small fry. Presumably you pushed the point?'

'Of course and, in the end, he said he'd look into it. This morning, just as we got to the church, he got a reply to his enquiry…'

'… which, presumably, wasn't very good,' surmised Beki, remembering the obvious acrimony resulting from that call.

'It was worse than that. According to Alistair, the shares he invested my money in are now worth nothing… the money's gone completely.'

'Gone!' Even Beki was flabbergasted by this revelation. 'How can that level of investment dwindle to nothing? Surely you kept a check yourself on how your shares were doing, Oliver?'

'That's the trouble; I've been so involved with my new constituency affairs that I was content for Alistair to look after all that. I didn't even know what funds he'd invested in, but I do remember him assuring me that they were low-risk.'

'You mean you did the whole thing on trust?'

'Yes. I figured, if you couldn't trust a friend and the son of the chief executive of one of the country's leading banks, then who could you?'

'I can see that, but what excuse has Alistair made for such appalling incompetence?'

Oliver shook his head again. 'None. Just said he was sorry, but that was how the stock-market went: downs as well as ups.'

'That's a pretty big "down", Oliver, but I would have thought, if Alistair had any scruples, he could pay you back out of his bonus alone.'

'I did suggest something on those lines, but he just laughed at me.'

'So much for friendship.' Beki shook her head. 'So, you've lost everything?'

'Yep, all my savings and, when the party realise I can't pay back my expenses deficit, probably my parliamentary career will be down the pan as well. If I'm lucky, I'll just be made bankrupt and, if not, I'll end up in court on fraud charges.'

'Oh, Oliver.' Beki put her arm around the MP's weary shoulders. 'What can I do?'

Oliver Stanhope managed to raise a little smile. 'Just teach me that astral projection you were talking about the other night. Achieving another dimension in deep space would be a pretty good option for me at present.'

'I don't think that would be the solution,' she replied, smiling back, happy at least that this old friend could still see some humour in his situation. 'But, you must feel very bitter against Alistair?'

'More bitter than you could ever imagine.' Oliver looked out to sea and frowned at his own dark thoughts.

* * *

Clarissa Hepscott's feelings weren't very much different as she sat in a pub on Marine Parade and considered her husband through a succession of G&Ts.

After leaving the cruiser, with the promise to join the rest at the pier later, she'd wandered down Regent Road, casting distasteful glances at the discount shops on either side, and onto the promenade itself. The popular holiday resort was heaving with people making the most of a glorious evening. The noise and razzmatazz all around, was an alien experience to Clarissa and she felt like a fish out of water. Ready for a rest, she found a seat overlooking the miles of golden sands and decided to spend a few moments people-watching, not to admire the latest fashions as in Saint Tropez, but to simply feel smug and superior. It wasn't long, however, before she became aware of the fact that these people were having such a lot of fun together. They weren't restricted by pretence and keeping up appearances, but were thoroughly enjoying the results of a year of honest toil and were making the most of every second. She began to reflect on her own life. Where had it all gone wrong? Before maudlin thoughts filled her head, she dragged herself up and made her way to the nearest bar where she found a small table, moved the second chair well out of the way, and began her lone binge.

But alcohol failed to lift her spirits and the knowledge that her husband was with Amy rankled her. She always knew that Alistair had married the wrong person and that she'd won his hand through foul means. Desperate to entrap this rich son of a lord, she'd lured him to her bed the night before their finals, knowing he'd drunk far too much. She knew he'd have never continued a relationship with her if it hadn't been for the baby, and that that loveless one-night-stand, was something Alistair had lived to regret every day of his life.

She'd got what she wanted but, in the end, it had brought neither of them any happiness. And now the past had come back to haunt her and she felt very insecure. The fact that Amy had retained her looks and spirit, and that Alistair had made little effort to hide his infatuation for her, only gave the knife of her jealousy an extra twist.

And, if her husband decided to leave her for this old flame, what would she get out of it? Nothing, was the blunt answer. Her ambition for a wealthy lifestyle had come to fruition, with Alistair's family connection ensuring one lucrative promotion after another.

And then had come disaster, the audits following his father's death, the close examination of all his dealings and the upset that the results of those investigations gave rise to. Doubtless, a few more weeks would see Alistair out of his job completely and the fraud squad taking over where the bank left off.

A few more weeks. Clarissa rotated her third glass in her hand and considered that time frame. Alistair had been officially suspended a month before, but was still nominally an employee of the bank. As such, he was still covered by the very generous bank insurance which, if claimed, would make her, his next-of-kin, very wealthy indeed.

Was that possible? It had been Alistair's idea for them to join this holiday afloat and she had been forced to come along as well, to keep him from making a fool of himself with Amy. Well, Alistair Hepscott, she thought to herself, you might well have sown the seeds of your own destruction.

For the first time in a long time, Clarissa found herself enjoying a sense of smugness. The simple fact was, that for only a little while yet, her husband was worth far more dead than alive.

* * *

One of Clarissa's concerns was certainly unfounded, for, as far as Amy was concerned, there would be no question of her entertaining any further feeling for Alistair Hepscott other than that of friendship.

Her father had dropped them both off on the seafront and now they were walking together down Yarmouth's Golden Mile. She sensed that Alistair, finally having got her alone, wanted this to be a more intimate evening, but one spin-off from this ill-omened reunion was that any feelings of a romantic nature that she'd fostered for this man, were now well-and-truly consigned to the past.

Amy wasn't quite sure what had triggered this welcome realisation. Partly, it was memories of all the hurt he'd caused her before, but more probably, a growing awareness of her feelings for Spencer Ovington.

She'd always liked this clever, energetic student with good looks and a taste for the outdoors, but his apparent shyness and her own reticence to push herself, even in the face of mutual attraction, had resulted in a disappointing stalemate. Alistair, on the other hand, had not been backward in coming forward. Certainly he was nowhere near as clever as Spencer, but he had charm, confidence and, until that awful night, apparent sincerity. She glanced across to the man walking beside her, still fresh-faced and youthful in his designer jeans and expensive blue check shirt. He appeared so seemingly-decent that Amy wondered yet again how he could have behaved so badly.

'Amy, what we were talking about the other night… you and I.'

She had been dreading this moment and now here it was again. 'There's nothing to talk about, Alistair. You've gone your way and I've gone mine, and that's an end to it.'

'Not necessarily…' he went to take her hand, but she managed to avoid contact by scratching her nose. Instead he took her arm, brought them to a halt and looked her straight in the eyes. 'All right, I know how bitter you must feel about me, Amy, but couldn't you give me one more chance? If some time in the future, I managed to start a new life without Clarissa, would you come and join me?'

'You're wrong, Alistair, I don't feel bitter any more. I did once, but the years have managed to clear my thoughts.' Amy wanted to terminate this embarrassing conversation as soon as possible. They walked on past the Hippodrome Circus, Sea-Life Centre, Reptile House and several amusement arcades full of noisy, flashing machines and the promise of easy winnings. Not for many years had Amy even considered entering such a place, but tonight they offered sanctuary from all that might be following. She steered him towards the nearest. 'Look, let's forget the past and, just for this evening, have some fun together.' She went inside, pulling him after her. 'I haven't been in one of these since I was a child. Come on, it's been a crap day, let's win some money.'

Alistair forced a laugh. 'All right.' The noise within was certainly enough to distract them. All around, people of all ages played the hundreds of machines. The atmosphere was far from relaxing with coloured lights flashing to the background thump of some appalling music, but it did provide distraction, and that was what Amy needed right now. 'Not quite what you're used to in the City of London,' she teased, in her effort to keep the mood light.

Alistair smiled back. 'No, but it's still preferable to an evening with Clarissa.'

'Well, enjoy it while it lasts,' she said, checking her watch and giving him a playful nudge of reprimand. 'Don't forget we're meeting the others at nine-thirty.' There was still time for her to play the machine she had enjoyed most as a child. She led him to the 2p machine, fed in a coin and watched while a sliding shelf pushed piles of such coins towards a precipice. None fell off this time, but she shared what two-pences she had and together they continued feeding them in. It was almost like old times and, on the few occasions coins came tumbling noisily out of the bottom of the machine, they both eagerly scooped them up for yet more goes. Eventually, with a stack of coins teetering tantalisingly on the very edge of the shelf, they had both run out of coins.

Amy glanced again at her watch: just a few minutes to nine. 'We'll have to go soon and meet the others, Alistair.'

'Time for a few more goes yet.' He took a wad of notes from his back pocket and extracted a fiver. 'Here, let's get some change.'

'It's all right, I've got some pound coins,' she said, leading the way to the change machine with Alistair just behind her. 'How much shall I get?' she asked over her shoulder.

But there was no reply. Amy turned to be met only by the flashing lights of one-armed bandits and stares from a couple of young studs out on the pull. She ignored the lot and went back to the 2p machine, convinced she would find Alistair there. He wasn't.

'Fancy a drink, love.' It was a young lad, not far out of his teens, taking her arm. She shook him off and went further back into the arcade. More lights, more noise, no Alistair but a female attendant, noticing her worried face.

'Something wrong?'

'It's… it's my friend… he's disappeared.'

He had indeed. It was just as though Alistair Hepscott had vanished into thin air.

*   *   *

Chapter Fourteen

'Amy... good grief... what's wrong?' It was Beki who came running to meet her, aware even at a distance, that her friend was in some distress.

Amy had spent more frantic minutes searching for Alistair around the amusement arcade, all the time telling herself that it was easy to lose sight of people in busy places. Perhaps, with all the noise, she hadn't heard him say he'd go on to meet the others. Yes, that must be it, she'd thought to herself, and had hurried down the prom to the pier to find the others waiting.

'It's Alistair... is he here...?' she panted.

'We've not set eyes on him since you both went off to the hospital,' answered Spencer, looking concerned.

'Well, he's just vanished into thin air,' replied Amy, anxiously, holding out her hands in a gesture of disbelief.

'Vanished?' Clarissa had joined them now, her face showing more an expression of suspicion than concern. 'Got lost, you mean?'

'No. One second he was there and the next he wasn't,' blurted out Amy, trying to impart the increasing unease she felt.

'He won't have gone far,' reassured Spencer, calmly. 'We'll just hang around here a bit longer and he's sure to join us.'

'I expect so.'

'Wretched man,' muttered Clarissa. 'Never there when you want him.' She cast another dubious eye towards Amy. 'I knew I shouldn't have left him alone with you.'

'What are you saying, Clarissa?' Amy's nerves were tense enough without this woman's snide remarks.

'Why don't we all go for a drink nearby and I'll try calling him on his mobile,' suggested Oliver.

'Good idea.' Beki led them to an open café where they sat in relative silence to the carefree banter of the holidaymakers around them. After a few minutes, Oliver returned.

'No luck, I'm afraid. He's just not answering.'

'We'll give him half an hour and then I'm going back to the boat,' stated Amy. 'If he can't find us, that's where he'll head next.'

Thirty minutes went by, but there was no sign of Alistair.

* * *

'It's no good. I think we should call the police.'

For the umpteenth time, Amy checked her watch. It was nearing eleven o'clock now, the gang were sitting around *Brookside*'s saloon table, trying to keep upbeat while waiting out their fruitless vigil for Alistair. After arriving back at the Yacht Station, they'd made enquiries on other boats with equally negative results and it was obvious no-one had been back to their cruiser since they left hours before. Now, only Clarissa remained unconcerned. 'Don't be ridiculous. He's a grown man and I wouldn't put it past him to have sneaked off to a casino unless he's picked up a girl and's having a one-night-fling.'

'I shouldn't think he's done that since he left uni,' muttered Spencer just loud enough for all to hear and getting a withering look back from Clarissa.

The others would have smiled if the situation hadn't felt so fraught, but it was Oliver who still urged caution. 'I'm not sure if the police would take it too seriously anyway after such a short time. My guess is they only start proceedings for adults after they've been missing at least twenty-four hours.'

'I think you're right,' agreed Spencer.

'Well then, I'm going to ring Dad,' decided Amy. 'He'll know what to do for the best.'

* * *

Jack had just put down his book and was nodding off when the bedside phone rang. Audrey awoke just as he was answering.

'Uh... hello, Amy love... what's the problem?... really?... okay then, I can tell you're worried so I'll ring the police myself... they'll listen to me, but don't upset yourself, I'm sure there's a simple explanation.'

'Good heavens, what's happening now?' asked Audrey as her husband replaced the phone.

Jack explained and added, 'Amy's right, unless it involves children or other vulnerable people, the police never take missing persons too seriously at first.

They've dealt with too many couples walking out on each other and disgruntled teenagers, to get overly concerned at first reports.'

'But Alistair doesn't seem that sort,' protested Audrey.

'I'm not so sure, Aud. Remember he walked out on our Amy once before.'

'But you said he seemed pleasant enough when you took him to the hospital earlier?'

'Yes, although there's some issue lurking in the background. I can't put my finger on it yet, but every instinct tells me nothing is quite what it seems.'

'Well, instead of listening to your instincts, perhaps you'd better be ringing the police like you promised Amy.'

'Right.' Jack dialled Norfolk Police headquarters and explained the situation. 'Nothing more we can do now,' he said to Audrey after ringing off and snuggling down again.

Audrey knew he was right, but that still didn't stop her lying awake worrying. So far, poor Amy's reunion had been one disaster after another.

* * *

It seemed that Jack and Audrey had only been asleep minutes before the phone rang again.

'Hello!' Jack glanced at the bedside clock and saw that it was actually five-thirty-five in the morning.

'Jack?' The voice on the other end was familiar. 'It's Bailey here… DS Bailey.'

'Bailey, I didn't expect to hear from you.' Jack was always pleased to talk to this young detective sergeant, but not this morning.

'Apparently you called in late last night to report a missing person?'

'That's right… chap called Alistair Hepscott… in Great Yarmouth. But I didn't expect CID to be involved so soon, Bailey.'

'Normally we wouldn't be,' agreed the DS, 'but things have taken a bit of a turn since your report, Jack.'

'In what way?'

Bailey explained.

'Strewth!' Jack became instantly alert and threw off the duvet. 'I'll go straight away and see them myself.'

‘Has there been a development?’ asked Audrey, as her husband tumbled out of bed.

‘There has indeed,’ acknowledged her husband, ‘and it’s not what any of us wanted to hear.’

*   *   *

Chapter Fifteen

'Dad… what are you doing here? … what's happened?'

Amy Fellows knew her father well enough to know that this was no social call when he came banging on *Brookside*'s cabin door so early in the morning. Great Yarmouth's Yacht Station was just showing signs of life as holidaymakers prepared for an early start in order to pass under the bridges at low water, when Jack's troubled face appeared at the door.

'Is Clarissa here, Amy?'

'Yes, but…'

'Don't tell me they've found him.' The lady herself had appeared, wrapping a dressing gown around her ample body, and blinking through eyes clouded by a hangover rather than any tears of anguish. If anything, her question carried a ring of disappointment rather than relief.

'Possibly.' Jack scanned the other members of the party already gathering in the saloon, anxious to hear of any development. He turned back to Clarissa. 'I think it would be better if we could talk alone.'

'Don't worry.' Clarissa swept a bored hand over the assembled group. 'Anything you want to say can be said in front of this lot. If my husband's been making a fool of himself, no reason why they all shouldn't know.'

'Okay…' Jack paused, not happy at the procedure, but keen nonetheless to get this painful task out of the way. 'The fact is, Clarissa, this morning the police recovered a body from the river. We can't be sure until you've done an ID, but indications, so far, are that it's Alistair.'

'Oh my God!' Amy put a hand to her mouth and even Clarissa seemed momentarily stunned.

It was a few seconds before she could even stammer, 'Body… in the river… where?'

'Norwich.'

'Norwich!' It was Spencer's turn to speak up. 'But that's miles from here.'

'Twenty-six, to be exact.' A police car had just pulled up outside the Yacht Station gates and a female officer was making her way towards the quay. Jack stuck his head out of the cabin door and hailed her over before turning back to

Clarissa. 'It's not a nice duty, I'm afraid, but they need you to come to Norwich to identify the body.'

'Can't someone else do that?'

'No, it has to be you.' Jack once again looked at the others. 'But you can bring a friend for support if you like.'

'I'll come with you,' offered Amy, blinking back her tears.

'I really think you should leave that to one of the chaps, Amy.' Jack had been in enough morgues to want to spare his youngest daughter the experience.

But Amy was determined. 'No, Dad, I organised this whole debacle, so *I* should face the consequences, whatever they are.'

'Okay, if that's what you want.'

They climbed out onto the quay, the female officer putting a sympathetic arm around Clarissa as she guided her towards the patrol car. Jack turned back to Spencer. 'They'll want to get the boats moving here very shortly. My suggestion is that you take these up to Reedham and moor there. Then you'll be that much closer to Norwich when we return.'

'Right, we'll do that.' Spencer turned to Amy and put his arm protectively around her. 'You sure you don't want me to come along as well?'

'I'd love you to be with me Spencer, but…' she kissed him briefly on the cheek and nodded back to the quay, '… better you stay and look after the boats.'

As she walked with her dad to the car, she just had time to voice her confusion. 'Like Spencer said, Dad, Norwich is miles from here. What on earth was Alistair doing there?'

'I don't know and there are even bigger mysteries than that to sort with this one.' Jack glanced about to ensure they were out of earshot of the others. 'The police pathologist has already done his preliminary examination, Amy. He put the time of death as nine o'clock last night.'

* * *

'Yes, that's my husband.' Clarissa Hepscott looked down at the still form before her and wiped away a tear. 'No doubt about it.'

'Thank you, Mrs Hepscott.' DS Bailey glanced to Jack standing at the widow's side and got a nod in return. Then the mortuary technician replaced the sheet over Alistair's face and led them back into the small waiting area.

Amy had been sitting there, head in hands, trying to make sense of all that had happened. As the door opened she jumped up to offer whatever comfort Clarissa needed, but the woman was remarkably composed for someone who had just lost her husband of twelve years. Instead, the widow turned to the Detective Sergeant. 'How, exactly, was my husband murdered?'

'We can't even assume it was murder yet, Mrs Hepscott. That's for the coroner to decide but, for what it's worth, initial examination showed death was probably caused by a blow to the head.' Bailey paused. 'You say you and your husband were spending a week on a boat, Mrs Hepscott. Accidents do happen, but it'll take a full autopsy before we're really sure.'

'Well, one thing it will establish is that the time of death can't have been nine,' insisted Amy, 'because Alistair was with me in Yarmouth at that time, so it must have been much later.'

Bailey held up a quietening hand. 'Miss Fellows… Amy… there's a lot about this that is going to need sorting, but right now isn't the time…' he glanced around the sombre setting of the city morgue, '… or place to be doing it. What I suggest is that we all go back to headquarters where I can chat to you both in greater detail.'

'Do I have to?' asked Clarissa. 'I am on holiday, you know, and I haven't even had my breakfast yet.'

Bailey gave a barely audible sigh. 'Yes, I think it's important you do, Mrs Hepscott. This is…' he glanced towards Jack, '… this *could* be a murder enquiry, and the sooner I get some details the better.'

'And presumably you want Amy there as well? asked Jack.

'I'm afraid so.' He turned to Jack's daughter, still wiping red eyes. 'Apparently you were the last person to see Alistair Hepscott alive, Miss Fellows, so it's *you* I particularly want to talk to.'

* * *

It was at Bethel Street Police Station, to the side of Norwich City Hall, that Bailey took the three of them through the formalities of the front desk and on to what were obviously the CID offices. Amy knew it was ridiculous, but somehow she felt all the sensations of an accused felon. She comforted herself with the thought that, once she'd had a good chat with Bailey, all those suspicions would be dispelled. As they were ushered into a small seating area , the DS turned to

Clarissa and said, 'I'll see you first, Mrs Hepscott. That way you won't have to wait so long for your breakfast.'

'Shouldn't I have my solicitor present or something?' In her bereavement, Clarissa had lost none of her old haughtiness.

'That's not normal for a preliminary interview,' explained Bailey, 'but there will be one of our female officers present and if you'd like your own witness, then I suggest Jack joins us as well.'

'If that's procedure, very well.'

Jack turned to Amy. 'Will you be all right?'

'Of course, Dad.'

'I'll get someone to bring you a coffee,' said Bailey before leading the other two into the interview room.

'Right,' he started, after the young female DC had taken a seat behind them, 'I'm DS Bailey and…'

But Bailey's youthful good looks hadn't gone unnoticed by Clarissa, who straightway cut in with, '… aren't you rather young to be a superintendent?'

Bailey looked up from his notebook. 'Sorry to disillusion you, Mrs Hepscott, but the S stands for *sergeant*, not superintendent.'

'Sergeant!' Clarissa looked around her in apparent consternation. '*Sergeant* Bailey, my husband was a senior executive in a leading bank and the son of a lord and you mean to tell me his murder is going to be investigated by a mere *sergeant*?'

'As I said earlier, we haven't established your husband's death as murder yet, Mrs Hepscott, and this is only a first interview unless…' he fixed Clarissa with questioning eyes, '… you're going to do something significant like make a confession.'

'What? … Confess to what? … I haven't done anything.' Just a little of the arrogance and some of the plummy accent had slipped from Clarissa's voice.

'Good.' Bailey reopened his notebook. 'Then I suggest you let *me* ask the questions.'

'If you must.'

'Like, where were you at nine o'clock last night?'

'I was walking through Great Yarmouth, from the Yacht Station to the pier. I'd arranged to meet the others, including my husband, there at nine-thirty.'

'On your own?'

'Yes.'

'And your husband was… where?'

'With…' Clarissa cast a glance sideways at Jack, '… Amy Fellows.'

Bailey's eyebrows rose just a fraction before Jack cut in. 'I'll explain that later, sergeant.'

'Okay.' Bailey sat back. 'Let me get a bit of background on your husband, Mrs Hepscott. You say he was the son of a lord.'

'That's right, Lord Hepscott, the bank's chief executive,' replied Clarissa, puffing out her chest slightly.

'Is his father still alive?'

'No, he died over a year ago.'

'But you are just plain *Mrs* Hepscott still?'

'That's right.' Clarissa's chest visibly deflated. 'Alistair was Lord Hepscott's *adopted* son, so he didn't inherit the title.'

'Okay.' The DS leaned forward again. 'That's just about it for now… except for one more very important question.'

'Which is?'

'Did your husband have any enemies… anyone who held a particular grudge against him?'

'Certainly not.' Clarissa shifted slightly in her chair. 'Obviously a man in my husband's position has to hire and fire and perhaps there's the odd investor with a grievance, but generally, Alistair was a most loved and respected man and I can't think of anyone who would want him dead.'

'Then, can you think of any reason why he should end up miles away from where he was last seen and at the very same time?'

Clarissa had obviously been giving this problem some thought. 'There's only one explanation as far as I can tell.'

'And, what's that?'

'Astral projection.'

'Astral… *what*?' Bailey had heard most stories in his time but this was a first.

'Astral projection. Apparently, it's a form of out-of-body experience in which people transport themselves to a different dimension.' Clarissa caught the detective's highly dubious expression. 'I know, complete crap, but it's something the Smith girl put into my husband's head and which seemed to fascinate him. All I can think of is that he somehow managed it and got himself killed in the process.'

'Yes… well… I think we'll keep our investigations in this dimension for the present,' said a slightly bemused Bailey. He put down his pen. 'Right, Mrs

Hepscott, that will be all for now, but please keep yourself available for more questions later.'

'You mean I can't go home?'

'Where is home?'

'London.'

'Too far. I'd prefer you stayed in Norfolk, Mrs Hepscott.'

'Why not stay on the boat for the rest of the week,' suggested Jack. 'At least there you'd be near at hand and amongst people you know. I'm afraid Alistair's body won't be released until after the inquest, so there'll be little you can do until then.'

'Good idea,' agreed Bailey before Clarissa could object. 'And I'll be wanting to talk with the whole group later anyway.' He stood up. 'Thank you, Mrs Hepscott.'

Clarissa was about to be shown out by the DC, when something occurred to her. 'Oh, yes, I *do* have a question, if you don't mind.'

'What is it?'

'My husband's death certificate… when can I expect that to be issued?'

For a second, Bailey seemed taken aback by the question. 'Er… sometime after the inquest I should think… why?'

'Because I'll need it for my insurance claim from the bank.' Even Clarissa seemed to suddenly sense just how crass she was sounding. 'Obviously I'm going to have a lot of expenses to meet and accounts to settle. You do understand?'

'Of course.' He nodded to the DC. 'Show Miss Fellows in now, please.'

With the rest gone, he turned to Jack and rolled his eyes in disbelief.

Jack nodded back. 'Yeah, I know, they don't come bitchier than that.'

'If there is one, *I* haven't met her,' agreed Bailey. 'Hard as nails, but I'm not sure she's capable of murder.'

'You're pretty sure it *is* murder?'

'I'd stake my pension on it, Jack. I saw that blow to the back of his head. Your good old "blunt instrument" if ever I saw one and the pathologist agrees.' Bailey gave Jack a grim smile. 'If Hepscott did project himself to another dimension, he chose a pretty violent one for his first visit.'

'So, where exactly in Norwich was the body discovered?' enquired Jack.

'In the old port area. A boat leaving early morning spotted something sinister wedged against one of the liveaboards. BroadsBeat investigated and that's when we found him.'

‘A long way from Yarmouth,’ observed Jack but, before Bailey could respond, a very nervous-looking Amy was being shown in by the DC. She gave her dad a forced smile and got a reassuring wink in return.

‘Right, Amy, just a few questions,’ said Bailey and once more opened his notebook.

* * *

‘So, Amy, one second he was there and the next he was gone.’ Bailey looked up from his notes. ‘And you say you searched the whole arcade?’

‘Virtually, though I can’t say I went in every back office and broom cupboard.’ Amy had spent the last fifteen minutes recounting her last evening with Alistair. It wasn’t difficult; it was something she’d done mentally a dozen times since last night.

‘But, the time was definitely nine o’clock?’

‘Yes, I remember checking my watch. We were meeting the others at nine-thirty and I didn’t want us to be late.’

‘Okay.’ Bailey checked his own notes. ‘Tell me again about Alistair offering to pay for some more change.’

Yes, he brought some notes out of his back pocket.’

‘A large amount?’

‘Yes, quite a wad.’

‘And, presumably, there were quite a few other punters around to witness this?’

‘Yes.’

‘Any… how shall we say… unsavoury types?’

‘Some.’ Amy remembered the lout whose attention she’d had to shake off after losing Alistair.

Bailey cast Jack a knowing glance. ‘Just one further point, Amy. You say you and Alistair Hepscott were good friends…’ Bailey once again studied the red circles around Amy’s eyes. ‘… how good?’

‘*Very* good.’

‘Lovers?’

Amy looked at her dad who nodded back. ‘Yes, at university, but not since.’ She straightened a little in her chair. ‘I’m not the sort who would go out with a married man, sergeant.’

'I'm sure you're not.' Bailey closed his notebook. 'Right, thanks Amy, that's all for now but I'd just like a few more words with your dad.'

The DC showed Amy out leaving Jack alone with Bailey, who shook his head. 'What do you make of it, Jack?'

'It's certainly a puzzler in many ways. But, one thing I do know for certain…' Jack looked the DS straight in the eyes, '… my daughter wouldn't lie.'

'I'm sure she wouldn't, Jack, but perhaps she could get things a bit confused… like the time she last saw Hepscott.'

Jack shook his head. 'Not my Amy. She was brought up to be punctual and that's how she's stayed.'

Bailey nodded. 'A pity really, because I'd have liked half-an-hour at least between her last seeing him and the time of death.'

'I agree, but you and I both know, Bailey, that these TODs are never as accurate as the path-chaps would have us believe.'

'True,' nodded Bailey, 'and we do now have a possible motive.'

'The wad of money being flashed around, you mean? Presumably you didn't find any cash on the body?'

'No, just his wallet containing bank and credit cards, and driving licence which gave us the initial ID. The fact is, Jack, Yarmouth's a great place, but like all popular seaside resorts with a huge influx of visitors, it's a perfect location for petty-criminals to blend in unnoticed. The amusement arcades in particular are a favourite for chummies to hang out.' Bailey closed his notebook. 'Not unfeasible that some of our lovelies spotted that wad of notes, lured Mr Hepscott away, clobbered him, stole the cash and dumped him in the river.'

'What, all in a matter of seconds and with dozens of holidaymakers milling around. And, why didn't they take his bank and credit cards while they were about it?'

Bailey shrugged. 'Perhaps not sophisticated enough to use them, but cash might be a different matter. And as regards the setting, it might not have been quite like that. Perhaps, for some reason, Hepscott wandered off on his own, was followed by his assailant and clobbered elsewhere.'

'Then how did he end up in Norwich?' Jack leaned forward. 'At the most, even allowing for six hours of tidal flood, a body dumped in the Yare at Yarmouth wouldn't drift further than Reedham.'

'And then it would start coming back on the ebb,' agreed Bailey, before returning to his notes. 'These other members of Amy's party… Ovington, Stanhope and the girl Beki Smith… I'll need to talk to them as well.'

Jack nodded. 'All old college friends, but good types as far as I know.'

'Any with a grievance against Hepscott?'

Jack shrugged. 'Who knows? They're all young and pursuing their lives.'

'Which brings me back to Amy, Jack… because she's the one who once had an attachment to Hepscott.' Bailey leaned forward. 'Was the parting amicable?'

'No, it wasn't.' Jack had been hoping he wouldn't have to discuss this aspect, but Bailey was a good copper and it was inevitable he'd soon suss the connection. 'Hepscott actually did the dirty on her and married Clarissa instead.'

'… while Amy's still single…' Bailey's eyebrows rose slightly, '… and perhaps harbouring bitterness.'

'What are you saying?' The ranger was half out of his chair before Bailey waved him down with a calming hand.

'I'm not saying anything Jack, but we have to look at every angle. You know how it is.'

'Yes, I do and sorry, Bailey; you're only doing your job.' Jack sank back into his chair. 'There is one other name though who you might want to add to your list of interviewees.' Jack felt a stab of guilt at what he was about to disclose, but if "the job" was to be done properly, then this young DS needed all the facts available. 'Harold Searby.'

'Who's he?'

Jack explained including why Amy and Alistair had ended up together in Yarmouth.

'What connection does this Searby have with Hepscott then?' queried Bailey.

'I'm not sure,' admitted Jack. 'Just my old copper instinct telling me that Alistair somehow recognised him when they were collecting the boat. Also, he behaved just a little strangely when we were visiting at the hospital.'

'… where, you say, Searby was kept in for the night.'

'Yes.'

Bailey shrugged. 'All right, Jack, I'll have a chat with him, if you think it's relevant.'

'I'm trying to trace his past myself,' admitted, Jack, 'but you'd have more muscle in some quarters… like the bank, for instance.'

'Hepscott's bank?' Bailey frowned slightly. 'What's that got to do with Searby?'

'I don't know…. just a hunch.'

'I'm running a murder enquiry, Jack,' protested the DS. 'I haven't got time to help in finding someone's past history.'

'It's more than that. Something tells me that Searby fits into this conundrum, but I don't know where.' Jack smiled slightly. 'Bailey, you and I have worked together before and we haven't done too badly as a result. Trust me on this one, and I'm sure we'll find it's relevant.'

'Okay, Jack. If that's what your gut instinct is telling you, then I'll go along with it.' Bailey was making a name for himself as a detective, but he still had a high regard for this ex-senior officer's experience and judgement. He flicked closed the file and shook his head. 'What a bag of worms. I guess anything that might shed a bit of light on it has to be worth a go.' The DS stood up and shook the ranger's hand. 'Good to be working with you again, Jack.'

*   *   *

Chapter Sixteen

'Oh my goodness, what a mess.' Audrey had been anguishing all day until Jack came home to tell her of developments. Now, over tea, he'd given her a full narrative of the day's events and they didn't make for good listening. Alistair Hepscott's death was distressing enough, but perhaps it was only natural that Audrey's first concern was for her daughter. 'But surely, Bailey can't imagine Amy has anything to do with it?'

'No, I'm sure he doesn't,' said Jack stretching his legs under the table and stroking Spike with his toes, 'but he can't let a personal friendship prevent him investigating every angle. If anything, he's got to look even harder at Amy's involvement.'

'But she wasn't *involved*, Jack. Amy just happened to be with Alistair when he disappeared.'

'… and, consequently, was the last known person to see him alive,' stressed Jack. 'To the police, that's always significant, Audrey.'

'What's *significant* is that a man vanishes into thin air and reappears miles away dead.' Audrey gave a little shiver. 'The whole thing is just plain… well… spooky.'

'I agree, but there has to be a rational explanation.' Jack scratched his head. 'But blow me if I can think of it.'

'Well, I'm sure the great detective will come up with something,' declared Audrey, 'and I reckon a good starting place is that Clarissa. The awful woman, fancy her worrying about insurance with her late husband meeting an untimely death only hours before.'

'That's what makes me think she had nothing to do with it. Anyone murdering their husband for insurance would surely be a bit more discreet about their motive.'

'Maybe but, God forgive me, I can't help hating her. She was determined to benefit financially from Alistair's life and now she seems just as resolved to do the same from his death.' Audrey turned an accusing eye on her own husband. 'And whatever possessed you, Jack, to encourage her to stay with the rest of them on the boat. I should think the only consolation the gang derived from poor Alistair's death was getting shot of his wife.'

'Yes, there were certainly degrees of enthusiasm when I dropped her back at Reedham this afternoon,' admitted Jack, 'though everyone was as sympathetic as they could be.'

'Only for Alistair's sake, I'm sure,' said Audrey, 'but I wish Amy had come home with you. After all that's happened so far, I don't think she should be cooped up on that boat an hour longer.'

'I think she feels she should stick it out with the rest. After all, the whole thing was her idea and, besides…' Jack looked into his cup and swirled around the dregs, '… she may have another reason for staying on *Brookside*.'

'Oh, really? What?'

'Spencer Ovington.'

'The pilot?' Audrey was leaning forward slightly. 'You don't mean…'

'Yep, I think they're both getting a bit sweet on each other.'

'Fancy that,' smiled Audrey dreamily, before putting on a more matter-of-fact expression and saying, 'Well, as long as Amy's happy.' She poured them both another cup. 'So, what are their plans now?'

'When I left them, they were about to motor back down to *Berney Arms* so they could do a bit of sailing on Breydon.'

Audrey wrinkled her nose. 'I can't think that remote spot will be Clarissa's idea of fun.'

'Don't worry about Clarissa,' answered Jack. 'She'll have the pub nearby and otherwise be quite content curled up in the cabin working out how to spend poor Alistair's insurance money.'

Bitch, thought Audrey, but didn't say. Instead she asked, 'What about Bailey wanting to interview the others? They'll need to be somewhere other than Berney for him to do that.'

'I know, but he's going to call me with a time and place… and this is probably him now,' said Jack, dashing into the hall to answer the phone.

Through the partly closed door, Audrey could only hear a succession of "good griefs", "when did this happen?" and "leave it with me, Bailey".

'Well, that didn't sound too cheery,' she said when her husband returned.

Jack sat down with a sigh. 'I didn't think this case could get any weirder, but it just has.'

'Why? What's gone wrong now?'

'It's Harold Searby… Bailey called the hospital as soon as I'd left this morning and, guess what? Harold's disappeared as well.'

'But he can't have. He's still unwell.'

'He's more than unwell,' sighed Jack, plonking back down onto his chair, 'He's been dead ten years.'

*   *   *

With *Brookside* moored close by the famous *Berney Arms* windpump, the gang made their way along the high riverbank to the pub.

As Amy ambled with them, the view of the old estuary caused her thoughts to return to the great afternoon they'd just spent sailing on Breydon, the perfect antidote to all the grief in the first part of the day. Certainly, they'd all been stunned by the loss of an old friend and Amy felt particular loss and a sense of guilt at enjoying herself so soon after tragedy but, as Spencer had pointed out, nothing could bring Alistair back and there was no sense moping about it.

They'd taken *Babbling Brook* out in pairs, Spencer and Amy first, beating against a brisk south-easterly on the still-ebbing tide. 'At least we'll be running back,' Spencer had yelled as they tacked through the narrower part of the channel, before entering the huge expanse of Breydon Water. Amy hadn't been quite sure what he meant. Apart from the first afternoon, she had never really sailed before and certainly not on her own, but Spencer had promised to teach her and now, with great mudflats opening up on either side and seagulls screeching overhead, he'd handed over the tiller and told her to "have a go".

At first, the sight of all that mud had made Amy nervous of running aground, but the marked-channel was wide and there'd been surprisingly few other boats traversing the two and a half mile estuary. 'That's because it's still a bit too early for passing through Yarmouth,' Spencer had explained. 'The strange thing is that, although the two rivers meet Yarmouth only a mile or so before the sea, the Bure ebbs for a full hour after the Yare, so you don't want to make a passage going this way, until an hour after slack water.'

'How on earth do you know all that?' Amy had asked, remembering that Spencer had never visited the Broads before.

'Because I took the trouble to read the pilot,' he'd said with a smile. 'Here, Amy…' he'd broken off, '… you can bring her up into the wind a bit more than this.' Spencer had been sitting opposite, his hand lingering on top of hers as he'd guided the tiller a little to leeward. *Babbling Brook*'s bow had pointed slightly more into the wind, but she'd still been sailing. 'And she'll keep going as long as the sail is filled.' Spencer had nodded up to the masthead where the burgee fluttered four points off their course. 'That's about as close as we'll get her.'

Amy had concentrated on holding this heading. 'Gosh, this is brilliant!' she'd exclaimed gleefully as the boat's stem had cut through the wash of a passing sea-going cruiser with great plunges of spray.

'Yes, in spite of everything, I wish this day could go on forever.'

Their eyes had met and, without looking away, Amy had mouthed: 'Me too.' It was one of those moments when time had indeed seemed to stand still, broken only by the angry slapping of the mainsail losing its drive. 'Whoops…' Amy had instinctively brought the tiller back towards her, filling the canvas and getting them sailing once more.

'Yes… sorry… I need to concentrate a bit more myself,' Spencer had confessed, laughing.

'And I can't believe what we just said,' she'd gasped sadly, as the other side of the channel approached. 'It's less than a day since Alistair died, and here we are talking about how much we're enjoying ourselves.'

'Life goes on.' They'd reached the marker posts again with Spencer judging the distance. 'Ready about… lee ho!' he'd shouted and Amy had pushed across the tiller to have *Babbling Brook* obediently bringing her bow through the wind and settlng on the next tack. Sitting to windward now, Spencer had once again taken the tiller. 'Okay, I've got her.'

Amy had sat back and relaxed. 'I'm really grateful for this. On such a distressing day, I can't think of a better way to take my mind off sad thoughts.'

'And what *are* those thoughts?' Spencer had asked, '… about Alistair , I mean.'

'Just sorrow really… the thought that he's wasted a life that showed such promise.'

'When it could have been spent with you?' Spencer had been looking well for'ard as he'd asked his questions. It had reminded Amy of driving to school with her dad and how awkward conversations were always that much easier when you didn't have to make eye-contact.

'He made his bed and had to lie in it… in more ways than one,' she'd added, almost to herself, before shaking away the pity such thinking provoked. 'No, I'm just sad he had such a miserable life with Clarissa and glad it's not me who's been left the widow.'

'Or still loving him?' Spencer had looked her in the eye as he asked this question.

'No, definitely not still loving him.'

'I'm glad of that.' The other-side posts had been closing up and he'd taken his hand once more from the helm. 'Here, you do this one.'

Amy had forced her mind back to sailing and managed a passable tack without any instruction from Spencer. He'd smiled. 'You're doing brilliantly, Amy. Are you really enjoying it?'

'No…' she'd frowned, before smiling impishly, '… I'm *loving* it.'

'Good.' He'd fixed her again with questioning eyes. 'Would you like to do more of it?'

'With you?'

'Yes.'

'I would, very much, Spencer.'

'Fantastic.' He'd glanced at his watch. 'We'd better be getting back if Oliver and Beki are going to have their go.' Spencer had kept the next tack going until they were running dead downwind, the big lugsail sheeted right out and *Babbling Brook* sliding effortlessly through the peaked wavelets rolling down the estuary. 'Wind against tide… always produces them,' he'd said, indicating the little white caps.

'Fun though.' Amy had watched them tumbling into their own wake. The marker posts had been going by much slower as they stemmed the tide, but it had been a relief not to have to keep tacking. She'd thought about what Spencer had just said about wind against tide. Life was much the same really: as long as you kept everything going along in the same direction, it stayed reasonably calm. It was only when you turned against the flow that things got choppy. Had Alistair "turned against the flow" and brought upon himself a fatal turbulence? Their own run before the wind had soon carried them back to the *Berney Arms* and…

… now the short walk had brought the group almost to its entrance. With a shock, Amy's thoughts returned to the present and she realised that she'd been in a world of her own, oblivious to those around her.

'Nice to have you back with us.' Beki smiled, but was it a knowing smile? Amy suspected it was.

'Sorry, just day-dreaming.'

'Probably working out what you're next going to tell that Detective-Sergeant,' grumbled Clarissa. 'I don't know about you, but just sitting in his office felt like being in court.'

'I haven't been in one… yet, so I wouldn't know,' chipped in Oliver.

'You *will* when he interviews you,' responded Clarissa, once again completely missing the point.

'I wonder when that will be?' Spencer had stopped just before the pub to look at the spectacular view of water and marshland, surrounding them. By climbing up the slightly elevated banks, you could see for miles.

'I don't know, but being here right now at the remotest pub in Norfolk makes me feel a million miles from all that's happened,' said Amy.

'Same here,' Oliver nodded towards the isolated, but welcoming building, 'and a good meal will make me feel even better.'

They were just about to file in when Amy's phone rang. While the rest carried on, she stayed outside to answer it.

* * *

They were all settling in with drinks around a big bare dark oak table in the main bar area when she joined them.

'That was Dad with one more twist to the tale I'm afraid.'

'Not another?' Spencer had jumped up to get Amy a drink from the bar. She waited for him to return before continuing.

'Yes, apparently a couple of hours after Alistair and I visited Harold Searby in hospital last night, he disappeared.'

'What, vanished you mean?' asked a shocked Beki.

'No, not exactly.' Amy took a sip of her gin and tonic. 'He did stop to grab his clothes and, soon after, a visitor noticed him slipping out through a back exit.'

'Sounds pretty furtive to me,' remarked Oliver.

Clarissa looked up from her double vodka. 'I never did trust that man.'

It was Spencer though who was doing the maths. 'That must have made his exit time about eight pm… just an hour before Alistair disappeared…'

'… and so giving Searby plenty of time to murder him,' completed Clarissa showing no sign of emotion.

'But, I was with Alistair right until the time in question,' repeated Amy for what must have been the hundredth time that day. 'And that still doesn't explain how he ended up in Norwich.'

'Oh, that's easy,' replied Clarissa. 'Searby's a dab hand with boats. Obviously he nicked one and escaped to Norwich with his victim.'

'For what reason?'

'How should I know?' The widow took another good swig of her vodka. 'Theft, probably. The man looked as if he hadn't two halfpennies to rub together and Bailey told us that all Alistair's cash was missing.'

‘This is your latest theory is it, Clarissa?’ Amy was tired of hearing this overbearing woman discussing the murder of her husband as though it were some parlour game. ‘Yesterday you were telling the police that Alistair had astral-projected himself.’

‘Really?’ Beki looked up from her drink. ‘Well, I’m afraid AP doesn’t quite work like that, Clarissa, but thanks anyway for putting me on the police radar.’

‘I think we’re all on it, actually,’ pointed out Spencer, ‘but let’s not start getting at each other. Obviously we’re all pretty uptight about what’s happened, but infighting isn’t going to help.’

‘I agree and… sorry Clarissa,’ apologised Amy. ‘But talking of the police, Dad also passed on the message that DS Bailey wants to see us *all* at Bethel Street tomorrow. If we moor at Norwich Yacht Station, a police car will pick us up from there.’

‘What time?’

‘Nine o’clock.’

‘A very early start then,’ said Spencer, ‘but, if we set sail at five, we should be there on time.’

‘Well, make sure you don’t wake me until we get there,’ ordered Clarissa. ‘Just the thought of more questioning makes me need another drink.’ She went to the bar. ‘How about the rest of you?… this round’s on me.’

It was almost as though she had something to celebrate, thought Amy.

* * *

‘Goodnight, Mrs Searby, and thank you again for talking to me.’ Jack replaced the receiver and went back into the lounge.

Audrey closed her book and looked up. ‘Did she mind you calling?’

‘No, a lovely lady, though it wasn’t easy to talk about it, even after all this time.’

‘But Harold Searby was definitely her husband?’

Jack nodded. ‘Oh yes… but he wasn’t *our* Harold Searby.’

‘Who was he then?’

‘The real Harold Searby was an employee of Alistair’s bank and held some minor position in one of his departments.’

Audrey put her book down. ‘So, what happened to him?’

‘The poor chap was diagnosed with a rare genetic disease at the early age of forty-five and died just a few months later, after a very short illness.’

‘Poor man.’ Audrey gave a heartfelt sigh. ‘And Bailey found all this out this afternoon?’

'Yes. He told me he was calling the bank about Alistair, so I asked him to also mention Harold's name.'

'So, what are you thinking, Jack: that this Harold Searby didn't actually die, but simply disappeared and started a new life up here on the Broads?'

But Jack shook his head. 'Not at all. It's obvious the Searbys were a devoted couple and she was with him to the end. In fact he died in her arms.'

'So, is it just coincidence that our Harold has the same name?'

'You know I don't believe in coincidence, not when you're talking murder,' declared Jack. 'No, I'm convinced this is a simple case of fraud. Someone took the identity of this dead man to create a new one for themselves or someone else.'

It was Audrey's turn to shake her head. 'Who would do such a dreadful thing?'

'My guess is Alistair Hepscott.'

'Alistair! Surely not.'

'He ticks all the boxes, Aud. Searby worked in his department and Mrs Searby remembers Alistair very kindly calling on her to give his personal condolences.'

'And a very nice gesture too, Jack. What can be wrong with that?'

'Nothing, except Alistair wanted Harold's birth certificate… made the excuse that it was needed to finalise the widows' pension she would be receiving from the bank.'

'That could have been true.'

'No it couldn't Aud. If they'd needed anything it would have been his death certificate. No, Alistair needed that to forge a new identity for someone and we know who that was.'

'The man we now know as Harold Searby?'

'Exactly.'

'But what for?'

'I'm not sure, but I'm forming a few theories.' Jack glanced at the clock. 'Bedtime, I think, because I'm off early tomorrow to the boatyard that *Fisher of Men* was brought from. Hopefully it might give me a few more clues.'

But just as Jack was snuggling down, the bedside phone rang. It was Frank Brooker.

'Jack, I heard on this evening's news about Alistair Hepscott… terrible business… and when I called the hospital to see how Harold was getting on, they told me he'd done a bunk last night and hasn't been found. What's happening, for crikey's sake?'

'I wish I knew, Frank. It's all a bit of a mystery.'

'You're telling me.' Frank paused, as though reluctant to appear insensitive. 'Is the boat okay, Jack?'

'Yes, from what they tell me she's running like a dream… no problems there.'

'Good. Without Harold I'd be a bit stuck to get out if they needed help. Where are they now, exactly?'

'At *Berney Arms* tonight, and then going up to Norwich tomorrow.'

'Right, well hopefully they won't have any other problems, but call me if they do. I'll get to them somehow.'

'Thanks, Frank.' Jack switched off and relayed the conversation to Audrey.

'Poor man,' she sympathised picking up her book and preparing for bed herself. 'He must feel he's lost his right arm now he hasn't got Harold… or whoever Harold really is.' She paused. 'I'm glad you didn't tell Amy any of this identity business. She's got enough on her plate without that.'

Jack agreed and hoped his daughter was making the most of the evening, far from the relentless investigations of the justice system. At least she was with good company.

* * *

Indeed she was. As their evening wore on, the old gang were enjoying good food and only slightly-muted conversation in *Berney Arms*' rustic atmosphere, where framed fish, model boats and assorted nautical memorabilia looked down on a scene that had changed little since its days as a watering hole for the wherry trade. Seated on a pew-like bench backing onto ancient wooden panelling, Amy pondered on the ways of human nature.

Here she was, only hours after the death of a man she had once loved deeply, sitting opposite his widow and secretly holding hands with the man beside her. She gave it a squeeze and got a smile back from Spencer Ovington. Was she being fickle? Of course she wasn't, she told herself. Her own romance with Alistair was history and the whole idea of this week was to wipe the slate clean. Nevertheless, Amy mentally winced at the thought of how brutally fate had done just that.

Laughter from a group at another table brought her out of her musings. The *Berney Arms* moorings were popular with boaters, and the pub could only be accessed by water, foot or rail. Obviously all in here tonight were holidaying afloat and having a great time ashore. Once again, Amy felt sadness that Alistair was not there to share it.

It was an emotion not shared by his widow, however. Clarissa, with none of her appetite dented by events, was just finishing tucking in to a huge plate of locally-caught cod washed down by a pint of lager. In fact, to Amy's eyes, she was the most relaxed she had been this whole trip so far. It was time to say something. 'Are you sure you don't think us insensitive for enjoying ourselves like this, Clarissa,' she asked, slightly concerned.

''course not!' Clarissa pushed away her empty plate on which not so much as a pea had been missed. 'What's the point of moping? Alistair wouldn't have wanted that.'

'But surely, you don't want to continue your holiday with us,' put in Spencer, crossing his fingers under the table and making Amy smile.

'Why not?' Clarissa was scanning the dessert menu. 'Widows' weeds wouldn't look good on me and, quite honestly, I'm even beginning to warm to this waterborne life.'

'But surely there are financial implications to what's happened?' queried Oliver from behind his lager. 'I mean, surely the loss of Alistair's income must mean you'll have to cut back a bit on your lifestyle?'

'Quite the opposite, actually.' Clarissa looked up from her menu, decision made. 'I'm expecting a large insurance settlement on Alistair's life. Also, the bank will be paying me a healthy pension, so I'll be quids-in. No, I expect to live better than I've done for a long time.' She passed the menu to Amy. 'When you've made your choice, order me a "Death by Chocolate" will you, sweetie… there's a good girl.'

* * *

Chapter Seventeen

The village of St Olaves lay on the River Waveney, six miles southwest of Great Yarmouth and named after the priory which once stood where a handsome windpump now surveyed the surrounding marshes. But local history was far from Jack's mind as he drove over the cast-iron bowstring bridge and turned onto a rough track that took him to the boatyard of J F Hendricks & Sons. After parking the car and entering reception, however, he soon found that neither J F Hendricks nor any of his sons still ran the yard.

'My husband bought them out about eight years ago,' explained the lady in her fifties, with glasses and a friendly smile, in response to Jack's enquiry. 'The Hendricks had decided to get out of the hire-boat business, so we bought it as a purely sales-and-maintenance operation.'

Not what Jack really wanted to hear, but there was still a chance he could hit lucky. 'Do you still have their old records, though Mrs…?'

'… Sculfer… Wendy Sculfer.' She frowned. 'There are some stuffed in boxes in the back room. What exactly are you looking for?'

'The sale of one of the Hendricks' old cruisers. I don't know what it was called back then, but here's its registration number.'

'I am quite busy right now,' said Mrs Sculfer. 'Perhaps if you rang me…'

'This is really important, Mrs… Wendy,' broke in Jack. He showed his Broads Authority ID and gave her his most winning smile. 'If you could look now, I'd be very grateful.'

She smiled back. 'Alright, let me go and see if I can find the sales invoices for…?'

'… ten years ago.'

After what seemed an interminable time, a somewhat dustier Wendy Sculfer returned, but waving a sales invoice as triumphantly as Chamberlain returning from Munich. 'Got it.'

'Brilliant.' Jack scanned the document, but, most importantly, the name this sale had been made out to. It was there, right at the top: Harold Searby. He choked back his disappointment. 'Would this Harold Searby be the one who actually *paid* for the boat, Mrs Sculfer?'

'Not necessarily, but I can't say for sure, Mr Fellows. All before our time and…'

'I understand, but will there be any other paperwork relating to the sale?'

'If the buyer paid in cash, there might be a receipt. I could get the receipt book for you if you want.'

'Please.'

Another wait and then a very dog-eared receipt book, obviously extracted from deep in the Hendricks' archives, was held up. 'Here we are.'

Jack checked the date on the invoice and thumbed through the copy receipts to that date and a figure corresponding exactly with that shown on the invoice. The receipt was made out to one M Biggs.

'Thank you, Wendy. You're an angel.'

'Oh well…'

But Jack was already out of the office and back in his car. He had no idea who this "M Biggs" was, but it was a start. He took out his mobile and, once again, called Henry Mayhew at Dragonfly House.

* * *

'Thanks for coming in, Spencer. Good trip?'

'Great, thanks.'

It had indeed been a delightful early-morning cruise, starting with the dawn departure from Berney Mill and covering the remaining twenty-three miles, to arrive at Norwich just before the requested time. This good progress had been made possible by carrying the river's flood all the way and leaving the half-decker on the moorings at *Berney Arms*. With the river devoid of other traffic at this early hour, all except Clarissa had taken a trick at the wheel between making coffees or frying bacon for a steady supply of butties in the galley. Clarissa remained oblivious to it all as she slept off the night's excesses in her bunk. They woke her just as they joined the Wensum, for the last few interesting miles into the city itself. At the Yacht Station, a police car stood waiting. Perhaps a meeting with the police wasn't the best of reasons for the journey, but it had at least given them a sense of purpose. Now, at nine-thirty, they were all standing outside Bailey's office at city headquarters.

'Let's do you first then shall we?' Bailey led Spencer in and ushered him into a chair. The same female DC who had sat in on the girls' interviews was already sitting to one side of the desk.

Bailey took Spencer's details, which were jotted down by the silent DC. That done, he seemed to relax slightly. 'So, you were one of the reunion party?'

'Yes, we were at university together twelve years ago.'

'And all good friends?'

'Then… yes.'

Bailey picked up the slight hesitation. '"Then"?'

Spencer shrugged. 'Inevitably you follow different paths in later life, so naturally don't remain as close.'

'And your path was…' Bailey checked his notes, '… aviation.'

'Yes, I'm a pilot with a long-haul charter operation.'

'A captain?'

'Yes, I'm glad to say. About three years now.'

'Very nice too.' Bailey leaned back a little in his chair and put his hands behind his head. 'So tell me, Spencer, what were your impressions of Alistair Hepscott?'

Spencer paused for a few seconds on this one while he felt the eyes of the two police officers piercing his very thoughts. 'On the surface, he seemed a nice enough chap, but he certainly showed a hard, unfeeling streak when I knew him as a student.'

'Oh, really. In what way?'

'Well… let's just say he could be heartless and callous.'

'Like when he cheated on Amy Fellows, you mean?' Bailey caught the look of surprise on Spencer's face. 'It's all right, she's told us all about it.'

'Well, it didn't do him any favours in the end, did it, doing the dirty on the nicest girl in the world for that dominating Clarissa.'

Bailey closed one eye as though taking aim and smiled slightly. 'Didn't harbour a few ambitions in that direction yourself, did you, Spencer?'

The pilot bit his lip. 'I liked Amy very much then, and still do.'

'O…ka…y…' Bailey strung out the word, before glancing back to his notes. 'Well, let's go back to nine o'clock Monday evening, the time of Alistair Hepscott's death. Where were you then, Spencer?'

'Walking north along the promenade towards the pier. I'd been spending some time on the South Denes.'

'Not the prettiest part of Yarmouth,' observed Bailey. 'Why there?'

'Because I wanted to see where my grandfather served in the First World War. He was a pilot at the naval air station there.'

'From stringbags to jet airliners,' said Bailey with a smile. 'You and your grandad certainly spanned a breadth of technology.'

'Yes, and my father flew jet fighters with the RAF during *his* National Service.'

'Aviation seems to run in the family then, Spencer.' Bailey raised questioning eyebrows. 'You didn't, by any chance, have access to an aircraft at North Denes last Monday?'

'*North* Denes?'

'Yes, that's the Yarmouth heliport, but they also have grass runways there for light aircraft. I was just wondering…'

'… if I'd bumped off Alistair, flown his body to Norwich and dumped it into the river there,' completed Spencer with a smile. 'An exciting concept, but…' he shook his head, '… sorry to disappoint you, sergeant, but my feet stayed firmly on the ground last Monday.'

'Or water,' corrected Bailey. He shrugged. 'Okay, then tell us what your actual movements *were* last Monday evening, Spencer. If they were as you say, then you must have been passing that amusement arcade just at the time Hepscott disappeared.'

The pilot nodded. 'Possibly though, like I said, I was on the prom and that arcade is well back on the other side of the Parade.'

'Which arcade?'

'The one Alistair and Amy were in.'

'How do you know which one that was? The name hasn't been mentioned.'

'No… I know, but Amy must have told me… and when I went from the boat *to* South Denes, I walked up on that side and stuck my nose in some of them just out of interest. From what Amy said, I'm pretty sure I know which one they went in.'

'Of course. Pilot's observational skills kicking in, I imagine.' Bailey stayed silent for a few seconds, fixing Spencer through suspicious eyes, before suddenly brightening and standing up. 'Well, I think that's *it* for now, Spencer. Keep yourself available for more questioning and send Beki Smith in now, will you please.'

* * *

The few minutes waiting for the Reedham Ferry gave Jack time to make another call, this time to his fellow Navigation Ranger, Tommy Taylor, who patrolled the upper Yare.

The call was answered immediately. 'Jack, what can I do for you? Not another day off?' There was the background murmur of a diesel engine showing he was already out on his beat.

'I wish.' Jack glanced down at his notebook and the name Henry Mayhew had given him. 'Tommy, I'm looking for a boat called *Ocean Venturer*. With a name like that, I imagine she's a big one.'

'*Ocean Venturer*... *Ocean Venturer*... yep, I know the one, and you're right, big sea-going job moored in Brundall Marina. In fact, that's the only place I see her. She never seems to go out.'

'That's all I need to know, Tommy. Thanks for your help.'

As Jack switched off, the chain-link ferry was clanking its way onto the slip. Cars drove off, he drove on, and soon they were rattling their way across the Yare. On the other side, it would only be a short journey to Brundall Marina.

*   *   *

'So, Beki, you were Amy's best friend at university.'

Beki Smith sat across the desk from DS Bailey. The detective was obviously trying to put her at ease but, in spite of all her stage-training, she felt uncharacteristically nervous.

'Yes, we were very close.'

'So you must have felt pretty aggrieved, when she was so hurt by Alistair Hepscott?'

'Yes, very.'

'So much so, that you might well have harboured some bitterness against him.'

'I wouldn't say that.' Beki felt even more uncomfortable at this pointed question so early in the interview. She'd come here thinking this was informal questioning, but clearly DS Bailey regarded her as a possible suspect. 'I didn't particularly like Alistair Hepscott for what he'd done to my friend, but that's all part of being young, isn't it? Heartache is just one of the hazards of growing up and I didn't regard it as more than that.'

Bailey glanced down at Beki's clenched fingers. 'Not married yourself?'

'No.'

'Never have been?'

'No.'

'But you were very pleased to arrange this get together with your old… friend, even though her ex- lover was going to be part of the party?'

'Yes.' Suddenly Beki could see where this line of questioning was heading. She straightened up in her chair. 'But let me make it quite clear, sergeant, that there was nothing like that in my friendship with Amy and neither was I jealous of Alistair Hepscott.'

'No, of course not.' Bailey smiled as though his question had been patently misunderstood. 'But you must have worried that it could lead to Amy being hurt for a second time?'

'I think he would have liked to try it on again with her if she'd been willing… if that's what you mean,' said Beki, 'but I didn't have any worries on that score as soon as I knew Clarissa would be there as well.'

'Ah yes, the wife.' Bailey gave a cynical smile. 'Not the most popular of shipmates I would imagine.'

'You could say that.'

'Obviously you two aren't close.'

'We certainly aren't.'

'Which would probably account for Mrs Hepscott holding you, in some strange way, accountable for her husband's death, so far from where he was last seen.'

'Oh that… that I somehow talked Alistair into trying astral projection and he used it to escape from her, the stupid woman.' Beki shook her head. 'I wouldn't blame him, being desperate to get away from that conniving bitch, but AP doesn't work like that, sergeant.'

'How *does* it work, Beki?'

'By projecting your astral body to the astral plane, and *leaving* your physical body.'

'A form of out-of-body experience?'

'Exactly.'

'And you've done this, Beki?'

'Only to a very small degree. I'm only in the very early stages of astral travel, sergeant, but I aim to achieve much better results as I reach the astral plane.'

'But there *are* reports of some people…' Bailey hit a key on his computer, producing a website on the screen, '… who report actually being *seen* in their astral-wanderings.'

'Yes, I've read those reports myself,' admitted Beki, 'but they are exceptional happenings to exceptional people and their physical bodies still never moved.'

She cocked her head on one side. 'Let me assure you, Sergeant Bailey, that there was no way Alistair Hepscott could have projected his physical body twenty-six miles to Norwich, either before or after his death.'

'I'm glad to hear that.' Bailey hit another key on his computer and turned the screen towards her. She recognised the website in front of her, as her own. 'You're an actress, Beki?'

'That's one of the ways I earn a crust… yes.'

'Can't be easy in this day and age.' Bailey leaned a little closer. 'But a little media attention might just help. Could this whole business have been a publicity stunt gone wrong? Let's take a possible scenario. Perhaps you pushed him into the water so that you could "save him from drowning". Plenty of media-coverage there to kick-start your career, only perhaps he sustained a fatal blow to his head as he fell.'

Beki couldn't believe what she was hearing. 'Are you telling me you think I was involved… that I actually conspired in Alistair Hepscott's death?'

'It's a hypothetical concept, Beki.' Bailey sat back again. 'Where were you at nine o'clock Monday night?'

'Sitting on the promenade just north of the pier.'

'Anyone who can verify that?'

Beki lowered her eyes slightly. 'I'm afraid not. I was with Oliver Stanhope until shortly before that, but he went off on his own until our agreed rendezvous at the pier at nine-thirty.'

'Pity.' Bailey seemed to relax slightly. 'So, if it wasn't you, Beki, who do you reckon had a motive to kill Hepscott?'

Beki Smith sat back herself. Now she knew what Clarissa had meant by Bailey's ability to make you feel just one step from arrest. Although desperate to divert suspicion from herself, she still retained sufficient integrity not to want to implicate any of her friends. So she simply said: 'We all had one reason or another to dislike Alistair.'

'What, even this MP, Stanhope?'

Just as quickly, Beki realised she'd been tricked into saying too much. Oliver was the only one still not interviewed and she knew the detective would use what she'd just said, to tease out his own problem with Alistair. All she could do now was mumble, 'I don't know; you'll have to ask him.'

'I surely will,' responded Bailey. 'That'll be all for now, Beki.' He nodded to the DC. 'Show Miss Smith out and Mr Stanhope in.'

As she joined the others, Beki knew DS Bailey wasn't allowing her the chance to warn Oliver.

* * *

The morning overcast was lifting slightly by the time Jack made his way down the seemingly endless rows of assorted marine craft in Brundall Bay Marina.

For the boat enthusiast, there was every type of vessel imaginable here, from small dayboats to large ocean-going cruisers, old Dutch barges to modern high-performance yachts. Jack knew where the boat he sought was moored, having already checked at the marina office, shown his ID and got the berth number.

It was a mooring at the end of a pontoon and well clear of the majority of other boats. In fact, *Ocean Venturer* was well clear of all of them at this time, because she wasn't there at all. The berth was empty.

'Damn!' This was something Jack hadn't foreseen, especially as Tommy Taylor said the boat never went out. If there had been liveaboards moored close by, he would have tried asking a few questions, but the other boats around were small and unmanned on this rather murky day. It was as Jack was just nosing around, that he noticed a man walking down the pontoon. Was it someone who might have some useful information?

The man got closer, though it was apparent that he still hadn't registered the ranger standing close to the spot he was so obviously heading for. Some instinct prompted Jack to slip behind one of the other boats on its finger jetty, and take in the man's features. He was good-looking enough, about thirty-five, slim, clean-shaven, casually dressed with short dark hair, and checking berth-numbers as though also looking for a specific one. Instinct told Jack which, and he wasn't surprised at the flash of disappointment on this stranger's face when he finally arrived at the empty space where *Ocean Venturer* once lay.

The stranger stood there for a full minute, looking about him, checking that the large cruiser hadn't just moved to another berth close by. Only when he made to move off did Jack step out from his concealment and then walk up to him with outstretched hand.

'Jacob Matson, I presume.' The man glanced quickly round, but Jack put the loosest of restraining arms on his shoulder. 'I don't know about you,

Jacob, but I could do with some breakfast.' He nodded towards the marina café. 'My treat.'

*   *   *

'We don't get too many MPs in here,' said Bailey.

'And I haven't been in too many police stations,' countered Oliver Stanhope. He glanced around him. Outside, other officers were coming and going, computer screens displayed meaningless data, coffee was being drunk and jokes exchanged. But, in here, with just the young female DC and Bailey, there was an air of intimidating purpose. 'Don't take it personally, sergeant, but I'm hoping I won't be in this one much longer.'

'That depends,' said Bailey without emotion. It wasn't the response Oliver had wanted to hear and neither was the next question. 'Tell me of your own relationship with Alistair Hepscott, Mr Stanhope.'

'We were just good friends at university.'

'You mean you haven't spoken to him since… until this reunion thing?'

Bailey's eyes remained fixed on Oliver's. Years spent in his own clashes with authority told the MP it would be futile to lie to this astute young officer. 'Well, we have had some occasional conversations.'

'About what?'

'Money actually… Alistair made some investments for me.'

'Good ones, I hope.'

'Not really.'

'Bad?'

'You could say that,' groaned Oliver.

'When did you first become aware that there was a problem?'

'Only since we met up for this reunion and I told him I needed to cash in the investment.'

'What was his reaction?'

'Almost confusion at first, as though he didn't know what I was talking about.'

'And then?'

'He said he'd make a call on Monday and sort it.'

'And…?'

Oliver shook his head. 'That's when he finally told me the money had gone completely.'

'Did he give any reason?'

'No, except to say that was how playing the markets sometimes went.'

Bailey leaned forward a little closer. 'Why did you so suddenly need to cash in these shares, Mr Stanhope?'

Oliver paused. Baring your soul was never easy, but now he was involved in issues deeper than he could ever have imagined.

'I'd been accused by the Independent Parliamentary Standards Authority of fiddling my expenses and I needed the money urgently to repay them, before the matter was taken to court.'

'That's interesting.' Bailey paused while assimilating this information, before continuing his questioning. 'How much have you lost?'

It was no good pretending any more. 'Everything.'

'That *is* serious.' Bailey narrowed his eyes. 'Presumably, bankruptcy would lose you your seat in the Commons?'

'Probably, but, anyway, I think it would only be right to resign.'

'And all thanks to Alistair Hepscott. That would make any man bitter, wouldn't it?'

'More than bitter, sergeant, but I assure you I didn't kill him.'

'Financial ruin, the end of your career, a possible prison sentence... I'd say they were pretty good motives for murder, Mr Stanhope.'

'If I were capable of such a thing,' argued the MP.

'But to have continued your holiday in such close proximity to a man who, seemingly without remorse, has just ruined you, and hearing his wife openly flaunt their well-heeled lifestyle, must have driven you insane. Could it be that need for revenge smouldered inside you until you could stand it no longer?'

'Ridiculous, and when could I have committed murder anyway?' asked Oliver, wiping away a bead of sweat from his forehead. 'I was sitting on the promenade with Beki Smith at the time.'

'Not *right* at that time, Mr Stanhope. Miss Smith has already told me you'd gone your separate ways by nine o'clock.'

'I don't know what the time was really,' Oliver whispered, almost to himself.

'And so, presumably, you have no-one who could confirm your alibi... for what it's worth?' Bailey responded.

'No.' Oliver shook himself out of his defensive attitude. 'Sergeant Bailey, I assure you, I have no involvement in Alistair Hepscott's death but, for reasons I've already told you, I'm desperate to preserve what little integrity I've got left.

I realise you, in turn, have a need to investigate this dreadful crime, but all I ask is that my name be kept out of it as far as the press are concerned.'

'As long as you stay out of court, your name will stay out of our press releases,' assured Bailey. 'He picked up his pen and opened his notebook once more. 'Now, tell me again, *exactly* where you were at nine o'clock on Monday night.'

* * *

'You haven't been entirely honest with me, have you Mrs Hepscott?'

It was now Clarissa's turn to face DS Bailey and, judging by the shaken look on Oliver Stanhope's face as she'd passed him in the corridor, this second interview promised to have all the warmth of an Eskimo's freezer. Bailey's opening statement did nothing to negate that feeling, but Clarissa decided there was still room for a bit of denial.

'I don't know what you mean.'

'I think you do.' Bailey tapped his notebook. 'Yesterday, I had a long conversation with a senior executive at your husband's bank. What he had to say was very interesting.'

'How dare you poke your nose into Alistair's personal affairs.' Clarissa was pulling out all the stops to appear the affronted widow. 'What's that got to do with his murder?'

'A lot… possibly,' answered Bailey. 'There's a motive for most murders, Mrs Hepsott, and what I found out from the bank could well be the one for your husband's.'

'And, what *did* you "find out"?'

'That Alistair and the bank were very shortly to part company. You know, of course, that ten years ago your husband featured in an enquiry into missing money.'

'Of course but, in the end, all the evidence led to another man in the department, Jacob Matson, who'd been working a fiddle and misappropriating bank funds abroad…'

'… where Matson himself disappeared to as the investigation got too hot,' completed Bailey. 'But, it's a more recent enquiry I'm referring to, Mrs Hepscott; one triggered by an internal audit ordered shortly after your father-in-law's death. Apparently, that's routine after the appointment of a new chief executive. Unfortunately, this one disclosed very large sums of money being unaccounted for. After a lengthy investigation, those shortcomings led right back to Alistair and his financial dealings.'

Clarissa sniffed. 'You wouldn't understand these things, sergeant, but when you're dealing in large sums, it's inevitable that some money… shall we say… drops between the cracks.'

'It must have been a pretty big crack, Mrs Hepscott… one capable of taking six-million pounds.'

'*How much*?' Clarissa shot upright in her chair. 'I didn't know it was that much… I mean, I had no idea of my husband's dealings.'

'Neither, it seems, had the bank until just recently, but you're quite right on one thing, Mrs Hepscott, I don't understand these things but, luckily, we have experts that do…' Bailey flicked a printed e-mail, '… the Fraud Squad and, from what they've just told me, a formal charge and arrest of your husband was only days away.'

'Well, thank goodness that's nothing to do with me.' Clarissa sat back again in her chair. 'Your fraud people can check my personal accounts as much as they like, Sergeant Bailey; they'll find there's precious little money there.'

'They already have,' said Bailey without batting an eyelid, 'and you're right again: personally you seem pretty skint.'

'Don't I know it,' scoffed Clarissa. 'Well, there you are then…' she got up, '… can I go now?'

'You certainly can't. Sit down.'

Clarissa wasn't used to being told to do *anything* and the experience was so alien that she found herself dumbly obeying. Perhaps the DC's hand on her shoulder also helped as she sank back into her chair.

'We were talking about motives a little earlier, Mrs Hepscott,' continued Bailey. 'Well, as far as *you're* concerned, they come by the bucket-load.'

'Me?' Once again, Clarissa's plummy accent was slipping. ' You think I bumped off my husband… why would I?'

'For a lot of reasons, Mrs Hepscott. For one, you're a woman who obviously holds social standing in very high regard. Your husband appearing at the Old Bailey on fraud charges wouldn't exactly pave the way to a Buckingham Palace garden party, would it? On the other hand, Alistair's untimely… or should we perhaps say "timely"… death, just before the charges became public, would leave you more an object of sympathy within your social network.'

'And still penniless,' countered Clarissa.

'Not at all. You know full-well that Alistair's sad demise will leave you pretty well off.' Bailey went back to his notes. 'The bank didn't have the specific details but, as your husband was only suspended and not actually fired, they would be obligated to make you a lump-sum payment and provide you with a pension for life.'

'So I gathered,' said Clarissa without emotion, before brightening slightly and asking, 'How much, exactly?'

'Probably a million up-front and at least fifty thousand a year.'

'That much,' gulped Clarissa. 'Even *I* could manage on that.'

Bailey smiled. 'You might not need to if you're living in Holloway.' He held up three fingers. 'Motive, means and opportunity: that's what we always look for, Mrs Hepscott. Well, we've established the first and, as regards the last, what were you doing at the time of your husband's death?'

'Walking from the boat to the pier to meet him.' Clarissa, ran a slightly frenzied hand through her hair.

'Alone?'

'Yes, of course.' She wiped away a tear and sniffed. She had never been the most sentimental of women, but now seemed to be the time to at least try. 'And you've missed out the "means" bit, sergeant, because you know a woman like myself…' she gave another loud sniff, '… wouldn't have the strength to kill a fit man like Alistair.'

'On the contrary,' said Bailey, 'you had all the means in the world, Mrs Hepscott, and we've just enumerated them. With the money you were going to make from your husband's death, you could afford to hire someone perfectly capable of doing the job.'

'A hit man… you mean?' There was mild hysteria now in her voice. 'Where would *I* find a hit man?'

The detective never got to answer that question, because the telephone at his side suddenly rang. 'Bailey speaking… he's got what?… right, tell him I'll be down in a sec.' He turned back to his suspect. 'I'm going to have to terminate this interview, Mrs Hepscott, because a significant development has just occurred.' He turned at the door. 'Carry on enjoying your holiday, but don't leave this area without my permission.'

Normally, Clarissa would have been demanding to know why. As it was, as Bailey door-slammed from his office, her predominant reaction was one of unmitigated relief.

* * *

'Jack… what's happening?… who's this?'

Bailey was down at the front desk, where the ranger stood with a youngish, rather nervous-looking man.

Jack presented his companion. 'Bailey, I'd like you to meet someone. This is Jacob Matson, late of Alistair Hepscott's bank, and someone who might well help you with your enquiries…' he paused while the DS took in this unexpected information, '… or, as I used to know him… Harold Searby.'

* * *

Chapter Eighteen

'I certainly prefer this to that dreadful police station,' said Beki letting out a relieved sigh.

The gang, minus Clarissa, had crossed the road and were sitting in the pizzeria at The Forum in the city centre.

'Yes, you all seem to have had a real grilling,' sympathised Amy, sipping her orange juice as they waited for their lunch to arrive. Through the spectacular curved glass frontage, they overlooked the magnificent gothic tower of St Peter Mancroft church, which provided a pleasing contrast to this award-winning, state-of-the-art civic building. Below them in the open space of The Atrium, they could see visitors wandering around a temporary photographic exhibition while, across the great void and at their same level, was BBC East's regional headquarters.

Oliver nodded towards it. 'No doubt Hepscott's murder's been headline news. Strange isn't it, we're at the centre of the investigation but, with no telly on board, have no idea what the media's been saying about us. In fact, I'm surprised we haven't had reporters sniffing around us before now.' He shrugged. 'I guess that's the advantage of being afloat on waterways that are almost entirely inaccessible by road. Thank God they haven't got wind of us being in the same building or they'd have a field-day.'

Amy looked around her nervously, half-expecting to see a camera and microphone heading their way. 'We've got enough to cope with without being hounded by TV journalists delving into our private lives and trying to prise information out of us. They stop at nothing for a good story.'

'Don't I know it,' groaned Oliver, still looking very pale from his interrogation. 'I came on holiday to get *away* from the press, not imagining for a moment that I could end up being named as the prime-suspect in a murder investigation. I really felt I was going to be charged, at one point.'

'I think we all did,' replied Spencer. 'A few minutes with Sergeant Bailey, and you feel like Public Enemy Number One.'

Beki nodded and replied, with just a hint of malice, 'It sounds as though Clarissa got the toughest grilling. Apparently, Bailey almost accused her of bumping off Alistair for the insurance payoff.'

'Which isn't such a wild hypothesis.' Spencer took a mouthful of lager. 'Where is she, by the way?'

'Shopping,' said Beki. 'She caught sight of Jarrold's Department Store when we were standing by the City Hall and she was off.'

'Not exactly the distraught widow, is she,' observed Oliver, disapprovingly.

'Probably thinks she can stop pretending to be upset now Bailey's got another likely suspect.' Beki's mouth did a downturn. 'She really must be as hard as nails, and it certainly seems that she and Alistair put up with a totally loveless marriage. Serves her right. She got just what she deserved for trading true-love for an open cheque-book and the opportunity of mixing with the rich and famous. I'd *never* marry for money. For me, a successful partnership means striving for common goals through good times and bad.'

Oliver's eyes met hers as he nodded slowly in agreement.

Spencer turned to Amy. 'Well, your dad appearing out of the blue with Harold in tow, certainly put an abrupt end to Clarissa's interview. The sergeant couldn't wait to get rid of us.'

'Thank goodness, but Harold looked so different. I hardly recognised him, did you? And I was sure I heard Dad call him "Jacob".'

'It was certainly very bizarre,' agreed Beki. 'But, hopefully, your dad can tell us what's going on. I managed to tell him where we were going for lunch and he promised to try and join us once he'd finished with Bailey. In fact, here he is…' she said as Jack came up the stairs and sat down with them.

'Quite a morning,' he said, sitting back and taking a first welcome swig of a beer brought by Spencer. He glanced round the assembled group. 'I gather you lot were given quite a bashing?'

'We certainly were,' agreed Oliver.

'That's how they get results, I'm afraid. The questioning has to be tough if they're to break hardened criminals. It can feel pretty intimidating though, to law-abiding citizens,' sympathised Jack.

'But what's this about Harold, Dad?' asked an intrigued Amy. 'Is it true that he's completely changed his appearance?'

'He's actually reverted back to how he *used* to look.' Jack put down his beer. 'His real name is Jacob Matson.'

'What, the bank employee who embezzled a fortune years ago and bunked off abroad?' gasped Beki.

'The very one.'

Amy frowned. 'But how did Harold get to Norwich and change so dramatically in such a short time?'

'Easy really,' said Jack. 'After sneaking out of hospital, he used the few pounds Frank had given him days before to buy a train ticket to Norwich, get a haircut and full shave at a barbers and a change of clothes from a charity shop.'

'And, in between, somehow murdered Alistair and dumped his body,' broke in Oliver.

'That's what Bailey thinks,' sighed Jack.

'What do *you* think, Dad,' asked Amy, noticing the look of concern on her father's face.

'Hard to say right now. He certainly had motive, means and opportunity.'

'Motive?' questioned Spencer, '… what motive, Jack?'

'Oh… things he told me, but I'll leave Bailey to make his own assumptions. As Jacob Matson is a wanted fraudster anyway, the police will have no problem holding him for questioning.'

Amy knew her father better than to press the point, so she changed the subject by asking, 'How did you recognise him, Dad?'

'Oh, just one little detail,' Jack disclosed but, frustratingly, didn't elaborate further. He took another swig of beer and made an effort to brighten. 'But the important thing is that Sergeant Bailey doesn't need to see any of you again in the immediate future, so you're free to wander off at will.'

'Phew, that's a relief,' breathed Oliver. 'For a while I thought we were all going to end up in police custody.'

'Not just yet,' laughed Jack. 'So, what do you think you'll do?'

Beki answered first. 'After lunch, Amy and I'll probably look around the shop in The Forum before moving on. I'm in the city most days, so I'm happy to go-along with whatever Amy wants to do.'

'In that case, I'm really keen to have a look round the market,' replied Amy.

'Great idea.' Beki was always up for a bargain and loved mooching around the permanent open-air stalls.

Spencer nodded in the direction of the Millennium Library at the back of The Forum. 'I see they have a section in there dedicated as a memorial to the US Eighth Air Force. I'd like to have a look at that.' He turned to the MP. 'How about you, Oliver?'

'Oh, I'll just wander round the shops and see if I can spot Clarissa. There's something I want to ask her.'

'Rather you than me,' laughed Amy. At this point their lunches arrived. She turned to her father. 'Are you going to have some with us Dad?'

Jack shook his head and stood up. 'Thanks anyway, but I'm going to meet Mum. I promised I'd give her ten minutes notice, so…' Jack was fumbling for his mobile, '… oh, no…'

'What's up, Dad?'

'Left my phone in the car,' admitted Jack. 'Can I borrow yours, Amy?'

'Of course.' Amy took her phone out from her bag and passed it over.

'Thanks.' Not wishing to disturb the diners, Jack went a little distance away to make his call.

'All sorted, Dad?' asked his daughter as he handed it back.

'Yep. Thanks, love.'

Jack left them tucking in with the relief of the reprieved. He wished his own thoughts were that untroubled.

*   *   *

An hour later and Amy and Beki were threading their way through the one hundred and ninety stalls of Norwich's colourful market-place.

'What exactly are you looking for?' asked Beki as they traversed yet another row.

'I need a new pair of sandals,' replied Amy, though already aware that she was being distracted by the vast diversity of goods on sale around her. Even as she spoke, she was thumbing through a bookcase-full of second-hand paperbacks.

The clouds had lifted now and the sun was coming out, making the two girls grateful for the cooling effect of the brightly-painted striped roofs over the stalls, and the covered walkways. They meandered happily through the labyrinth of connecting aisles, enjoying the hubbub generated by shoppers and stallholders. Much to her delight, Amy spotted racks of shoes and was soon squatting beside a selection of sandals. She found just what she looking for and turned round to show Beki, but her friend was nowhere to be seen. Her heart sank and she felt physically sick. Surely, this couldn't happen a second time.

'Beki!' She found herself uttering the name aloud, raising several bemused glances. 'Where's my friend?… what happened to her?…' She thrust her way through the crowds, but couldn't spot her anywhere. Amy became increasingly distraught as she continued her frantic search.

‘What’s the matter, love,’ asked a stallholder as she wound her way through his displays of costume jewellery. In her panic, she backed into another stall, where a hand clutched her shoulder. She spun around.

‘Amy, what on earth’s the matter?’ It was Beki.

‘I… I thought you’d vanished into thin air, just like Alistair.’ Amy was well aware she was stammering like a lost child at the seaside.

‘I only slipped off to try and find some old play-scripts.’ Beki ran a comforting hand down Amy’s cheek. ‘You silly old onion, you look scared to death.’

‘I was.’ Amy was pulling herself together now. She glanced around and was relieved to see she wasn’t the centre of attention and that everyone around her was carrying on as normal. ‘Let’s just move on shall we; I’m feeling pretty stupid right now.’

Beki led her to a snack bar selling hot drinks. She wasn’t hungry so soon after lunch, but the hot sweet tea had a calming effect. ‘Thanks, Beki. I made a bit of a fool of myself back there.’

‘Understandable.’ Beki sipped her black coffee. ‘You’ve had a pretty traumatic experience, so no wonder you’re so easily freaked out.’

‘I guess so. I really felt I was back in that amusement arcade and you’d just disappeared like Alistair.’ She gave a little shiver. ‘I thought I must be going mad.’

‘No you’re not. Just badly shaken, and I think we can all relax now, in the knowledge the murderer has been detained.’

Amy nodded. ‘I suppose you’re right… though I somehow don’t think Dad’s convinced they’ve got the right man.’

* * *

‘That was a long ten minutes, Jack Fellows,’ said Audrey, looking up from the corner table as her husband hurried in.

‘Yeah, sorry love. Just remembered some last-minute shopping on the way.’ Jack settled into the chair opposite his wife. They were sitting in the tearoom uniquely set in what had once been a courtroom in Norwich’s historic Guildhall.

‘Right, Jack, tell me all that’s been happening,’ said Audrey as soon as the waitress had taken their orders.

‘Okay, but there’s a lot to tell.’ It was a long narration, broken only to allow the waitress to deliver their soup.

‘My goodness… Harold… a wanted fraudster and, possibly, a murderer?’ Audrey put her soupspoon down and tried to assimilate the results of her husband’s eventful day. ‘I can’t believe it. He seemed such a devout man.’

‘And still is, and younger than even *he* imagined.’ Jack began to tear open his roll. ‘When I first met Harold, he said he was forty-five, but I was sure he was a lot younger than that.’

‘… which made you a bit suspicious at the time, I remember. But why lie about your age when it might only raise suspicion?’

‘Because, he genuinely believed he *was* that age, as it corresponded with the real late Harold Searby’s date of birth.’

Audrey gave a sigh and handed Jack the butter. ‘So, not only did he steal millions from his employers, but he also took on the identity of a dead man. That really *is* unforgivable.’ She took a sip of soup. ‘How on earth did you recognise him, Jack?’

‘I had my suspicions that Alistair and Harold had met before, when we went to see Amy and the gang off at Brookerboats. When the two men met then, I glimpsed a look of recognition in Alistair’s face, just as if he’d seen a ghost. Alarm bells began to ring during my celebration dinner in Norwich with Amy and Beki. Do you remember, Aud, Beki told us about the enquiry into missing funds which the bank had conducted two years after Alistair started there? And how the evidence had led to Jacob Matson, who’d disappeared abroad?’

‘I do… except now we know he hadn’t, but had come to live on the Broads instead,’ reasoned Audrey.

‘Exactly, and that time-frame, coinciding with Harold’s accident, seemed too much of a coincidence for me. And then Alistair seemed determined to visit Harold in hospital with us, which aroused my suspicions still further. Now, as you know, this second blow to Harold’s head brought back his memory and he regained consciousness as Jacob Matson once more. You should have seen the fear in *his* face when he was confronted by his former boss.’

‘… because Harold… I mean Jacob… knew he was going to be exposed as a fraudster?’

Jack shook his head. ‘No, because he’d come face-to-face again with the man who’d tried to murder him.’

‘Murder… Alistair!’ exclaimed Audrey. ‘Why, for heaven’s sake?’

'I'll come to that later and it wasn't difficult to recognise Jacob Matson as Harold? As I said, Aud, I was already considering the two were one-and-the-same. Harold said that when he was recovering from that first head injury, he was cared for on a boat by a woman he knew as "Mary". When I visited Hendricks, the boatyard from where *Fisher of Men* was bought, the receipt for the boat was made out to M Biggs. I reckoned this had to be the mysterious "Mary", so I got the office to check if they had any boat registered to M Biggs.'

'… and…?'

'… they had. *Ocean Venturer*, and guess who had been the previous registered owner of this big sea-going cruiser?'

'Go on…'

'Alistair Hepscott, until two years ago, when he'd sold it to this M Biggs.'

'Who is this Mary Biggs then, who seems to have a penchant for buying boats?'

'I don't know,' admitted Jack, 'but it did confirm that *Ocean Venturer* was the boat I wanted. Tommy Taylor told me she was moored in Brundall Marina, so I went straight there, found it gone, but with Harold just arriving himself. With my deep suspicion that Harold was actually Jacob Matson, I greeted him with that name and he responded accordingly.'

'But, how did you know it was Harold when he was clean-shaven and dressed completely differently?'

'Easy. Do you remember Harold wearing a gold crucifix, given by one of his followers? Well, Jacob Matson was wearing that same crucifix.'

'He can't be all bad, then,' declared Audrey.

'I don't think he's bad at all,' said Jack. 'Jacob Matson was already a committed Christian in his old life.'

'He told you that?'

'He told me *everything*. He looked pretty hungry so, after getting over the shock of being recognised, I took him for breakfast and, over a big fry-up, he poured out his story.'

'That must have been interesting.' Audrey had finished her soup. 'Presumably he really did work for the bank?'

'Oh yes, in Alistair's department where they were both graduate trainees. They were very different in many ways: Matson came from an ordinary family, deeply committed to their church, whereas Alistair was the son of the Chief Executive and very much for the high-life.'

'No doubt prompted by Clarissa, to whom he was already married.'

'I'm sure,' agreed Jack. 'In fact, according to Jacob, Alistair's considerable income was inadequate for his wife's expensive tastes and he often complained that Lord Hepscott refused to cough up more money.'

'I don't blame him. They must have sussed Clarissa for the money-grabber she was, and realised it would be money down the drain.'

'I'm sure, and apparently she was so embarrassing that Alistair kept her well-away from the office anyway. By now though, Jacob had noticed something even more disturbing.'

'Money disappearing?'

'Exactly, small amounts at first, but rapidly escalating into considerable fortunes. Ostensibly, these were funds being transferred overseas to pay for foreign government bonds. It was almost a year before Jacob discovered that there were no bonds and that the money had gone into obscure offshore accounts.'

'Didn't anyone else notice this?'

'Apparently not. Being the chief executive's son, Alistair had been given considerable responsibility and Jacob was loathe to question these dubious transactions with the management.'

'So, what did he do?'

'Simply confronted Alistair to his face. He liked him as a person and, if it were a genuine mistake, he didn't want to cause his colleague unnecessary grief.'

'So, how did Alistair respond?'

'Said it was something they needed to talk over and invited him up to Norfolk to spend a weekend on his boat.'

'*Ocean Venturer*?'

'The very one, but it turned out to be no pleasure cruise. For starters, Alistair was very different to the congenial colleague he'd known at work, being very off-hand and aggressive. At first he denied any wrongdoing and then, when Jacob confronted him with photocopied evidence, tried to bribe him into keeping quiet.'

'Which, presumably, he refused to do?'

'Of course. His Christian ethics would never allow him to even consider condoning theft. The only leeway he gave was the option of returning the funds to the bank, for which he'd turn a blind eye to the whole business. At first, Alistair appeared to agree but, later that evening when they were well down the Yare and far from habitation, Jacob happened to turn his back on him, felt a stunning blow to the head, and that was the last he remembered.'

'But what of all those years spent as Harold Searby, evangelising on the Broads?' asked Audrey, completely baffled by this incredible story. 'Has this Jacob no recollection of those at all?'

'None. As far as he's concerned he was bashed on the head and woke up in Gorleston hospital three days ago.'

'So, why did he go on the run from there?'

'Reaction to the shock of meeting Alistair, seemingly so soon after he'd attacked him. As far as he was concerned, in his mind, the bank had been defrauded by Alistair and the evidence for that still lay where he'd left it on *Ocean Venturer*, only days before. He knew that no would believe him without the photocopies, and headed back to the boat to recover them before Alistair got at him again.'

'… little realising that ten years had elapsed between that attack and his waking in Gorleston. The whole series of events sounds totally unbelievable, but I've read before of people regaining their memory after another knock on the head. Alistair must have been horrified when he realised what had happened,' surmised Audrey, pouring them both a glass of water. She sat back. 'So, what do you think really happened all those years ago, Jack?'

'Good question.' Jack sat back himself. 'I certainly think there was an attempt made on Jacob Matson's life, but that it failed to kill him outright. When it was realised that he'd only been knocked unconscious, it caused a dilemma. A cowardly blow from behind is one thing, but to strike an injured man lying facing you is another. When Jacob came round, I bet Alistair couldn't believe his luck when he realised he was suffering from acute amnesia and had no recollection of what had happened, or of his former life. Alistair must have arranged for this Mary Biggs to come to the boat and nurse Jacob back to full-health. During that time, she managed to convince him his name was Harold Searby, with documents taken from the deceased man to prove the fact. Alistair completed the deception by buying him an old cruiser to live on, and then launched him off with his new identity for a life away from it all on the Broads.'

'He was taking a bit of a risk though,' Audrey pointed out. 'There was always the chance that the man now known as Harold would recover his memory and spill the beans.'

'I imagine Alistair monitored the situation at first, but after a few months he must have felt pretty safe. Even now, Jacob has no idea that back then he'd been wrongly accused of fraud, with all the evidence showing that he'd scarpered overseas to live off his ill-gotten gains.'

'I suppose we can presume that it was actually Alistair who planted false evidence at the bank to steer suspicion away from himself and incriminate Matson.'

'Yes, and he must have made a pretty good job of it.' Jack shook his head. 'That's just another aspect of this whole mess that Jacob found hard to understand. No-one at the bank held Alistair in great esteem professionally. His performance was generally mediocre with only the odd flash of brilliance.'

'His whole life seems to have been a series of contradictions,' said Audrey. 'He was the son of a lord, but wasn't; he loved Amy, but married Clarissa; he struggled at university, but came out with a first; he was a mediocre banker, but pulled off some news-worthy deals and now, it appears, he tried to kill Matson, but ended up caring for him. It's all very strange, Jack.'

'Yes, his life has been far from straightforward,' agreed Jack.

'Anyway, I'm just relieved he didn't end up as our son-in-law. Amy had a lucky escape, as it turned out.' Audrey paused for a moment, thinking to herself how the most upsetting of events, often worked out for the best. 'To get back to poor Jacob, what's happening to him now, Jack?'

'I told him he was on the Fraud Squad's "wanted list" and that the best thing was to go to the police with me and make a clean breast of the whole matter, which he agreed to do.'

'Good for him.' Audrey smiled. 'Hopefully, with retraining, he could even take up his old bank job once this awful business is sorted out.'

Jack grimaced. 'I wouldn't count on that, Aud. The problem is, Bailey is now convinced that Jacob Matson killed Alistair Hepscott and I feel bad because *I'm* the one who made him hand himself in.'

'But you don't think he did?'

'No, I don't.' Jack looked around at the period fittings of this old courtroom and hoped Jacob Matson would not have to face a similar scene for real. He turned back to Audrey. 'There are still some loose ends here that need sorting.'

'Like the mysterious Mary Biggs, for instance.' Audrey paused while the waitress came and cleared their table. In keeping with the setting, she was wearing traditional tearoom black skirt and shirt and a white pinafore. 'I'm sure you'd like to know who she is… Jack… are you listening?'

But Jack wasn't. Instead, he was watching the waitress with more than comely scrutiny. Finally, he turned back to his wife. 'Sorry, Aud. I've just had an idea and need to go talk to Bailey.' He stood up, took out his wallet, went to extract a note, but paused.

'What's the matter, Jack… not enough?' asked Audrey, already puzzled by this sudden burst of activity.

'No, just another piece clicking into place,' he said, smiling and taking out a twenty-pound note. He laid it on the table. 'Settle up for us, please love. You go shopping and I'll meet you at the car in an hour.'

Another minute he was gone, leaving his wife wondering what on earth was going on now.

*　　*　　*

Chapter Nineteen

'Come on, Jack.' DS Bailey tapped the recording of his recent interview with Jacob Matson. 'He's told me all about that earlier financial scam and we know Hepscott must have set him up as the fall-guy, so *there's* a motive for revenge if ever there was one.'

Jack shook his head. 'But, he didn't know he'd been set up until *I* told him, Bailey. All that was done at the beginning of the ten years when he genuinely thought he *was* Harold Searby.'

'That's what he wants us to think,' insisted Bailey, 'but it would take a psychiatrist to be sure all that supposed loss of memory wasn't faked.'

It had only been a few minutes walk back from the Guildhall to Bethel Street Police Station and up to CID. The DS had just finished a long interview with his new suspect and wasn't in the mood to hear protests of his innocence. But this wasn't the prime reason for Jack's revisit. 'Bailey, I'm sure this man is the victim rather than the offender.'

'You're the only one that thinks that, Jack.' The DS nodded to a pile of recent e-mails. 'Since they heard we've got Matson, the Fraud Squad's been itching to get their hands on him as well.'

'Then hold them off as long as you can, because I've got just one more line of enquiry for you to pursue.'

'What's that?' groaned Bailey, who was up to his neck in work.

'The Hepscott family… I mean the old family… Lord and Lady Hepscott… I want you to delve a little into their affairs.'

'They're dead Jack,' disclosed Bailey. 'When they fished Alistair's body out of the river we made enquiries of all next-of-kin, but Lord Hepscott died a year ago and his wife, soon after that.'

'Did you find out where they lived?'

'Yep…' Bailey glanced into his notebook, '… some grand place in Berkshire.'

'Right, well get someone to nose around a bit there… perhaps the village Post Office. Find out if anyone knows of someone called Mary Biggs.'

'Who's she?'

'The woman Harold reckoned cared for him when he was recovering from what we now know was an assault.'

Bailey sounded rather dismissive. 'A waste of time, Jack. That was all some tale to get out of the fraud charge. And, even if this Mary Biggs does exist, how's that going to help my murder enquiry?'

'Perhaps more than you think.' Jack nodded towards the computer. 'And, while you're at it, find out the *exact* antecedents of Alistair Hepscott and then you might see where I'm coming from.'

'All right.' Bailey sighed. 'The things I do for you, Jack…' he paused to smile, '… but you haven't let me down yet.'

'And I don't think I will this time either.' The ranger sat back. 'The thing is, Bailey, I now have an inkling how this whole nasty business was engineered and, believe me, there's far more to it than the settling of old scores.'

'Well, if you've got a theory, I'd like to hear it…' said Bailey, before adding, '… that's if you're prepared to share it.'

'Of course I will.' Jack stretched his legs towards the DS's desk. 'And then I'm going to tell you how we prove it.'

* * *

'Come on, Beki,' said Oliver, taking her hand, 'let's give this one a go.'

The gang were enjoying a night in Norwich, letting their hair down at a Riverside night-spot where the strobe lights made the gyrating figure of Clarissa on the dance-floor, look decidedly bizarre.

'What, and make a fool of myself like her?' protested Beki, indicating the widow's ample figure nuzzling up to some complete stranger. 'I like to think I've got *some* dignity left.'

'Well I'm game if you are,' persisted the MP. 'We *are* on holiday, Beks. Just this one night we can let it all hang out.'

'I suppose I haven't got quite as much to "hang out" as Clarissa,' she conceded, 'so why not.'

'Go for it, Beks,' said Amy laughing, as the two went onto the dance floor, hand-in-hand.

'They seem to be hitting it off,' commented Spencer. He pointed towards the two enjoying some uninhibited close contact. 'How about it, Amy… shall we join them.'

'Not just yet.' She was still feeling a bit jaded after her silly panic of the afternoon. It had gone against the grain, but she'd told Spencer the whole embarrassing tale.

'Don't worry about it, Amy, the mind's a funny thing and it's been a traumatic few days. I'm sure it'll never happen again.'

'I hope not,' she said, forcing a smile. 'But I guess there is just one other thing holding me back tonight.' She looked towards the unseen river. 'It's only three days since Alistair's body was pulled out of there. Somehow it's not right for us to be enjoying ourselves so soon.'

'I know what you mean, but it doesn't seem to be worrying *her*,' Spencer said as he glanced in the direction of a sudden squeal from Clarissa, who'd somehow managed to slip to the floor in a tumble of flailing limbs and exposed flabby flesh.

'No I guess not,' laughed Amy. The scene was so hilarious that she couldn't do anything but see the funny side of it. She put her hand in his. 'Thanks, Spencer. You're just the company I need right now.'

'Only "right now"?'

She shook her head coyly. 'No, I'd like to keep seeing you even after we get back. It's just that somehow, I feel we have to close this chapter before opening the next.'

'In what way?'

'Hard to define… just the feeling that there's more to this than we yet know.'

'Now you *are* imagining things,' joked Spencer, standing up and pulling Amy to her feet as he did so. 'Come on, you'll soon forget your worries when you see how well I can dance.'

She allowed herself to be led onto the floor. He was right, she should try and forget and, anyway, there were some things that she couldn't even start to explain. Like her suspicion that, perhaps, she'd inherited just a little of her dad's instinct for incipient evil.

* * *

While their daughter was attempting to relax in Norwich, Jack and Audrey were making the most of the evening's light to walk Spike along the riverbank close to their home.

'This is so lovely,' breathed Audrey as the river stilled to a silence broken only by the "click" of some nearby coots. 'A million miles from police HQ and that whole sorry business.'

'I know, love,' admitted Jack, conscious of his wife's pointed remarks. He wanted to explain his sudden inspiration back there in the restaurant, but showing his hand before he'd established the facts was something he never liked to do and Audrey knew him too well to ask. Instead, he threw a stick for Spike and watched as the border collie dashed off in playful pursuit. 'Just a few more pieces now, Aud, and the jigsaw might be complete.'

'I thought it already was.' She took the stick Spike had brought back for them and threw it again. 'You mean there are some revelations yet to come?'

'I'm certain of it, but I'll know for sure when Bailey calls me back.'

'Well that's probably now,' grumbled Audrey, hearing the ring of her husband's phone.

'Hi, Bailey, what have you got?' she heard him ask, as he slipped a little further away to talk to the DS. There was much nodding before he said, 'Right, Bailey, I'll be in touch.' Then he was switching off and rejoining her further up the bank.

'Well, I hope that's what you wanted to hear and that you're happy now, Jack.'

'I don't know about "happy", but it certainly explains everything.' Jack turned and, for a few seconds more, enjoyed the peace of the scene. 'This whole business is far deeper than anyone thought, Aud, and the sooner we bring it to a head, the better.'

* * *

Chapter Twenty

'It'll be lovely to see you, Dad. Five minutes then.' Amy switched off her mobile and laid it on the saloon table. They'd been approaching Reedham, en route to *Berney Arms* where they'd left *Babbling Brook*, when Jack had first called to ask if he could have a quick chat. Amy had said they'd try and moor up and give him a call back to confirm, which she'd just done.

'What does your dad want?' asked Beki.

'I don't know, but we'll soon find out,' she replied as she saw Jack's car drive onto the staithe. Minutes later, and the ranger was onboard, gratefully accepting a mug of hot chocolate. 'What's happening to Harold, Dad?' Amy asked as Oliver and Spencer joined them in the saloon.

'Still detained, pending further enquiries.' Jack shrugged. 'I think they'll be able to hold him almost indefinitely, seeing as there was a warrant out for Jacob Matson's arrest long before this murder investigation.'

'But nothing further with that?' enquired Spencer.

'Actually there is,' admitted Jack without giving further details, 'which is why I wanted to speak to you this morning.' He nodded vaguely to the east. 'Are you planning to stop at Yarmouth again on the way back?'

'Not really, Jack. We thought the place would bring back painful memories, especially for Clarissa.' He glanced for'ard to where she was obviously sleeping in after her night of clubbing.

'Which makes what I'm about to ask all the more demanding,' admitted Jack, because what I want is a complete reconstruction of Monday night.'

'You mean the murder?' gasped Amy. 'What, *all* of us?'

'Yes. I need you all to do exactly what you did on the night and, as far as possible, at exactly the same times.'

'Gosh.' Oliver gulped. 'This is a bit dramatic isn't it, Jack?'

'Not really.' The ranger swigged back his drink. 'In some countries, France for instance, it's standard procedure in any murder enquiry.' He frowned. 'There's still a lot of mystery involved in Alistair's demise and you all going over it again will help the police work out who did what.'

'I thought they knew "who did what",' said Spencer. 'Surely Harold… or whatever he's called now… is their man.'

'Possibly,' admitted Jack reluctantly, 'but you all played a part and we need to know how.'

'Are the police going to be in on this?' asked Amy.

Jack nodded. 'Yes, but you won't notice their presence. They'll just be in the background observing.'

'Let me get this right, Dad… you want me to go back into that amusement arcade just as I did with Alistair.' She shook her head. 'I'm not sure I'm up to that.'

'I know it'll be a bit of an ordeal, Amy, but I'm sure it will help.'

'How?' queried Beki. 'Surely the idea is to find out the way Alistair was abducted, but how can you do that if he's not with us anymore?'

'There were a lot of bystanders in that arcade,' explained Jack. 'What we're hoping is that seeing Amy again, dressed just as she was on the night, will at least jog someone's memory.'

Amy ran a hand through her hair. 'Okay, Dad… if you really think this will help, I'll do my bit.'

'And so will we,' added Spencer. 'And don't worry, Amy… we'll *all* be there for you.'

'But not until that nine-thirty rendezvous at the pier,' insisted Jack. 'Everything's got to be *exactly* like last time…' he turned to his daughter, '… especially you, Amy, even down to the cash you have with you.'

'I'll try.'

'Good girl.' He nodded for'ard. 'I'll leave you all to brief her ladyship.'

'We will.'

'That'll be great… excuse me, I need to call Bailey…' Jack produced his mobile and keyed in a number, '… Bailey… all on for tonight… we'll see you there.' He finished his call and turned back to the others. 'Right, you lot need to get going if you're to be on your mooring and in town on time.'

'Yes, especially as we have to collect the sailing boat on our way,' agreed Spencer.

Jack went to climb ashore.

'I'll walk with you a bit, Dad,' said Amy, jumping off the boat at the same time.

As they got to the car, Jack turned and gave his daughter a hug. 'I know I'm asking a lot of you, Amy. If you want to back out…'

'I'll be fine, Dad,' she confirmed with determination. 'I only hope, in the end, it'll be worth all the trouble.'

'We'll see.' He kissed her goodbye and was gone.

Amy wandered back to *Brookside*, mulling over all that had happened and still wondering what results this re-enactment could possibly produce.

The rest were waiting for her there, Spencer obviously keen to get going again if they were to be in Yarmouth for the appointed time. He gave her a reassuring wink. 'Just bite the bullet on this one, Amy, and then it'll all be over. We're all behind you.'

It was good to know that. This last act was going to be more of a trial than anyone realised and having her old chums around would make all the difference.

* * *

'Well, Jack, I just hope you know what you're doing, making poor Amy go through with this charade you've got planned.' Audrey was unhappy at the idea of Jack persuading their daughter to act out the whole upsetting scenario again. 'Are you sure it's safe… Amy on her own like that… and is it necessary anyway?'

'It's worth a try at least.' Jack went to pop a slice of bread in the toaster. 'It's surprising how people's minds can be jogged by a little play-acting.'

'Only if they know about it, surely,' replied Audrey. 'You're talking about Yarmouth, Jack, where people come and go all the time. What are the chances of the same people being in that amusement arcade as were there last Monday?'

'The staff will probably be the same,' pointed out Jack, 'and they, more than anyone, will keep their eyes open for anything out of the norm.'

'But why have all the others replicating their movements as well?' persisted Audrey, who was making no secret that she thought the whole idea was daft. 'Surely the police don't still suspect any of *them*?'

'No-one is ruled out until the curtain comes down, Audrey…' Jack glanced at his watch, '… and I'd better get shifting myself if I'm going to be around to help.'

As her husband went upstairs to change, Audrey couldn't help wishing this whole rotten business could come to an end.

Perhaps tonight it would.

Chapter Twenty-one

True to the plan, once again Spencer Ovington sat on the beach, close by where the old naval air station had once stood. It had been a good afternoon afloat, but somehow he felt this evening wouldn't be quite so enjoyable.

After collecting *Babbling Brook* from *Berney Arms*, they'd made good time crossing Breydon Water on the last of the ebb. Then they were turning once more into the Bure and stemming its outgoing tide at a snail's-pace as they pushed the last half-mile to the Yacht Station. Secure alongside, they'd had some quick refreshments and then set off on their separate ways to re-enact the strange events of four nights previous. Jack had wanted everything just as it had been, so here Spencer was, dressed in the same clothes and at exactly the same time.

But those were the only things that *were* the same. For one thing, the sea was different. When he'd sat here before, it had been a gently rolling, almost benign, expanse in the warm evening air. Tonight though, there was a fresher breeze with waves big enough to curl into breakers on the hard shingle shore. Spencer wondered how those airmen of a century ago had coped with even worse conditions than these? He could imagine those early ground crews struggling to recover flimsy flying boats up the slipway with seas breaking all around them. And this evening there was a slight mist hanging over the water, possibly the start of a sea "fret", as warm moist air moved over the colder ocean. With the land also radiating its heat of the day, the breeze had turned to on-shore now, bringing the sea-mist ever closer. Pilots must have dreaded this phenomena, returning to this base after long hours patrolling, only to find it "socked in" by the elements.

How different was flying now and how different was his own personal life since the last time he'd sat here. Then he had been agonising over his feelings for Amy, but now those feelings were known and… joy of joys… reciprocated. That gave Spencer the only warmth he was feeling at this time as a cool breeze licked at his bare arms… that and the thought of all the happiness yet to come.

Ah, that anything should happen this evening to blight that prospect. Amy was alone at this time, replaying her own role in the drama, but how he wished he were with her. Her father had requested this strange exercise, and he hoped-against-hope she were safe. Surely Jack Fellows wouldn't allow his daughter to be exposed to any danger? This, after all, was only play-acting.

But Spencer couldn't get it out of his mind that there was something far more sinister in this whole dark procedure than a simple play.

He got up and made his way towards the pier

*   *   *

'I just hope this whole business is worth while.' Oliver Stanhope was wishing he could have brought a warm fleece, as a decidedly chilly mist swirled around the same sea-front bench where he and Beki Smith had sat on Monday evening.

'I'm sure Jack must have some good reason for it,' Beki assured him, 'though it is a bit eerie thinking we might all be being observed.'

'Doing what?' questioned Oliver. 'I mean, if one of us did bump off Alistair, we're hardly going to re-enact *that*, are we?'

Beki shrugged. 'I suppose not, but it is amazing how much has changed since last Monday. Like your financial problem, for instance.' She turned to face the MP. 'Where does Alistair's death leave you with that?'

'I'm not sure,' confessed Oliver. 'With him gone, I might have lost any chance I have of seeing the money again. I tried to find Clarissa in Norwich yesterday to ask if she could help. I never did, but I'm still hoping that, if she's going to benefit from a widow's payout as much as she thinks, then I might prevail on her good nature to recompense me.'

'"Good nature"!' scoffed Beki. 'When have you ever seen her showing so much as a glimmer?' She shook her head sadly. 'No, I'm sorry, Oliver, but if you're relying on Clarissa Hepscott's good nature to get your money back, then you're doomed to disappointment.'

'You're probably right,' admitted Oliver, gloomily. 'But how about you, Beks? Where will all this leave you?'

'Probably carrying on the same old life as I had before.' The sea fret had a real nip to it now and Beki moved closer to Oliver for warmth. 'Getting what acting parts I can in local theatre and trying to survive on the little extra I earn at the restaurant and Brookerboats.'

'In some ways I envy you, Beks,' said Oliver. 'I know you're not going to get rich, but I've lived politics since I was a teenager and, when I was elected to become an MP, my life's dreams were fulfilled. I thought I'd be walking the corridors of the House of Parliament with the opportunity of making a *real* difference to people's lives, but instead…'

'… but instead, you've just towed the party line?'

'Exactly. I feel a complete fraud, made even worse by these expense charges still hanging over me. I genuinely didn't realise I'd made unauthorised claims, but once my name was linked to the scandal, no-one wanted to be seen siding with me. Westminster can be a very lonely place, you know, especially when you're single.'

Beki gave his arm a squeeze. 'Well, Oliver, if you feel you may lose your seat because you can't repay the money, you've little to lose, so now's the time to speak out for what you truly believe in. Appease your conscience and try and make a difference, fight for those reforms you've dreamt about and blow the consequences.'

'Anything sounds possible when you say it, Beks, but I don't know if I've any fight left in me.'

'So you need the right person to back you up.' She took his hand. 'Me, for instance?'

'You?'

'Yes. Alone, living in London, fighting your solitary corner, must be pretty grim, but what if I were there to support you?'

'But you've no experience of legal or parliamentary procedures.'

'No, but I *am* an actress and I can play any part you want.' She smiled. 'Actually, I think I'd play a pretty good assistant.'

'But I already have people for that,' protested Oliver.

'Not ones who love you, you don't.'

The words took Oliver completely off guard. 'You… you mean that Beks. You mean *that* wouldn't be… well… just an act?'

'No, of course not. Haven't you sensed the way I feel about you and how much I admire all you've achieved?'

'Like bankrupting myself, for instance.' He gave a wry smile at his own naivety, but Beki shook her head and squeezed his hand even tighter.

'If the worst comes to the worst, we can face it together but, as long as we have our health, nothing's impossible.' She glanced at her watch. 'Nine o'clock, Oliver… we need to be wending our different ways towards the pier.'

Suddenly, even this rather macabre situation had all the joy of a dream come true, and Oliver stood up to play his part. 'I know we're supposed to act exactly as we did on Monday, Beks, but I'm sure one discrepancy won't matter.' And with that he gently pulled her to her feet and kissed her longingly.

Reluctantly, they drew apart, aware of the promise they'd made to Jack. 'It's going to seem a long time 'til nine-thirty,' Beki said, grinning mischievously. She stood on tiptoe and gave him a quick peck on the cheek. 'Only half an hour, so off you go…' she glanced south down the prom, now sheathed in translusent mist, '… but don't go asking *any* favours of Clarissa Hepscott.'

* * *

That would have been a futile exercise anyway, for Clarissa had already mentally spent all her forthcoming wealth. It had been a pleasant way to while away some of the time spent back at the bar she'd visited on Monday, sitting at the same outside table looking incredibly hardy to all the other punters, who were warm inside. Planning how to get through a million quid had taken up all of the first G & T quite nicely, but this second was prompting her to question what on earth she was doing, sitting in a sea fret wearing inappropriate clothes and feeling very cold. The police already had the man who'd somehow done away with Alistair, so what more did they want? Whatever his motive, this Harold chap had done her the best of favours and Clarissa only hoped tonight's exercise would do nothing to upset what were now her very agreeable plans. She suspected this whole daft thing was probably the bright idea of Amy's father and concluded he must be as mentally deluded as his daughter.

Clarissa glanced at her watch. Presumably Amy was now playing out her own role in this ridiculous farce. Well enjoy the play, Amy, she thought, making a mock toast with her glass and enjoying an inward smirk. Because this fantasy is as close to Alistair as you'll ever get again.

* * *

In fact, Amy was feeling full of doubt as she once again wandered into the amusement arcade where she'd last seen Alistair four nights before.

Was it really only four days and nights? After all that had happened, it seemed closer to four years. Amy wished it really was that long, but this strange replay was bringing it all back in vivid recall. In her heart-of-hearts, she wished her dad had never thought of it.

But Amy knew her dad never did anything without good reason, and so she'd entered into the spirit of the activity by wearing the same clothes, taking the same route and even ensuring she had the same cash in her purse as her dad had requested.

She was glad to get into the arcade this night, with the cold fingers of a sea-fret now starting to stroke the landward side of Marine Parade. In the arcade, the thumping music, flashing lights, rows of jangling machines, even the crowds of people, at least gave a little warmth to the scene. And there were certainly more of the latter tonight, no doubt driven undercover by the dismal conditions outside. Were any of these laughing youngsters actually there to witness her performance? Her dad had said this replay might jog someone's memory, but whose? Apart from the odd member of staff, most of the current crowd must be completely different from those on Monday. And who was around to ask them anyway? She glanced about her and saw no-one she recognised.

Slightly bemused, Amy made her way to the 2p machine with its constant shovelling blade. She took out her purse and from it, a handful of two-pences. Her luck tonight turned out to be no better than Monday's and soon her coins were exhausted and with no windfall to show for it. This time, though, there was no Alistair Hepscott taking out his wad of notes and offering to pay. Amy swallowed slightly, and once again got out her own purse. 'It's all right,' she said aloud, 'I've got some pound coins.' Self-conscious of appearing to be talking to herself, she made her way to the change-machine, determined to play her part to the last. As she neared the machine, she asked over her shoulder: 'How much shall I get?' and a heart-stopping voice answered, 'As much as you think we'll need, Amy.'

She spun around and felt her legs giving way as she did so. For there, smiling and as seemingly full of life as ever, was the figure of Alistair Hepscott.

*   *   *

Chapter Twenty-two

Was it his ghost? Was she dreaming? Was she simply awakening from a ghastly nightmare that had spanned four whole days and nights?

'Alistair… what are you doing here?' she found herself stammering as she leaned against the change-machine for support.

'To take you with me,' he answered, still smiling. It was almost as if the shock in her face was giving him amusement.

'Take… take me where?'

But Amy never got an answer to that question. By now, a scruffy figure playing one of the machines had detached himself and rapidly sped to join them. Beneath the baseball cap with its "Tomb Raider" logo, Amy recognised the fresh face of DS Bailey.

'Alistair Hepscott,' he said placing a firm hand on the banker's shoulder, 'I'm arresting you for the murder…'

A kaleidoscope of questions surged within Amy's mind, as confused as the flashing coloured lights around her. How could anyone be arrested for murdering themselves? How had this resurrection manifested itself when even Clarissa had identified the body as her husband?

Clearly there was to be no immediate answer to these questions, for uniformed officers were now entering the arcade and, right behind them, the burly figure of her father.

Was this the end of her nightmare or only the beginning?

*   *   *

'Will Amy be all right, Jack?'

It was an hour later and Bailey and Jack were standing on a large sea-going cruiser moored at Town Hall Quay, close by and just to seaward of Yarmouth's Haven Bridge. With the sun set and the creeping sea fret now filling even the docks, the whole scene was one of eerie opaqueness punctuated only by the ghostly glow of street and harbour lights. This boat though was well-illuminated, lit by hastily assembled floodlights that reflected off the encircling CRIME

SCENE tape and yellow jackets of the policeman guarding the entry-port. Combined with the fog, it made the hooded, white-coveralled figures of the CSI team even more wraithlike than ever.

Detective and ranger were similarly attired, the latter pausing to stroke the black lettering engraved into the bell that hung just abaft the cabin: **OCEAN VENTURER**

Fog was condensing now onto its surface, the shine of the brasswork misted over and rivulets already forming and dropping from the rim. Jack looked up. 'Amy'll be fine back on *Brookside* with all the gang there to support her.' He gave a little chuckle. 'Actually, I suspect it's Clarissa who might be the more upset.'

'I think you're right,' agreed Bailey. 'Her reaction was certainly odd for a woman just told her husband wasn't dead after all.'

'I think we can say that disappointment was the predominant emotion there,' confirmed Jack. 'For a woman like Clarissa, suddenly discovering you're not going to be handed a million quid after all, must come as a bit of a blow.' He nodded to the doorway leading into the big cruiser's main cabin. 'Shall we take a look?'

Inside, the forensic team was already hard at work, photographing every inch of the interior, taking samples from the plush carpets, lifting fingerprints from every likely touch-spot. Jack scanned the walnut panelling, the real-leather upholstery and the shining brass fittings. 'Not exactly going to rough it, our Mr Hepscott, was he?' Further for'ard, the galley displayed copper pans, best crockery and finest cut-glass. The ranger nodded to a companionway leading below. 'It's the machinery spaces I'd like to look at.'

He led them down and aft to where a watertight bulkhead door gained entry to the engine-room. Once again, well-ordered cleanliness reigned supreme. All the metalwork of the hull was freshly painted, as were the cylinder-heads of the two big diesels. Between them, a diesel generator purred its steady revs. Jack scanned the whole scene with admiration. 'As well-found technically as she is domestically.' He glanced at the oil and fuel filters with the date of the last change scratched onto their surface: one week ago. At the head of each main engine, the alternator pulley wheels caught his attention. Here the protruding thread of each studbolt had been drilled through and locking-wire inserted to prevent any loosening or loss of the nut. 'Very neat.'

'It's not neatness I'm worried about, Jack,' said Bailey with just a hint of impatience, 'it's evidence of what's gone on here that I need.' He nodded back up top. 'I suggest we leave the CSI lads to do their thing and go and have a chat with Alistair Hepscott.' He gave a grim smile. 'There's an awful lot I need to ask that young man.' He raised questioning eyes. 'Want to join me, Jack?'

The ranger smiled. 'Try and stop me.'

*   *   *

'Right, let's start right at the beginning, shall we?'

DS Bailey sat in the interview room of Great Yarmouth Police Station together with a young DC. Facing him, across the table and appearing more weary than concerned, was Alistair Hepscott. He sat alone, having declined his right to have a solicitor beside him. To Jack, standing outside the room viewing the whole proceedings through a one-way screen and listening to the words via an audio link, it seemed that Alistair Hepscott was almost resigned to his fate. Bailey was now extracting a document from a file and pushing it across the table. All this would be captured on the installed CCTV, but for good measure, Bailey was describing just what it was. 'I'm showing the accused a copy of his birth certificate,' he uttered for the recorder before saying, 'Just confirm that is *yours*, Alistair.'

The banker nodded. 'Yes, that's mine.'

'Interesting reading isn't it?' Bailey sat back. 'Because it shows quite clearly that Lord Hepscott, who it was always thought was your adopted father, was in fact your *natural* father.'

'That's right.'

'Would you like to enlighten us on that?' requested Bailey.

Alistair blinked just once. 'It's quite simple, actually. Lord and Lady Hepscott couldn't have children of their own. Working in the household, however, was a young maid.'

'Mary Biggs,' interrupted Bailey.

'Yes, attractive as a girl apparently, and someone my father subsequently had an affair with.' Alistair shrugged. 'Eventually, Mary declared she was pregnant by Lord Hepscott and left the household to have the baby. His Lord and Ladyship were both keen to adopt a child, so an arrangement was made by which I would be handed over to them at birth.'

'Did Lady Hepscott know that the father was her own husband?'

'I'm not sure,' admitted Alistair, 'but my guess is she suspected, but didn't want to know the truth.'

'Did they ever discuss your adoption with you?'

'No, in my early years I was led to believe I was their natural son.'

'So, who told you that you were adopted?'

'My brother…'

Bailey pushed across another paper. '… Malcolm Biggs, whose copy birth certificate this is. Will you confirm that, Alistair?'

'Yes, this is Malcolm's,' acknowledged Alistair.

'The interesting thing about that certificate,' continued Bailey, 'is that it shows his date of birth as the same as yours. In other words, you were twins?'

'Yes.'

'*Identical* twins?'

'Yes.'

'So, your natural mother, Mary Biggs, gave birth to identical twins, but the Hepscotts only adopted *you*. Why was that?'

'Simply because my mother didn't want to lose *both* her sons,' explained Alistair. 'So, the agreement was that she would keep one, Malcolm, and allow me to go.'

'Did Lord Hepscott continue to support Malcolm?'

'Oh, yes,' emphasised Alistair. 'It was an entirely amicable, though secret, arrangement.'

'And did it stay that way?'

'At first, yes, though I imagine Lord Hepscott soon realised he'd got the worst of the bargain.'

'Explain that.'

'Only that his own keen financial brain seemed to have been inherited by Malcolm, whereas I'd inherited my mother's more limited intellect.'

'Some things can't be helped,' sympathised Bailey. 'When did you learn all this?'

'Quite late into my teens, when I was fifteen. My natural mother had told Malcolm the whole story, and he searched me out and told me.'

'That must have been a bit of a shock: suddenly finding you had a twin-brother.'

Alistair shrugged. 'Yes and no. I think some instinct told me before I ever knew.'

'Is that why Malcolm searched you out, do you think?'

'What, natural brotherly love?' Alistair gave a humourless laugh. 'It would be nice to think so, but no, with Malcolm I'm sure it was a simple case of his knowing the money lay on my side of the family, and being determined to get his hands on some.'

'You don't seem to have a very good opinion of your twin,' commented Bailey.

'He was evil,' said Alistair with no hint of leniency. 'Malcolm had a brilliant mind, but couldn't be honest if he tried. My natural mother was a good kind woman, but I suspect somewhere in *her* family was some bad blood and Malcolm inherited more than his share of it.'

'So, how did you allow yourself to get ensnared into his devious ways?'

'By the simple fact that he was so much more intelligent than I was. Lord Hepscott, my natural father, was also a kind man and had great plans for my future. I was sent to a good school and from there it was ordained that I'd go on to university and eventually enter his bank.'

'Which is exactly what happened.'

'Yes, but only with Malcolm's help.' Alistair sighed. 'He was so bright that he left his comprehensive and went up to university a whole year before me. I, in the meantime, realised I'd be pushed to get the A-levels to go to university at all. That was when Malcolm came up with his scheme.'

'Which was?'

'That he'd take my A-levels for me.'

'Not a particularly honest way to embark on a career,' said Bailey.

Alistair nodded. 'I know, but my main concern was that I didn't let my father down, as he so wanted me to succeed and follow him into the bank. In the event, it was simplicity itself. Being identical twins, no-one even questioned Malcolm's identity when he turned up to take them. He got me four A grades.'

'Didn't this sudden change in your academic ability raise a few eyebrows?'

'Yes, but only in a gratified way. Everyone just assumed I was a late-starter.'

'So, off you went to university?'

'Yes, to study accounting and finance but, of course, I soon found myself way out of my depth with the course work. To avoid being sent down, the solution was the same as the A-levels. Malcolm was also studying the same course at his university, but still a year ahead. So, each year he came and took my exams for me.'

'Including your finals, when he got you a First-Class degree?'

'Yes.'

DS Bailey leaned forward. 'But that's where it all started to go wrong, isn't it Alistair? Because it was all such a doddle for Malcolm that he didn't even have to stay in and swot. Instead, while you kept your head down in your room pretending to cram, he went into town in the evenings and lived it up. And that, presumably, was how he met Clarissa.'

'Or how she met *him*, to be more precise,' corrected Alistair. He shook his head. 'Knowing I was from a wealthy family, she'd been trying to get her claws in me from the day we started.'

'But *you* were in love with Amy Fellows?'

'*Deeply* in love with Amy, yes,' Alistair confessed sincerely. 'But Clarissa, seeing who she thought was me on the loose at that nightclub, took her chance and captured her prey.' Alistair frowned. 'Of course, of all the rotten luck, Amy's best friend, Beki Smith, saw them together and told her.'

'And Amy, being the girl she was, straightway ditched you?'

'Yes.' Alistair put his head in his hands. 'I tried to tell her that Clarissa was the last girl in the world I'd be attracted to, but she wouldn't believe me and, of course, I couldn't explain the true story as that would have blown everything and I'd have been slung out in disgrace.'

'Wouldn't even that have been worth it, to keep the girl you loved?' asked Bailey.

'It would to me,' agreed Alistair, but I had my father to consider. With all he'd done for me, I couldn't see him humiliated like that.'

'So, instead you married Clarissa?'

'Not by choice, I can assure you,' protested Alistair, rubbing his forehead. 'A few months later, she rejoiced in telling me she was pregnant. My father couldn't believe I'd been so stupid and, even then, was very dubious of Clarissa's morals. So he insisted on paying for a DNA test to prove it was mine...'

'... which of course the test did,' deduced Bailey, 'because identical twins have the same DNA and, presumably, your father knew nothing of Malcolm's involvement?'

'None at all. To the day he died, he was under the impression that I was unaware I even *had* a twin-brother.'

'So, at least, you got your position in the bank.'

'Yes,' acknowledged Alistair, 'but at the price of being condemned to twelve years marriage to a woman I couldn't stand and all the time, never falling out of love with the girl I'd always wanted.'

Bailey merely nodded and then glanced at his watch. 'I think we're both ready for a break, Alistair. Have a coffee and then you can tell me all about the bank frauds.'

* * *

'Just like you surmised so far, Jack,' said Bailey, leaning against the coffee-vending machine and holding up his plastic cup in a mock toast. 'Do you get the feeling he's almost glad to get it all off his chest?'

'I think he is,' agreed the ranger. 'Don't you find, Bailey, that it's often the case with villains who've been caught long after the crime? Living with guilt, it seems, can often be as hard as taking the punishment.' Jack looked back to the interview room. 'And the upsetting thing here is that Alistair still comes across as a basically decent type who, in the end, was a victim of circumstance.'

Bailey nodded. 'I agree, Jack. I get the distinct impression that his downfall's entirely due to the fact that he was prepared to go to any lengths to avoid letting his father down.'

'Absolutely, and I think there's little doubt that brother Malcolm was a thoroughly bad lot and that we'll find his sticky fingers in every evil pie.'

'I'm sure we will, but don't forget, Jack, that what I'm investigating here is murder, and there's *no* excuse for *that.*' The DS screwed up his plastic cup and threw it into the waste bin. 'Come on, let me go and nail him.'

* * *

Chapter Twenty-three

'It all started soon after I began working for the bank,' explained Alistair, as the questioning resumed. 'Once again, I was struggling to keep up with all the high-flyers who were intent on out-shining the son of the chief executive. Then, as always, Malcolm came up with a solution. Like I said, he'd inherited father's financial acumen so he started making deals on my behalf, earning good profits for the bank, which boosted my own apparent performance and enabled me to at least hold my own in such a competitive environment.'

'How?'

'Sometimes he would actually come into the bank and pose as me,' confessed Alistair. 'It wasn't difficult: we really were identical and if he wore my clothes, no-one even suspected I was being impersonated. Usually though, he would do the deals over the phone or on-line using my name and passwords and I would simply get the pat on the back.'

'… and, more often than not, he'd get the money,' presumed Bailey.

'Something like that,' nodded Alistair. 'I was only too pleased to take him up on his offer to help me, not realising his real motive was to make himself a fortune, safe in the knowledge that if anything went wrong, I'd end up carrying the can. At the start, I checked on his every move, but all his initial deals were perfectly legitimate, so I soon left him to it. It wasn't very long though, before he started feathering his own nest…'

'… by transferring large sums of the bank's money overseas to buy foreign government bonds,' completed Bailey. 'We know all about that from what Jacob Matson has already told us.' The DS paused. 'Whose idea was it to murder him when he rumbled you?'

'No-one's,' protested the banker. 'When Matson first realised there were, in fact, no government bonds to show for all the money that was going out, he spoke to me directly, said he couldn't understand what was happening and asked for an explanation which, of course, I couldn't give.'

'So, what happened?'

Alistair glanced despairingly at Bailey. 'The fact was, I really didn't understand what was happening myself, but I *was* beginning to suspect that my twin brother was working some fiddle to his own advantage. The only option I had was to tell Malcolm he'd been rumbled and ask what he was going to do about it.'

'... which was to invite Matson up to your boat and deal with him there,' continued the DS.

'Yes, but the idea was for Malcolm to pose as me and offer Matson a bribe to stay quiet. There was no suggestion of physical violence as far as I was concerned.'

'But Matson's silence couldn't be bought, could it? He was a completely honest chap and told you... or so he thought... that he couldn't entertain dishonesty. That's when your brother decided he had to be murdered. Presumably, you knew nothing about it?'

'Of course not,' answered Alistair, indignantly. 'The first I knew of the assault was when Malcolm called me to say Matson was unconscious on the boat and what did I want him to do? He made it quite clear that he was all for finishing the poor chap off, but I pleaded for him to wait until I got there. I raced to the boat, told Malcolm to clear off and did my best to nurse Matson round.'

'Without considering calling for medical help?' challenged Bailey.

Alistair dropped his head slightly. 'No. I could see Matson was gradually recovering, but it was only when he regained consciousness and started talking gibberish that I realised he'd had a complete loss of memory.'

'Perfect for you.'

The banker nodded. 'Yes, but I knew that he'd need looking after until he'd fully recovered... physically, at least.'

'So, you got your natural mother to come and care for him on the boat?'

'Yes, that was Malcolm's idea. He coerced her by implying we'd both be in gaol if the doctors took over, so she came and stayed with Jacob until he was up and about...'

'... when you decided to give him a boat to live on, an allowance, and a new identity?'

Once again Alistair nodded. 'It seemed the safest course. There was a middle-aged chap in my department who'd just died so...'

'... Harold Searby... yes, we know all about stealing his identity,' interrupted Bailey. He sat back again and put his hands behind his head for a couple of minutes, deep in thought, before continuing. 'So, let's now fast-forward several years to when your father, Lord Hepscott died, and the bank became aware that millions of pounds were unaccounted for. That's when you must have finally realised your actions were about to be exposed.'

Alistair nodded. 'Yes. After Lady Hepscott's death, which sadly soon followed my father's, I inherited a lot of money which I used to try and pay back the huge sums Malcolm had embezzled, in the hope of making amends. Unfortunately, after death duties, it wasn't nearly enough and, together with debts continually accumulated by Clarissa, the net was closing in on me. I was suspended by the bank and I knew I'd be facing a long, drawn-out court case, no doubt leading to a substantial prison sentence. My "death" seemed the only alternative, but I had *no* intention of committing suicide.'

'You're wrong,' argued Bailey. 'Another alternative would have been to come clean completely, expose Malcolm for what he was and let justice prevail.' The DS put his arms on the table and leaned forward. 'You'd have certainly been fired from the bank, but I doubt if the Fraud Squad would have prosecuted you if they'd got their hands on Malcolm.'

'I often thought of having the courage to spill the beans, but there was more to it than that,' went on Alistair. 'For one thing, I didn't want to sully my father's impeccable reputation, but I also had another reason to start a new life abroad.'

The DS merely raised his eyebrows.

'Clarissa,' continued Alistair, as if in reply. 'My marriage was a nightmare and home-life, almost as intolerable as work.'

'The child you'd married her for,' asked Bailey with genuine sympathy, 'was still-born wasn't it?'

'Yes and Clarissa always blamed my family for that. When my father insisted on a DNA test, the doctors warned there was always some risk to the unborn baby. So, when my son was pronounced dead at birth, she was quick to point the finger.' Alistair shook his head. 'The marriage had been loveless anyway, but after that we really grew to dislike each other.'

'Why not simply divorce?'

'Because it suited Clarissa to be my wife, even though in name only, and I couldn't risk leaving her. Not only would she have taken me to the cleaners financially, but would have taken revenge by dragging down the family name.'

Bailey could see the predicament Alistair had got himself into, but now was not the time for sentimentality and he continued his interrogation. 'Let's return to the present. Now the fraud had been exposed and, unlike the first time when a poor innocent took the blame, you'd been suspended with the prospect of a lengthy gaol sentence ahead of you. So instead, you decided to disappear by killing off your brother and taking on *his* identity.'

'Yes, no-one knew of him.' Alistair gave a grim smile. 'My natural mother died six years ago and it came to me that Malcolm, who had brought me nothing but grief in life, could now at least help me in death. By this time I'd been able to track down all the foreign bank accounts he'd stashed his millions in and so all I needed to do was pose as him and I'd be set for life.' The banker allowed himself a little smile. 'Seemed poetic justice really. He'd made that money posing as me and now I'd be the one to use it. All I needed was for him to die in an accident and everyonc to think it was me.'

'How was this "tragic accident" going to happen?' asked Bailey.

'I still hadn't worked that out,' confessed Alistair, 'but I knew how I'd get out of the country. I'd told Clarissa years ago that I'd sold *Ocean Venturer* but, in reality, I'd only transferred the registration to Malcolm without even his knowledge. Fortunately, Clarissa was only interested in *spending* my money and not in what I did with it. In essence, therefore, the boat was still mine and I could use it as a bolthole without raising a single eyebrow and with Clarissa believing I was away on business. I was still trying to work out how my twin's demise could be engineered when Beki came up with her reunion idea, and I knew that would be the perfect scenario for "my accidental death". So, I invited Malcolm up to the boat, did the dreaded deed, dressed him in my clothes with my wallet and ID in the pockets and disappeared myself.'

'Not very convincingly, actually,' commented Bailey. 'It really wasn't that smart to choose Yarmouth to make your exit, when your body turned up in Norwich.'

'No, things got a bit hurried in the end,' admitted Alistair. 'I had that MP Stanhope suddenly pushing me for money he'd invested with Malcolm and which I knew nothing about. Worse still, right at the start of the holiday I'd had the shock of finding Jacob Matson actually working in the very yard we'd hired the boat from. Even that wouldn't have been so bad if my stupid wife hadn't caused him to have an accident. When we visited him that evening in hospital, I realised his memory had returned and that the game would be up even sooner than I thought. I knew I had to act fast and bring my plan forward to that very night and then disappear.'

'But you didn't "disappear" did you?' Bailey frowned. 'What on earth possessed you to return to Yarmouth?'

'Love.' Alistair shrugged. 'As soon as I saw Amy again this holiday, I knew I was still besotted with her. I tried putting it to her that we could be together soon, but she was emphatic we could never be more than friends. So, after finishing off Malcolm, I took *Ocean Venturer* to Lowestoft with the idea of heading for the Med the next day.'

'So why didn't you?'

'Because, I just couldn't get Amy out of my mind. Although, earlier in the week, she'd made it clear she'd moved on, we seemed to be getting on well when we were alone together in Yarmouth and I wondered if there might still be hope of winning her round. Then, out of the blue, I received a text from her. Well, it was actually a text she'd sent to everyone in her address book giving her new mobile number. She obviously hadn't got round to removing my name. Somehow, that seemed a good omen and I decided to have one last chance. So, I risked everything by sending her a reply, begging her to tell no-one I was still alive but, if I could see her alone just once more, I'd explain everything. I was sure, being the loyal girl I knew her to be, she'd at least hear me out. And my hopes were raised when she replied, suggesting we meet at the spot we last saw each other.' Alistair shook his head and smiled cynically. 'The things we do for love, but what fools it makes of us.'

* * *

'What on earth made you think Alistair would show up when he did?' asked Amy.

It was early morning and all, except Clarissa, were enjoying hearty breakfasts in a transport cafe by the docks. In a couple of hours, *Brookside* would begin heading back upriver for home waters, but first, over big fry-ups, Jack had related in full, last-night's confessions in Yarmouth Police Station. Now it was time for a little confession of his own.

'Ahh… that's where I was a bit devious,' he admitted. 'Back there in Norwich when I joined you in the Forum, I told a little fib and said I needed to borrow your phone to ring your mum. What I did at the same time though, was to get Alistair's mobile number from your address book.'

'How sneaky, Dad,' protested Amy. 'Why didn't you just ask me?'

'Because I wasn't ready to air my theory at that time and still needed proof. So, after getting his number, I bought a cheap mobile from the market, en route to your mum, and sent him a text pretending to be you.'

'But surely that would arouse his suspicion, Dad?'

'Not the way I did it, it wouldn't. I pretended you'd got a new phone and were notifying everyone in your address book of the new number. Of course, I sent it to *only* him, but he didn't know that.'

'That was crafty,' said Amy, 'but it was a long shot that he'd ever reply.'

'I was banking on his feelings for you overcoming caution, and that he'd take the bait,' admitted Jack, 'and it worked. He texted back asking for a meeting and I suggested the place you'd last seen him.'

'I'm not sure I like the idea of you using his affection for me, Dad…' Amy swallowed back her uneasiness, '… but, I suppose extreme measures were called for. It upsets me a bit though to find out that Alistair hadn't done the dirty on me with Clarissa all those years ago at uni.'

'… and thereby condemned himself to a loveless marriage,' concluded Jack.

'Strangely, I also feel sorry for *her*,' sympathised Amy, glancing in the direction of the unseen Yacht Station. 'Marrying Alistair really brought them both unhappiness.'

'And gave you a lucky escape,' added her dad. 'It could be you instead of Clarissa facing the ignominy of seeing a husband in court.'

'… or being done out of a million-pounds worth of life insurance,' added Beki. She allowed herself a little smirk. 'No wonder Clarissa drank herself into oblivion last night after dear Alistair resurrected himself. It'll be a few hours yet before she surfaces to face reality.'

'In a way, I'm relieved just to have a line drawn under the whole business.' Amy squeezed Spencer's hand a little tighter. 'Life usually turns out for the best, doesn't it?'

'Not for Alistair, it won't,' said Beki. 'This twin-brother thing is a real shocker. What made you first suspect it, Jack?'

'I suppose it was all the inconsistencies of Alistair's behaviour that started to ring alarm bells.' Jack glanced towards his daughter. 'His doing the dirty on you, Amy, seemed very out of character and then there was his unexpected First-Class degree after everyone noticed he really struggled with the course work. Even when he started at the bank, Jacob Matson couldn't understand how he worked all those complicated frauds when he appeared really stretched with the day-to-day work. Schizophrenia is one thing, but Alistair's two lives seemed so diverse that I finally came to the conclusion he must actually *be* two different people.'

'Suspicion's one thing, Jack,' said Spencer, 'but how did you come up with the proof?'

'Almost accidentally,' admitted the ranger. 'This woman Mary who'd looked after Matson after his attack by Malcolm intrigued me. When I saw the name of "M Biggs" on the receipt for *Fisher of Men*, I was pretty sure the M was for Mary, and was keen to find out who she was. In actual fact, I found out later that I was wrong and that the M was for Malcolm and that Alistair had used his brother's name for the transaction. Anyway, when Audrey and I had had our lunch in Norwich, I noticed the waitresses traditionally dressed and that triggered the thought that Mary Biggs *might* just have been a maid in the Hepscott household. Bailey made enquiries at the old estate and found I was right, but the greatest breakthrough came when Bailey got a copy of Alistair's birth certificate which not only showed Mary Biggs as Alistair's natural mum, but also Lord Hepscott as his *real* father. He then tracked down Mary to where she'd been living in the West Country. Sadly, she'd died, but the locals were only too willing to explain how she'd had a son called Malcolm and that he must have been virtually the same age as Alistair. When Bailey obtained a copy of *his* birth certificate it proved he was Alistair's twin brother and, suddenly, the mystery of disappearance and death so far apart was solved. We already knew of Alistair's problems with bank and marriage, so the motive was already there before we found the solution.'

'And so Alistair was off in his boat to live the rest of his life on Malcolm's illicit spoils,' deduced Oliver. 'How much money are we talking about, Jack?' he asked with effected nonchalance.

'Millions, according to Alistair.' Jack sat back and smiled. 'At least the bank will be able to recover the missing money once they're given all the facts and there'll be no need for further investigation.'

Spencer glanced at his watch. 'Time to get going if we want to make full use of that tide. It's a shame our week's up tomorrow.' He turned to the ranger. 'We thought we'd head for Thurne Mouth today and that way we can enjoy a bit more sailing *and* not be far from Brookerboats.'

'Good idea.'

'But one thing you haven't explained, Dad,' queried Amy as they stood up to leave. 'How did Alistair manage to kill his brother at nine o'clock when he was with me in Yarmouth at that very same time?'

'Times-of-death are always approximate,' explained Jack. 'He could have caught a train from Yarmouth directly to Riverside in Norwich where, perhaps, his brother was meeting him. Somehow, then, the murder was committed.'

For a second time in as many days, Jack had chosen not to tell his daughter what he surmised to be the *whole* truth.

*　　*　　*

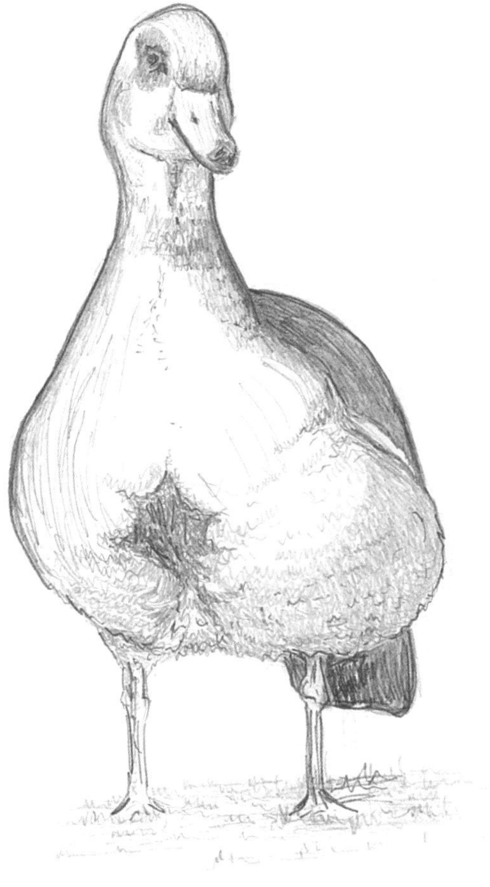

Chapter Twenty-four

'Is it only a week since we were here waving them off, Jack?' Audrey stood with her husband at Brookerboats, watching as *Brookside*, towing *Babbling Brook*, neared the yard.

'Yes, it's amazing what can happen in just seven days.' Jack returned Amy's wave, given only momentarily, as she edged *Brookside* into the basin. Spencer and Oliver stood fore and aft with their lines at the ready. Soon the two boats were gently and safely alongside.

'Nicely done,' commented Frank, who was standing with them. 'Gained some experience and confidence as well.'

'Yep, and I think you'll find your boat in just as good a nick as when she left,' added Jack. He raised his brows. 'Just as well, as you haven't got Harold… or Jacob, as I suppose we should call him now… to help get her ready for the next hirer.'

'Actually I will,' responded the yard-owner. 'He rang me last night to say he was being released today and he'd be back in the yard just as soon as he could get here.'

'I suppose, in a way, this *is* still his home.' Jack nodded towards *Fisher of Men*, still tucked in amongst Frank's fleet. 'At least he'll have somewhere to live until he sorts his life out.'

'And he can take as long as he likes,' said Frank, who had already been told the full story by Jack while they waited. 'From what he said this morning, I gathered he quite liked the idea of still living and working on the Broads. Although he's no memory of his evangelising days afloat, he reckons it sounds better than going back to the bank.'

'I can believe that.' Jack was watching as Amy made a heartfelt reunion with her mum, but it was Clarissa who had his closer attention. Already she was handing down her bags to Frank.

'Here, take these and then help me off this bloody boat.' The yard-owner was obviously biting his tongue, and it was Jack who took Clarissa's arm as she struggled down onto the quay. She took a second to steady herself before fixing the ranger with jaundiced eyes. 'Oh, it's you.'

'Afraid so.' Jack did his best to sound sympathetic. 'I expect you'll have a lot to sort out now, Clarissa?'

'Yes… thanks to all your interfering.' Her features hardened. 'Why couldn't you have just left things as they were?'

'Because that's not the way justice works, Clarissa.'

'To hell with justice… you cost me my nest-egg.' She turned to Frank with a nod to her bags. 'Take those to the car and then bring me the keys. The sooner I'm out of this place, the better.'

The yard-owner hesitated. 'Ah… well… bit of a problem there…'

'Problem… what sort of a problem?'

'Just that I don't have the keys anymore and you don't have the car,' admitted Frank. 'Some chap turned up here first thing this morning and took it.'

'And you let him?' wailed Clarissa. 'What right did you have?'

'A letter from your husband's bank,' explained Frank, 'authorising its repossession.'

Clarissa sank down onto her bags and pushed back the brim of her straw hat. 'That's all I need. How the hell am I going to get home?'

'We can give you a lift to Potter Heigham,' offered Spencer. 'From there you'll be able to get a bus to Norwich and then a train for London.'

'Buses?… trains?…' Clarissa spat out each word as though it were a profanity, 'I haven't used public transport since I was a student.'

'Well, you'd better get used to it again,' suggested Beki, unsympathetically, 'because that's how you'll be travelling for the foreseeable future. Come on,' she said, heaving a bag from beneath Clarissa's ample backside, 'you grab the other two. The exercise will do you good.'

'You're not kidding,' said Frank with a smile as Clarissa struggled with her bags to the car-park. 'That'll teach her not to pack so much in future.' Then he nodded towards *Nordic Princess*, lying serenely at her mooring. 'Trip's well-booked for tonight, Jack. Can you skipper it?'

'If you want me to, Frank, but you'd better show me what needs doing to get her ready.'

Frank led Jack to the *Princess*. 'She only really needs a good clean and I'll get Harold to help with that when he arrives,' he explained as they toured the decks. They'd just reached the wheelhouse when a police car pulled into the carpark. 'In fact, here he is now.' Jacob Matson climbed out and looked about him in slight bewilderment, having no recollection of ever having been in this yard before. Frank sighed. 'Must be strange when a whole section of your life is just a complete blank, poor devil.'

'Yes, very, but I'm sure with our support, he'll soon pick up the pieces,' Jack replied, as Frank's old yard-hand wandered down the jetty and stood gazing at *Fisher of Men*.

'You sure you're happy doing tonight's trip, Jack?' asked Frank again. He nodded back in the direction of *Brookside*. 'All that business last week must have been pretty disruptive.'

'Not as much for me as it was for Alistair Hepscott.'

'No, I guess it's not,' said Frank, pushing back his cap and scratching his head. 'Difficult to believe someone in his position could commit murder.'

'If in fact he did,' said Jack.

'No doubt about it, is there?' Frank sounded confused. 'You told me he made a full confession last night at Yarmouth.'

'So he did, but the confession was only part-true, Frank. Alistair was protecting someone. He couldn't have committed the murder himself because he was with Amy in Yarmouth at the time of his brother's death.'

'So… if *he* didn't do it… who did?'

'You did, Frank.'

'What… what are you talking about, Jack?'

'I'm talking about all the work you did on Alistair's boat, *Ocean Venturer*, to get her ready for his big escape abroad.'

'I don't know what you mean.'

'I mean, that I'd twigged on to the fact that you and Alistair had met before he arrived at the yard last Saturday.' Jack leaned back against the steering console.' Do you remember, days before, when Amy was looking at *Brookside* and saying she hadn't much boating experience? You told her not to worry, because "Mr Hepscott had". Now, I knew full-well that Amy hadn't given you the other people's names at that time, so how did you know Hepscott was one of the group or that he was a competent boat-handler? Because you must have already had some contact with him and, on the Saturday they departed, I knew you must have actually *met* because when he saw *Brookside* he said, "She looks great, *Frank*." How did he recognise you?'

Frank Brooker shook his head. 'You're just guessing, Jack… this whole business has gone to your head.'

'No it hasn't. That morning, before the gang sailed, you were dejected about a very large, unexpected tax bill, but later you seemed to have come up with a possible solution. My guess is that when Alistair brought you his car keys, he offered you a lot of money for services to be rendered.'

'Services... what services?... what are you talking about?'

'Another very special job. He must have already paid you for giving *Ocean Venturer* a complete refit. She'd only done local trips for years, but now Alistair was planning on using her to escape to a new life. Taking her to sea, he needed to know she was in good shape. All those days you were away from the yard, you were uncharacteristically secretive about what job you were working on. Now we know why.'

'You're still only guessing, Jack.'

The ranger shook his head. 'Not anymore, Frank. I was on *Ocean Venturer* last night and saw the work that had been done on her.' Jack folded his arms and pursed his lips. 'Very neat.'

'So what.' Frank shrugged. 'There's lots of marine engineers round here Jack who could have done that.'

'But not quite so thoroughly. Whoever had worked on that boat had even lock-wired the alternator pulley wheel studnuts to ensure there'd be no slackening on a long trip.'

'What does that prove?'

'Only that whoever did it was a cut above your average engineer, Frank. Usually the only engineers who lock-wire components are *aircraft* engineers. Aviation regulations require it. The only aircraft mechanic *I* know who now works on boats around here is *you*. You told me so yourself, of how you'd served in the Fleet Air Arm before coming back to the yard. Remember?'

Frank Brooker seemed to fold slightly. 'All right, Jack, I admit it. Alistair Hepscott did come and visit the yard as soon as he found out where the cruiser was being hired from. He explained that he already had a boat at Brundall, which his wife didn't know about. He said he needed it looked at and would I do the job for cash and a lot of discretion.' Frank looked out over the rotting quay-headings and leaning boat-shed. 'It didn't take much savvy on his part to see the yard was run down and that I was in desperate need of money.'

'But for more than just *working* on the boat, Frank. You also took it to Lowestoft for him.'

'How did you know that?'

'Because you rang me the evening before to ask where *Brookside* was. You needed to know you wouldn't meet her en route. As soon as you knew she was at *Berney Arms* and that she'd be heading for Norwich on the flood, you set off early via Haddiscoe New Cut and through Oulton Broad, thereby avoiding the possibility that Alistair's wife might recognise the boat or that the youngsters might recognise you. My guess is that Alistair lay low in Yarmouth the night of his disappearance and only rejoined *Ocean Venturer* once she was safe in Lowestoft.'

'None of which is illegal on my part, Jack,' protested Frank. 'I did some work and the relocation of a customer's boat, yes, but how was I to know he was plotting a murder?'

'Because you were *part* of that plot, Frank.'

'You're crazy.'

'Not yet Frank. I'm a good enough judge of men to know the likes of Alistair Hepscott haven't got it in them to kill a man. He needed to hire someone to do his dirty-work and he chose *you.*' Jack softened his tone. 'Give up, Frank. Forensics are going through *Ocean Venturer* with a fine-tooth comb. They're bound to find something to link you to the crime. Better you come clean now and save yourself a lot of worry.'

Frank sank back, shaking his head. 'I must have been mad to take on an ex-detective as skipper.' He turned again to the ranger. 'It was only my desperate need to keep the yard that made me do it. Yes, you're right Jack, on that day *Brookside* sailed, he made the excuse of leaving me the car keys to ask if I'd like to earn some *real* money.'

'In exchange for murdering his brother?'

'Exactly.' Frank took off his cap and ran a shaking hand through his hair. 'I know, Jack, I was mad to even consider the idea, but I'd just had that damn tax demand and when he told me how much he'd give me, and how worthless his brother was, I was tempted. Who wouldn't be?'

'*Very* few, actually… but what did you tell him?'

'That I'd have to think about it. I still wasn't sure.'

'So, when I came back into your office after the gang had gone, the reason you were so preoccupied wasn't your financial woes, but the torment of deciding whether to make the most significant decision of your life.'

'Exactly. I've never knowingly committed a crime before, Jack… let alone murder.'

‘So, when did you tell him you’d do it?’

‘On Monday when he rang to tell me about Harold’s accident. He probably realised then it could cause complications and once again upped the ante. I’d already thought long and hard and decided it was an offer I couldn’t refuse. I agreed. He was certainly glad to hear it and said he’d get onto his brother to come to the boat at Brundall that same night. The original plan was that I’d do the job the next day when I went to work on the boat.’

‘But events suddenly turned more urgent, didn’t they,’ persisted Jack. ‘That night at the hospital, when Alistair realised Harold’s memory had returned, he knew the game could be up even quicker than he thought. So his disappearance and brother Biggs’ murder had to be suddenly brought forward. My guess is, when he met you briefly in the hospital entrance just as we were leaving, he told you it had to be done that night. You and him had a few minutes alone before Amy and I joined you and that’s when you got your orders. Am I right?’

‘Absolutely.’ Frank seemed to be almost glad to get it off his chest. ‘After briefly visiting Harold, I went straight to *Ocean Venturer* and found Biggs already there and throwing his weight about. He was one of the most obnoxious men I’d come across and told me in the foulest of language, to sling my hook. Instead it was a spanner I slung and he was dead. Waiting until the early hours to lower him into the inflatable, I had plenty of time to wonder what the hell I’d done. But it was too late then for regrets, so I covered the body with fishing gear to look like I was night-angling, took it to Norwich port and heaved it over. I’d have got away with it too if Hepscott hadn’t taken *Venturer* back to Yarmouth, the idiot.’

Jack shook his head. ‘No, it was you who was the idiot, Frank, or at least naïve in trusting a man you hardly knew.’

‘Yes, but I thought I knew *you*,’ said Frank, stroking the gleaming varnish of *Princess*’s wheelhouse with a shaking hand. ‘I’m appealing to you now as a friend Jack, to please not take this any further. Let’s just keep it between ourselves… eh?… and enjoy working together on this boat like we planned.’

Jack glanced shorewards. The police car was still in the car-park and a familiar figure was making his way towards *Nordic Princess*. ‘It’s gone beyond that now, Frank. You took your chances, and now you’ve lost.’

There was a slight movement of the hull as someone stepped aboard, and then the figure of DS Bailey appeared in the wheelhouse doorway.

‘Frank Brooker, I’m arresting you for the murder of Malcolm Biggs. You don’t have to say anything, but…’

The caution given, Frank was led to the gangway where two uniformed constables waited. At the top he turned towards the ranger. 'I really did think we were friends, Jack.'

'We were, Frank. I'm just sorry you let yourself down. We could have pulled things together with Jacob's help, and turned the business around but, because you thought you saw a quick fix to your problems, you've ended up losing the lot and your freedom too.'

Minutes later, the police car was pulling out of Brookerboats, leaving the rest of the group to watch in stunned amazement.

It was a while before Jack's saddened gaze left the yard's empty gateway. Then he shook his head as if to clear unwanted memories, turned, smiled and went to join the gang.

*   *   *

Epilogue

'Thanks for coming, love. I'm glad of your company this evening.'

They were in *Nordic Princess*'s wheelhouse, rumbling across the broad on the evening's trip. Audrey wrinkled her nose affectionately and smiled. 'Yes, after what happened, I thought I should be with you.' She glanced at her husband, seemingly content at the wheel. 'Actually, I'm surprised you could bring yourself to do the trip at all.'

Jack turned round to see the passengers obviously enjoying their evening cruise. 'You can't let people down, Audrey. As Beki would tell you, "The show must go on".'

'Which she's certainly done with her usual brilliant commentary,' acknowledged Audrey, smiling as she watched the girl herself put down the microphone and join Oliver, Amy and Spencer on the after deck. 'Hopefully this trip will take their minds off what's happened.'

'Or at least help,' said Jack. Certainly, it was one of those magic summer's evenings when Broadland looked at its very best, brightening everyone's spirits, including the figure who now appeared smiling at the wheelhouse door. 'Come in Harold… I mean, Jacob,' beckoned Jack. 'I'm glad you could join us.'

'So am I,' admitted Jacob. 'After a few days locked up, you've no idea how wonderful fresh river air really feels.'

'I think I do.' Jack gave a questioning glance. 'I hear you're going to stay up here and not go back to work for the bank?'

'That's right.' He nodded across the broad to where a flight of swans was just making a formation landing against a backdrop of what promised to be a spectacular Norfolk sunset. 'Who could work in London again after experiencing this?'

'But, you've got no memory of all those years you spent on these rivers, so how could you miss it?' queried Audrey.

'One thing a man doesn't lose with his memory is his faith.' Matson took another long, lingering look across the shimmering water. 'I can quite believe my Harold feeling at one with God and nature in a place like this, so why should I feel any different.'

'Faith's one thing,' pointed out Jack,' but you've got to live. How will you do that with no money?'

'Good point…' for a few seconds, Matson seemed lost in thought. 'You know, Alistair can't have been all bad if, as you tell me, he supported me financially all those years.'

'No, not *all* bad. Just someone caught up in circumstances.'

'Like Frank.'

'Yes, like Frank.' Jack shrugged. 'Like so many transgressors, it was money that led him astray.'

Audrey closed her eyes. 'Poor man, you could understand him doing that work for Alistair, but he must have taken leave of his senses to agree to murder. That was indefensible.'

'Why were you so sure, that it *was* Frank who'd done it, Jack?' asked Jacob.

'It was that night we went to visit you in hospital,' explained the ranger. 'Amy chose some flowers for you and Alistair paid with a twenty-pound note from his wallet. But later, when he was with Amy in the amusement arcade in Yarmouth, she had a clear recollection of Alistair taking a *wad* of notes from his back pocket. Where was his wallet? We know now it was being planted on his brother's body in order to get the false identification.'

'But I still don't see how that implicated Frank,' said Audrey.

'Because the only other person to speak to Alistair between his paying for the flowers and taking out his cash in Yarmouth, *was* Frank. He admits that it was then that Alistair told him to go ahead with the murder that night and that he knew he was making the biggest mistake of his life.'

'But in the end, the only mistakes were Alistair's,' concluded Jacob. He made an effort to brighten. 'I do have got some good news though, Jack. The bank has already been in touch with me. Details have still to be ironed out, but they've hinted that, as I got injured the first time trying to protect their interests, I'll probably be getting my back-pay for all those ten years.'

'Phew,' whistled Jack. 'That's going to add up to a tidy sum. No need to be asking for donations from your congregation anymore.'

'Not if I invest it wisely,' agreed Jacob, 'and I already know how I want to do that.'

'How?'

'By making Frank an offer for Brookerboats. From what I've just seen today, there's an awful lot someone with a love of boats, a business brain and a surplus of cash could do to improve that yard. I reckon I could make it pay.'

'I'm sure you could,' agreed Jack, 'and certainly Frank will be out of circulation for many years yet.'

'Sadly, yes,' said Jacob, wistfully. 'You say he was good to me when I needed help, so I hope, if he accepts my offer and the money is wisely invested, he'll have a healthy bank balance when he's released.'

'Sound's good to me. So…' Jack, gave the wheel a thump, '… very shortly this boat might be yours.'

'Just possibly, but I'll need you to help skipper it, Jack. Just this evening though, I'm going to mingle with the passengers, enjoy the trip from their perspective, and work out what improvements I can make.'

'Seems a good arrangement,' said Audrey, once Jacob had disappeared below.

'Yes, he'll make a good owner and it probably won't take long for him to regain all those skills he picked up during his years in *Fisher of Men*. That might all be a blank page to him now, but he's obviously got technical aptitude and he'll soon get things running right.'

'Especially with the capital the back-pay will provide.' Audrey glanced to where Oliver stood at the rail with his arm around Beki. 'I hope, when the bank's got all their money back, they'll also see fit to recompense *him* for all he lost.'

'They should do,' said Jack. 'It wasn't the bank's fault, but Oliver *thought* he was dealing *through* them with Alistair. We know now that it was Malcolm posing as Alistair who made that first call of congratulation and subsequently pocketed all Oliver's investments. Pure identity fraud really, for which the banks are compensating people all the time. I'm sure they'll be desperate to keep this one and the sort of bad publicity an MP could orchestrate, well away from the press.'

'No, they won't want their reputation dented in any more courts,' agreed Audrey. She noticed the MP now hugging Beki just a little tighter. 'Not that he needs to worry. He's struck gold anyway, with a girl like that. She'll be really good for him.'

Jack nodded. 'And London will be good for *her*. Through Oliver, she'll mix with influential people who may well provide the kick-start she needs to get her foot in the door of the West End.'

'She deserves it, she's a good actress.' A short distance away, Amy and Spencer were also enjoying each other's company, hand-in-hand by the stern-rail. 'It's nice to see Amy content again as well.'

'Yes. If this week's achieved nothing else, it at least allowed her to put the past behind her.'

'They'll make a good pair,' said Audrey. 'I haven't seen Amy look so happy for years. I reckon we'd better start saving for another wedding pretty soon.'

'Oh no,' groaned Jack. 'Everyone else looking forward to coining it in, and I'm going to be thoroughly skint.'

'That's daughters for you.' Audrey looked ahead. The end of the broad was coming up now and she'd go and join the others. 'Well, that's everyone happy, Jack, but how about you? Seeing Frank going for trial, after all you've done together, can't be easy.'

'No,' agreed her husband. He throttled back slightly to slow down for the turn. 'But it's water under the bridge, Audrey…' he put the wheel hard over and *Princess* started her turn, '… all just water under the bridge.'

THE END

Other books
in the
Jack Fellows
series of murder-mysteries

WaterProof

ISBN 978 0 903094 23

is the first in the Jack Fellows series of Murder Mysteries set on the Norfolk Broads.

Patrolling the Norfolk Broads as a Navigation Ranger is, to ex-Scotland Yard detective Jack Fellows, the perfect job.

That's until the cold hand of violent death touches even this idyllic corner of East Anglia. Murder on the Broads is rarer than a bittern, but the police soon have their man. Or have they? Jack is sure they've got it wrong and sets out to prove it. Amongst the tranquillity of this unique setting he discovers a simmering cauldron of bitterness and deceit with suspects aplenty.

Relationships, livelihoods and reputations are in jeopardy, but whose will be sacrificed as he pursues the truth.

The WaterProof can be obtained from your local bookseller, price £5.95, or direct from the author via his website:

www.chriscrowther.co.uk

or by sending a cheque for £5.95 + £1.50 p&p to:

Chris Crowther
PO Box 1239
Norwich
NR12 8XF

Still Waters

ISBN 978 0 903094 24 5

is the second in the Jack Fellows series of Murder Mysteries set on the Norfolk Broads.

Backpacker Sally Becket has inherited a boatyard she didn't know existed from a grandfather she never knew she had. But these are the least of the mysteries confronting her when she comes to live in a small Broadland village. Who really was "Captain Charles", and was his drowning an accident, suicide... or murder?

Even Ranger Jack Fellows' deductive skills are stretched to their limits as he seeks to separate myth from reality in this tale of family secrets and love beyond the grave.

Still Waters can be obtained from your local bookseller, price £6.95, or direct from the author via his website:

www.chriscrowther.co.uk

or by sending a cheque for £6.95 + £1.50 p&p to:

Chris Crowther
PO Box 1239
Norwich
NR12 8XF

The Water Frolic

ISBN 978 0 903094 26 9

is the third in the Jack Fellows series of Murder Mysteries set on the Norfolk Broads.

A month's secondment to the southern rivers finds Ranger Jack caught up in local discords of bigotry and suspicion. A joint endeavour might just bring harmony between two very different communities but, as plans go ahead, old grievances surface as surely as a sinister secret from the broad itself. Tensions run high, but no one can predict just how tragically events will ultimately turn.

The Water Frolic can be obtained from your local bookseller, price £6.95, or direct from the author via his website:

www.chriscrowther.co.uk

or by sending a cheque for £6.95 + £1.50 p&p to:

Chris Crowther
PO Box 1239
Norwich
NR12 8XF